M Y
G H O S T S

ALSO BY MARY SWAN

The Boys in the Trees
The Deep
Emma's Hands

MY GHOSTS

MARY SWAN

Alfred A. Knopf Canada

PUBLISHED BY ALFRED A. KNOPF CANADA

Copyright © 2013 Mary Swan

All rights reserved under International and Pan-American Copyright Conventions. No part of this book may be reproduced in any form or by any electronic or mechanical means, including information storage and retrieval systems, without permission in writing from the publisher, except by a reviewer, who may quote brief passages in a review. Published in 2013 by Alfred A. Knopf Canada, a division of Random House of Canada Limited, Toronto. Distributed in Canada by Random House of Canada Limited.

www.randomhouse.ca

Knopf Canada and colophon are registered trademarks.

Grateful acknowledgement is made for permission to reprint from the following:

"Site of Ambush," by Eiléan Ní Chuilleanáin from *The Second Voyage*. Revised edition. Published January 1986 Wake Forest University Press. Reprinted by permission of the publisher.

The Selected Poetry of Yehuda Amichai, by Yehuda Amichai, translated by Chana Block and Stephen Mitchell, © 1996 by Chana Bloch and Stephen Mitchell. Published by the University of California Press.

The Wild Iris, by Louise Gluck. © 1993 Louise Gluck. Published by Harper Collins.

Library and Archives Canada Cataloguing in Publication

Swan, Mary
    My ghosts / Mary Swan.

Issued also in electronic format.

ISBN 978-0-345-80783-0

    I. Title.

PS8587.W344M9 2013   C813'.6   C2013-901554-X

Text and cover design by Kelly Hill

Cover image by Adam Fuss from the series "My Ghost" 1998. © Adam Fuss. Courtesy of Cheim and Read, New York. Used with permission. All rights reserved.

Printed and bound in the United States of America

10 9 8 7 6 5 4 3 2 1

For George.
Always remembered.

A house can be haunted by those who were never there
If there is where they were missed.

—LOUIS MACNEICE

MY
GHOSTS

I

1879–1905

ABSENCE

September

In her room at the top of the house, Clare is thinking about time. Thinking with her eyes closed in the poky little space up under the roof, where things scuttle and rustle. Stifling in the summer and far too cold in winter and not anything like the room that will be hers a few years from now, when they all move to the new double house on Pembroke Street. The one where the scent of lilacs drifts through all the open windows.

But that's in the future, and the future, like the past, is nowhere in her mind. Instead she's thinking about time in a different way. Thinking about what it is, and why it is. Thinking about how it can be Eternal, and yet gone forever. About how it is a thing that has carried on for everyone else these past hours or days while she was lying in her narrow bed, thinking nothing at all.

The room has two small windows, east and west, and when the word *morning* floats into her mind she knows that it's there because of the faint bar of light that falls on her quilt through the panes to her right. The patchwork glows along that bar, a watery blue block at the edge of it. They each have a quilt their mother has made, sleep beneath patterns of worn-out clothing. The blue is from a shirt Wee Alan wore before he died on the crossing. Before he was sewn into a tiny shroud and tipped into the cold sea, while even Clare's father wept. That's a story they all know, although she doesn't remember anyone telling it. In her bed she realizes how far one word has brought her, and she closes her eyes and falls back down into the dark.

At some point she uses the chamber pot. When she gets up to use it again it is clean and that means someone has been there, her mother or her sisters. Maybe while she slept, if that's what she's been doing. Sometimes the light falls through the window to her left, sometimes to her right, and she has no idea where she's been in between. A thing that might worry her, if she wasn't so very tired. She wonders, idly, if this is what it is to lose your mind. Or maybe it's her body, the thin white hands she holds before her eyes; maybe her body is the thing that's been left behind.

Clare thinks that thought and then it's gone, and she finds herself in a moment when the light is neither left nor right; she is standing on legs that feel like India rubber, then walking a few paces. Sometime after that she sips broth from a white bowl, her sister's face wavering and strange through the steam. "Eight days," Kez says, when she asks. "You missed your birthday, we had to eat all sixteen tarts without you." Then she says, "Are you feeling any better?"

"I don't know," Clare says. "I don't seem to know anything at all."

———

Quite suddenly she remembers that her mother is two years dead, and not emptying anyone's chamber pot. Not sitting beside the bed before dawn, not placing a cool hand on Clare's forehead, nor singing that quiet song. Her leaving was so easy that it's always felt that she hasn't really gone. That she's somewhere just out of sight, standing by a window before the lamps are lit, or sitting on a chair in the next room. Maybe holding Wee Alan on her knee, while he pats her face with his baby hands. It's not a thing she's thought before, but it makes sense to Clare if that's what Heaven is. Not a place, exactly, but something like a fold, like the part of a let-down hem that has stayed as bright and clean as it was in the beginning, while all the rest fades and fades. Maybe there is a fold like that in time, a sort of sidestep that lets you stay with the ones you loved, lets you watch them and hold them up. But no work to be done, no fretting or cares. When they opened the bedroom door that morning, only the white curtains moved in the light. Their mother's eyes were closed, all the lines in her face smoothed away.

At one time it could barely hold them all, this tall, narrow house where Clare lies thinking, cheek resting on her folded hands. Like a dance, the way they moved through the rooms, turning sideways, stepping forward and back to keep from crashing into each other. Her brothers' thundering boots and the way they knocked and cuffed each other, up and down the stairs. Her sisters singing and her mother calling one name or another, and always underneath the *snick* of heavy scissors and the sound of the treadle from the front room where her father cut and stitched fine suits, by the only window that let in enough light.

Clare is the youngest and for so long it seemed that everything happened over her head. Talking and joking and secrets passing back and forth up above her. Some laundry days the sheets were boiled then draped all over the kitchen to dry and she liked to sit under them, steamy at first but cooling fast, a muffled white world and nothing outside but empty land and sky. Her brother Ross told her once about the Eskimo who lived in the frozen North; it's the only thing she really remembers about him. Even when she was older, and knew differently, she had the idea that was where Ross went when he left. Pictured him dressed in skins and furs, no sound but the snow squeaking under his heavy feet.

She tries now to remember how the Eskimo tell time, and decides that she never knew. Only that their days and nights are different, long periods when the sun never sets and others when there's nothing but dark. The reason for that a thing she did know once, and she squeezes her eyes shut, trying to bring it back. She thinks of those problems she used to love at school, the ones that came with a story: *If a man travels 150 miles in 5 days when the days are 12 hours long, in how many days of 10 hours each will he travel 500 miles?* Easy enough to solve, once she'd learned to close her mind to the picture of the man and the road he walked, winding through a forest, and between bare summer hills. His jaunty pace slowing and his boots wearing thin, the sun beating down on his dusty cap. Easy enough if she stopped wondering just where the man was going, that the days were becoming shorter. Who he had left behind, and if he ever missed them.

Ross was already gone when their father took sick, but even though the mails were slow where he was, there would have been plenty of time for him to come home. When their mother read his letter out, their father said, "He has so much to do, land to clear and a cabin to build, of course he can't come back." Then he coughed and coughed, his hair stuck flat to his sweating forehead.

Kez and Nan muttered across Clare, in the bed they all shared, saying, "That Ross, he always did think only of himself." There was a time when she thought his leaving was like one of those old songs, a great quarrel and a disowning, the details hidden somewhere in the words that bounced around above her head. But it may have been as her sisters said, that Ross just turned his back, and walked off into a life all his own. No care for their father's long death. No thought for their mother and the way she sat down at the table when his rare letters came, her fingers tracing each word before she read them slowly out loud. How many trees cut and split, and the cow stumbling into a mire. The birth of a baby girl, named for his wife's dead sister. And the boys who came after, that she'd never hold in her arms.

Clare wants to keep thinking about time, but the past keeps intruding, and she wonders if that's a clue. Like the hints her teacher used to give, trying to draw answers from their blank faces. "Think about it this way," he would say. "Think about what you know." The same teacher who showed them a card with a drawing of a girl, an old-fashioned cap perched on her head. Long hair flowing over her shoulders and a dark line of ribbon around her neck. "Keep looking," Mr. Dunbar said, and suddenly it became a picture of an old crone; the same white cap, but the chin now a hooked nose, the necklace a dark slash of mouth. Once you had seen that, your eyes switched back and forth, but you could never see them both at once, could never catch whatever it was that made the picture change.

She doesn't know why she feels as if there's a puzzle to solve. Steps to take, questions to ask. But remembering the magic picture makes her think of Aunt Peach, who lived with them before Clare went to school. Not really an aunt, but some kind of cousin with nowhere else to go. Always cold, her crooked hands clutching at her grey shawl, a whistle in her breathing, in her voice. She used to wander out in the street, calling the long dead in for supper. Set off for the shops in the middle of the night, her bony feet bare and bruised by the stones in the road. A sudden cry in the house—*Peachey's out, she's out!*—and everyone running to search for her.

Even in her chair by the stove Aunt Peach didn't know anyone's right name. Clare's mother said that her memories were all scrambled up, like a big mess of eggs. Now she thinks that Aunt Peach was somehow cut loose from time, the way she herself has been. "What's my name?" Aunt Peach used to say. "What's my name?" And when they told her, she'd repeat it again and again, like the name of a town, or a river in Africa. Something to memorize, something just as removed.

"You had a fever, that's all," Kez says. Clare isn't sure that was all, but it's enough to know for now. Kez climbs the stairs with a bowl and spoon rattling on a tray, with the pale china jug. She helps Clare wash, waits while she spoons in soup or stew, tears off small pellets of bread. It's not like Kez to be so patient, to speak so soothingly. Nan is the soft one, the one who will listen to anything. The one who used to whisper, "Sorry lovey, so sorry honey," as she cleaned and bandaged a scraped shin. More motherly than their own mother if that was how you measured it, but maybe she just had more time. Clare's mother was always in motion, and she fretted about the rent, about the accounts her father took so long to collect. The price of sugar, and how quickly the boys grew out of their boots. Always food to prepare and washing to do and mounds of mending, her needle held close to the light. A pat on the head, a quick touch on the shoulder, but no time, or not that Clare can remember, to sit quietly with her arms wrapped around a child on her lap.

"Where's Nan?" she thinks to ask. "She's not caught my fever, has she?" Kez tells her that Nan hurt her knee, that it's swollen up like anything and she can't do the stairs. She says it happened when they were dancing in the kitchen, that Ben was there, that Charlie had stopped by and was showing them some steps he said were all the rage. "I'm surprised you didn't hear us all the way up here," Kez says, "we were laughing so hard."

It might be true. Their brother Charlie usually brings some wildness with him and he always has the latest knot in his tie, the most fashionable collar. She can picture her brothers and sisters dancing all over the kitchen, the table and chairs moved aside and steam hitting the dark windows, running down in streams. It might have happened, and Nan might have twisted her knee, but she thinks it more likely that Kez is making it up, a cruel reminder that all kinds of things are going on without her.

Her sleep is still sudden and deep; days pass, and when she's awake her floating mind snags on thoughts that she tries to examine. Something has happened to her body, she knows that. A walk across the room wears her out, her limbs at the same time so heavy and so weak. She's not sure why, but she senses that it's important to keep her mind tethered to this notion of time, to rein it in when it scatters and wanders too far. Another kind of exercise, like the way Kez makes her shuffle from her bed to the doorway, so her feet don't forget what it's like.

Clare doesn't think there's anything in her books that will help, and besides, someone has taken them away. The little wall shelf empty, except for the doll her father made from bits of wood and knotted string, a faceless circle for its head, topped with a mess of fine woollen hair. She's puzzled by the doll, doesn't think that it has always been there, but that's not what she wants to be thinking about, so she closes her eyes and tries to remember, instead, all the things she knows about time.

People used to believe that the sun rode the sky like a fiery horse and chariot, dragging the night behind; she remembers learning that. An answer to a question that was satisfying enough, that let them live their lives by the broad rhythm of light and dark, free to eat when they were hungry, rest when they were tired. Now she asks herself why that wasn't the end of it, why someone felt a need for more order, and then more. For sundials and church bells, for school bells and ticking clocks and watches. For the time-ball that dropped like a slow stone, her father lifting her onto his shoulders to see over the tall people in front of them. All of it marked out, ticking away, days and hours and minutes, the present divided into smaller and smaller pieces, as if that could keep you from looking into the great black expanse of the future. Darkness on the other side as well, years and years, thousands of them, millions, it's said, since the world began. Time that existed so long before there were men to think of it.

Clare imagines that kind of time as the inky black cloth her father rippled out onto his long table. A dark, flowing mass that he measured and cut, tamed to take on the shape of a man. She used to hide under that table, too, listening to the stories he told himself as he worked, the songs he sang so softly. Not even thinking until much later that he had known she was there, of course he had, and the stories were for her. Tamlane with the Elfin Queen, and Thomas the Rhymer. The long song about the cold blowing wind. "Little pitchers," she remembers him saying sometimes, when her mother stood, cross, in the doorway.

She can't picture her father's face, except at the end. Those last days at his bedside, when the time between his eyes flickering open grew longer and longer, as if he was getting used to how it would be. But she remembers how strong his arms once were, lifting her through the air. And she remembers his foot tapping when he played his old fiddle, and how she loved the times when the neighbours came with more fiddles and drums, when the music was loud in the crowded kitchen, everything a swirl of colour and sound. Hands clapping and her father's eyes closed, his knee bent and lifting and his boot crashing down.

After he died they had to sell the long table and the sewing machine, the box of chalk his fingers had held. Their mother wrapped his fiddle in a baby-sized quilt and sent it to Ross, even though Charlie was the one who made music from everything he touched. A pair of spoons or sticks of kindling, the battered squeezebox he spent hours cleaning and patching, and working the stuck buttons free. He must have minded about the fiddle, but that's just how it was, everyone in their place and things decided. Ross the eldest, if you didn't count Wee Alan, and entitled to certain things, even though he'd walked away. Ben, the next son, stepping into Ross's place, handing his pay envelope to their mother and later to Kez and Nan, who cooked and cleaned, who walked together to the shops every day and always came home with something they'd found, even if it was only a story to tell. No question but that Charlie would apprentice to the jeweller on King Street, a man from the same church, who dressed in plain suits their father had made. Or that Clare would become a teacher; what better way to earn her living, to make use of all she'd learned. A girl always top of her class. A girl who loved everything about going to school, loved even the smell of the classroom. The sleepy, chalk-dust light that fell through the tall windows.

October

The season is changing, autumn-blue sky hard against the attic window. There's a perfect red leaf on the tray Kez brings; "It's glorious outside," she says. Clare keeps the leaf until it dries and curls, crumbles it to powder and watches how it hangs in the air when she blows. Thinking, *That's time too, what it does.*

Later, her brother Ben climbs the stairs, to tell her that Principal Thomas has stopped by. That he drank a cup of tea, ate two pieces of Nan's seed cake and said he'd had to hire another teacher to take Clare's place. Perhaps next fall, he'd said, when she had completely recovered, perhaps then he could find her a new position. "He left this for you," Ben says, tugging a thin green book from his pocket. "He said you'd been discussing it."

Clare has no memory of that discussion, but when Ben is gone she runs her fingertips over the cover of the little book, a beautiful deep green, like the trees in Moss Park when the light is beginning to fade. It's called *Elementary Astronomy*, and she turns the clean pages slowly, looking at the simple illustrations.

Circles and ovals and lines with arrows, a tiny man on a hill with a telescope. The patterns of the fixed stars that you can only see when you're told what they're meant to be.

She knows it's not right, but all she feels is relief at losing her place. As if she's put down some heavy thing she hadn't even realized she was carrying. She remembers, but distantly, how proud she was of her first class certificate, how happy when Principal Thomas opened the door and showed her the empty classroom that would be hers. She remembers counting off the days last summer, waking earlier and earlier as the time drew closer.

But when the first day of school finally came it was hard to open her eyes, and the bedclothes seemed an impossible weight. She remembers how carefully she began to brush her hair, and then her arm was so tired and she realized that she'd been brushing and brushing for who knew how long, staring at herself in the mirror. "Pull yourself together," she said then, and the moment she said it she felt as if she was fraying at the edges, sliding away. The dishes Nan set on the table made a hollow sound, and the buildings she walked by on her way were all sharp lines and colours, like the rows of thin-shouldered children, their piercing voices. She understands now that her fever was coming on, but that day all she knew was that things were not quite right, and she thought that she just needed to *concentrate*. But the next day was the same, only more so. Like a dream, in the moments before you realize that it *is* a dream, that terrible feeling of everything sliding out of control. Next fall is a long way off, but it feels as if a door has closed quite firmly; she can't imagine herself trying to do it all again.

———

Kez has brought her the old brown sewing box, the button jar and the smooth darning egg Clare loves to hold in her hands, along with a pile of things to be mended. "Nothing too tiring," she says, as she leaves with the tray, "but it will give you something to do." Clare thinks for the first time of how much extra work she's causing, how it's not only her days and nights that have changed. She will do the mending, make herself useful, and she thinks that she might even learn something from the tears and frayed seams, messages from the lives going on in the rest of the house. They're none of them the mud-slinging, tree-climbing children they once were, but Ben still sheds buttons almost daily, and his jacket pockets often tear from the notebooks and sharpened pencil stubs he stuffs them with. Nan's blue dress has a pattern of tiny singed holes near the hem, sparks scattered from their father's old pipe when she knocks it on the sole of her shoe. Sitting on the back steps in the dark, having her quiet smoke, her body in their father's shape, elbows on her knees and right hand cupped around the bowl. They all know not to say a word, if they happen to open the door to a curl of scent that reminds them of another time.

The clothes in the mending pile have only the usual types of damage, tell her nothing she doesn't already know. She concentrates on her neat, small stitches, the tiny snap of the thread in her teeth. "Was it Rumpelstiltskin?" Kez says, when she picks them up in the morning. She gives a little jump and tries to click her heels, laughs the witchy cackle their mother used to do when they begged for one of her stories, a thing Clare hadn't known she remembered. She thinks of something Ben told her once, a trick he used when he studied for examinations. He said that he imagined the tall old dresser in the kitchen, that he lined his facts up, put them in different spots in different shelves and drawers, and he said that he could always call that picture to mind, find anything he needed that way. It never worked for Clare, but she thinks now that maybe her mind is something like that dresser after all, drawers and compartments swollen shut by age and weather; she wonders what else might be hiding there, waiting to slide suddenly free.

Clare's sister Nan has a very round face, and her sister Kez has ears that stick out. They call each other Moon and Jug, but no one else does. They were born as close together as they could be, without being twins; impossible to think of one without the other, even though they're nothing alike. Nan's round, kind face hides a secret sorrow, another thing Clare knows, though she doesn't know how. She has two friends from church, the Misses Simp, Kez calls them, although one's a widow and they aren't related at all. But they both have long, thin noses and pale faces, sit very straight and hold their saucers up in front, set their teacups down with the tiniest of sounds. Long pauses in their conversation, while the clock ticks. Kez says they make her want to break wind loudly, she says one day she'll pin them down, knees on their bony shoulders, and smear rouge on their sagging, pale cheeks. "Oh stop!" Nan says, through her laughing, and Kez does stop, although she wouldn't for anyone else.

Kez is a joker, like Charlie, but with a meaner edge, someone who would tickle you into nothing but pain. She can't let anything go and it's worse since their mother died, no one to check her tongue. "For Heaven's sake, I'm only joking," she'll say, as if words shouldn't cut within the walls of your own house. Still, she's the one you'd want with you if there's a dull, hard job to be done. Her arms are skinny but strong and she pushes up her sleeves and jumps in, something like their mother in the way she's rarely still. "Pretend this carpet's the mean old landlord's face," she says, when it's draped over the line outside. "Take that," Kez says, giving it a whack with the beater. "Take that and that." And they do it until their arms are so tired, the dust that's left only a shiver in the air. She's good at thinking up games while they wring out the laundry, knead and peel things at the kitchen table. What kind of animal would the fat man next door be, the grocer's wife, the butcher with his missing fingertips. What would be the best meal you could ever eat, every single ingredient. Or what do you think the princess would do, if the prince never came to the tower?

"A fever," Kez says, "a collapse—what does it matter? This is where we are, and soon you'll be better, and that's that." She tells Clare not to *think* so much, tells her the doctor said that too, just like their mother always did. "The doctor came?" Clare says, but Kez bats the question away. "Only a few times," she says, "only those first days. Just rest, is what he said, and he left a nasty tonic for your heart, but we couldn't get you to take it." She puts on her witchy voice and says she poured the bottle out the back door, says it bubbled and seethed and burned the ground black, and Clare knows she'll hear nothing more about the doctor, how worried they must have been to call him.

"I'll try," Clare says. She knows she can't explain it to Kez, how safe she feels in her dark-walled room. How it's beginning to feel like a gift, this time with nothing to do *but* think. Although it must be what wears her out; she does nothing else but sew a few buttons and walk the room end to end, read a paragraph about the changing face of the moon.

Nan's knee is better and she's sometimes there when Clare opens her eyes. Other times Kez is sitting in the chair by her bed, or Ben, and sometimes even Charlie, who brings her a book on repairing clocks and watches. That's not really the kind of time she's been wondering about, but when he's gone she turns the pages, looks at the diagrams, all the tiny parts hidden beneath the plain face. Trains and bridges and pinions, levers and springs and jewels. The escapement, which regulates everything, makes the wheels turn at a steady rate that equals the passing of time, shown by the moving hands. She covers the page and tries to see it in her mind, each part of the mechanism, and what its purpose is. In one of the illustrations the pieces are exploded out, each one separate with its own neat label. But you can see that they are all in order, that at any moment they could fall back into place with a tiny sound and become whole again, and then time will go ticking on.

When Charlie comes next there's been a first, early snow; he bends his head so she can feel it in his hair. Then he sits in the chair, fidgeting with his cuffs, his open collar. Scratches at his earlobe. His nails are bitten down, there are dark smudges under his eyes, and Clare thinks that he looks like the person he might be if he wasn't always so lively.

Charlie is next to her in age, and there was a time they were always together. Wandering through alleyways and the wilder parts of the park, climbing over fences and up through the branches of swaying trees. Once they tried to rig a tightrope, but the knots didn't hold, and after they saw the Wild West show they galloped down all the back laneways for days, on their way to rob the two o'clock train. Clare was the lookout, her job to peek around the corner and then give the special whistle that would bring Charlie thundering past, a torn-off sleeve tied over his nose and mouth. Noisy bullets flying from his cocked thumb and finger. She doesn't remember exactly when it changed. When she began to spend the sleepy afternoons scrubbing potatoes at the battered table, or whispering behind her hand with the other girls at school. Charlie fixing his part just so with a wet comb and stroking the soft hairs above his lip, walking with a new, lazy slouch and not telling her anything that mattered.

Clare knows, they all do, that he's not happy where he is. Always complaining about the fine, close work and the bad temper of Mr. Howell, and about his tiny room above the shop. Looking at him now there's barely a trace of the smooth-skinned boy, but she remembers sitting beside him, throwing stones that gulped into a pond, the smell of wild grass all around. And she remembers sitting on the hot roof of a shed while he told her what they'd do with all their stolen gold. The fine house they'd live in together, soft green lawns through the window where horses chased each other and shook their manes, their long brown heads. Heavy linen napkins snapped out in their hands when they sat at a long table spread with covered silver dishes, each one holding some food they'd heard of but never tasted.

She wonders now where that picture came from, nothing like a life either of them had ever seen. And she wonders if there's another kind of sidestep, like the one she's decided Heaven must be. A place where she and Charlie still sit in the hot sun, chewing on blades of fresh spring grass with their shoulders touching, not one sad thought in their heads. She's just about to ask him what he thinks about that when he gives a huge sigh, and his hands fall open, palms up on his splayed-out thighs. "I don't want it," Charlie says. "A little life like this."

———

After he's gone, his footsteps fading on the stairs, Clare smooths
the rucked-up chair cover and thinks that in a strange way those
few words are the most Charlie's ever said to her. As if he slipped
out of a cloak as he came through her doorway. She thinks that
maybe Kez does too, something softer showing, that Clare never
thought was there to be seen. Even Ben, who climbs the stairs
most evenings and talks about what's gone on at the Telegraph
Office, tells her about an idea he's working on, switches and
currents and relays. It doesn't matter that it's nothing she can
follow; as he talks he pulls out his notebook and begins to draw,
to scribble down figures, and soon the only sound is the scratch
of his pencil, and the soft *pss pss pss* of breath through his teeth.
But lately he drifts, with a little smile on his lips, and once he
asked her about hair combs, and was that a gift that a woman
might like. What kind, did she think, for hair that was lighter
than hers, and straighter. Hair that had a sort of *gleam*.

Arranging the cover she thinks of the chair too, a gift from
Kez and Nan when she got her certificate. Something they
found on one of their prowls. Walk with them to the shops or
down any street and you'll notice how their heads swivel, how
they see the worth in all kinds of things other people think
they no longer want or need. A dented fire screen, the old
squeezebox that made Charlie's eyes open wide, a bouquet of
flowers, barely wilted.

Somehow they dragged the heavy chair home, found a
place to hide it while Ben fixed the broken leg, the wobbly arm.
They dyed a sheet deep blue and draped it to cover the leaking stuffing, huffed it up the stairs for Clare to find when she
came home, a sign pinned on that said *Teacher's Chair*. When
she thinks of that, she feels a wash of shame at the way she
keeps herself apart. The fever itself is long past, and maybe

she's not as weak as she feels, maybe she needs to make herself get up, make herself set aside whatever it is that keeps her from the stairs. That keeps her from taking her place at the kitchen table, from going on with her life like a normal, happy girl.

November

The hard blue sky has turned a gloomy grey. Day after day a rainy light, although it must be falling softly, no sound on the roof that slants above her. No difference in the hours of the day. Clare thinks what it would be like to be trapped in an eternal, hazy present. Like the man in the problem, walking his endless road. Maybe that's why someone began to think about measurement. Maybe someone understood that being able to mark time in a different way could keep you from going mad, from thinking that nothing would ever change.

She wonders if that's what it was like for Aunt Peach, who was buried with the only things she owned. A dark grey dress and shawl, a thin gold ring on her crooked little finger. They used to say that she was content enough, that she didn't know; a blessing, really, that she had no idea at all. But maybe it was a choice, that wandering of mind and body. Leaving the chair by the stove, one way or another, to look for the place, the time when she lived a real life, when her mind worked as well as anyone's. Clare wonders what she would choose, if she became an old woman in a house of noisy strangers. Where she would go, while she twisted her ring around and around. Maybe she'd run down those laneways with Charlie, or perch on her father's shoulders, holding her breath while the time-ball fell. Maybe she'd choose the classroom, Mr. Dunbar's boots squeaking as he paced the oiled floor, while her pencil flew over the page. Or the very first one, kind Miss Bell with her pitted cheeks, soft hands. Trailing the faintest scent of flowers when she walked between the rows, or looked over Clare's shoulder and whispered, "Oh, very good. Very good."

Minutes and hours are the same length, and days have twenty-four hours, even when the light changes according to the seasons. The same length everywhere in the world, although Clare knows that the actual hour varies. Knew that even before Ben's stories from the Telegraph Office, a man in Toronto receiving word of a death in Edinburgh, that in some way hadn't happened yet. And then there is time that seems to go on forever, yet on looking back has vanished in a blink. For so long the house could barely hold them all, and then it went quiet; she could walk into a room and find no one there. A dancing of motes in the light, disturbed by no one alive, although at those moments Clare has always felt that if she can only listen hard enough, she will hear her mother's voice. That she has just left the room, a flicker in the doorway, that she's always almost there.

It's not the same with her father. Wherever he is, it's not here, and she wonders if that means he didn't love them enough. Or if maybe he's somewhere deeper, a fold within the fold, another layer where he stays apart with her mother and Wee Alan. Because Wee Alan was the first of them, from a place not even Ross remembers. From a time glimpsed when her father used to play his fiddle, his head bobbing and a lost look on his face. A time when his heart was all open.

Clare's friends came calling, she's been told, when she was far too ill to see them. They still do, though not as often, and she tells Kez that she's still too tired to see anyone, that she fears a lively visit will wear her out, undo all the slow progress she's made. Easier than trying to explain how that life they were part of feels impossibly distant. She's used to her drifting days, doesn't want to be *cheered up*, to be distracted from things she needs to think about. Though sometimes now her eyes open in the middle of the night. She turns her head toward the window and looks at a sliver of moon, the rest of its pocked, dark circle. Wonders if that's really what she sees, or if her mind fills in what she knows must be there. It's terribly quiet and she suddenly thinks that maybe they've all gone away. That they've either forgotten her or had enough of her, nothing but empty rooms left below. If she could make her legs move down the stairs, there'd be nothing at all to find.

Or maybe she died from the fever, if it was a fever; maybe she's as much of a ghost as her mother is, as Wee Alan, as all the wandering souls. She pinches her thigh, but what good is that? Who knows if the dead still feel pain. At those moments she longs to be back in her warm place between her sleeping sisters, even if Kez sometimes flings out a sharp elbow and Nan's long toenails scrape her shins. She folds her hands together and squeezes, tries to focus on that, and just in time she hears the creak of someone turning in bed, the faraway tick of the old clock in the hall.

December

She knows they're becoming shorter, but the days feel longer. She tries now to keep herself awake, so the nights will be unbroken, sews or reads in the Teacher's Chair. The book about watches, the book about the skies, and even a terrible novel the Misses Simp have sent over, all ringlets and sighs and God's tests and forgiveness. Her thoughts still go around and around, but they all seem familiar, as if she's reached the end of where her own mind can take her. When she hears Kez and Nan leave for the shops, the door closing loudly behind them, she stands on stronger legs and carries her tray downstairs, washes the dishes and leaves them dripping in the rack.

At first she climbed straight back up the stairs, but now she walks through each small room, her eyes taking in clues from the lives going on without her. Ben's damp trousers are draped over a chair and that means he was home very late the night before, walking through the sudden sleety rain that clattered on the roof over Clare's head. He used to use the same attic space for his tinkering, his inventions. Drawings in coloured ink tacked up all over the walls. Until once when Kez helped him do something with glass and two wires; there was a loud bang, a singed smell growing stronger as the rest of them ran up the narrow stairs. Ben and Kez were sitting on the floor where they'd landed, laughing so hard. "Are we dead?" Kez said. "Are we dead?" Laughing with a sooty streak on her cheek, a thin trail of blood near her eye.

Their mother didn't laugh. She tore all the drawings off the wall, leaving tiny white flags that still flutter, stood with her arms folded while Ben packed everything away. He was already working at the Telegraph Office and had asked for the use of a basement storeroom; that's where he would have been until late. Barely noticing the slush that soaked his pant legs as he made his way home, his head filled with diagrams, with arrows and letters and possibilities.

There are more signs in the kitchen; the sugar tin empty and three cakes cooling on wire racks mean that Nan is a little sad about something. And Kez must be having trouble sleeping again, the good silver teapot gleaming on the kitchen table, beside a puddled, blackened cloth. It's as if they've all left messages for her, or not *messages*, exactly, but things set out to tempt her. A plate and fork beside those cooling cakes, a magazine open to an article about sundials, a clipping on the table about distant stars. The intention making her think of that black and white dog Ben tried to tame, years ago, and how patiently he worked at it. Leaving scraps of food in the yard, luring it closer and closer to the back steps, any sudden noise or movement making it bound away. An angry bite on his hand, kept wrapped and hidden, from trying to pat its head too soon. Remembering that, she snaps her teeth together twice, a startling sound.

In truth she is ready to let herself be coaxed. Sometimes now she can see her breath in the attic room, reminding her what it's like in deep winter, the need to fall asleep before the last bit of warmth leaves the cloth-wrapped bricks at her feet. She'd claimed the space when Ben's things were gone, said it was too crowded in bed with her sisters, said that now that she was at the high school she needed a quiet place to do her lessons. She'd forgotten that, how she suffered the cold but wouldn't complain. Wrapped in blankets, making notes with the pen in her thick, gloved fingers. Her mother holding Clare's face in her hands, giving it a little shake and saying, "My stubborn girl, where do you get it from."

So one evening she comes down to supper, and then every one after that. She doesn't have much to say at first, but the others talk about the usual things, pass her the salt and fill her glass, and no one behaves as if her presence is a thing to be noticed. And maybe it isn't, but she knows how all of them, especially Nan, are good at playing a part. That time their neighbour came banging and shouting, Nan just smiled her sweet smile and told him that he was mistaken. That Charlie had been home with her all day and couldn't have broken the window; it must have been a completely different boy he saw, running away.

After the meal Clare helps with the washing-up, sits for a time with the day-old newspaper her sisters have carried home, climbs the stairs like she used to, after saying good night. She remembers, as she slides toward sleep, how that scruffy dog came to know Ben, sat up with its ears perked when he opened the back door. Let him scratch behind those ears and even let himself be brushed with Nan's good hairbrush, until she found out. But one day they heard a terrible whining and found the dog lying, splayed, at the base of the step, trickles of green bile from its mouth. Poison taken from someone's hand, that's what their mother thought. Better for him if he'd stayed fierce and wild, not been fooled into thinking that one kind hand meant that all were, but Clare knows that's only one way of looking at it.

No one has said, but she knows her small salary is missed. The price of everything is going up and they feel the pinch; they always have. There's talk around the table of taking a lodger; it's been a luxury really, the way they've kept their parents' room as it was. The quilt on the bed, the watch and the brush on the dressing table, the silver hatpin. The white curtains they wash every spring and fall, a clean scent rising with them when the window is open.

Charlie pushes away his empty plate and says that he has a key that will unlock gold and jewels enough for all of them. "Of course we'll have to light out for the West," he says, and then it's a joke, Kez saying that first they'll have to learn to ride horses. She rummages through the jumble in the dresser drawer, pulling out bits of twine, and Charlie knots them together, fashions a loop. They take turns twirling it, trying to throw it over the high stool and then over each other's heads, until Ben's glasses go flying, a crack in one lens that gives him a desperate look. "I'm just joking," Charlie says, when he meets Clare's eye, and she hopes he means it.

There are still days when she's too tired to leave her bed, times she's swept under, no way to know if for minutes or hours, except for the slanting light. But mostly she comes downstairs when she knows the others have gone out; there's nothing to fear in the familiar rooms, though she keeps her eyes away from the world that seems to breathe and press at the tall windows. So different from those in her own room, the small squares of sky in different shades, with wisps or crumples of cloud.

She's been coaxed this far, but she knows it will go no farther. Shakes her head when Kez asks her to come along to the shop, when Ben says why doesn't she walk with him to his office, or Charlie buys tickets to that new play. Things she once would have done without a thought. She knows she must be the same person, but it feels as if she's peeled away from that life, from the girl with the clear path to follow. She tries to remember what it felt like to be that girl, but it's difficult.

What comes into her head instead is a leaf-tossed day, a wind that roared and howled like something from the frozen North except that it was warm, that wind, though just as fierce.

She remembers walking down a street with her parents, holding on to their hands. All kinds of things flapping and tumbling past them, newspapers and twigs with green leaves still attached. A battered black hat, pieces of flimsy fruit crates, even a small child rolling over and over, though when she thinks of that now she's sure it couldn't have happened. Maybe a joke someone made, or a dream she had, but she can see the child, trailing a grey blanket, buffeted right past them and away down the street. She has no idea where they were going, or why it was just the three of them. No idea how long it lasted, but she remembers how her body felt, how solid. Her parents bent forward, her father's eyes half closed against the grit and her mother's skirt fluttering out behind, while she herself was quite steady, held firm to the ground by their warm hands.

January

Nan says she's looking better every day, "More like your old self." The others agree, and must think they're helping by talking about the future, about the note Principal Thomas has sent. As if this time is just a short side line that will soon link up with the main track again. Clare knows it's not like that, but she hasn't said, trying first to have a plan, some other way to earn money and add her share. The difficulty is that her sewing skills are basic, nothing anyone would pay her for, and she has no talent for music or drawing, can't think of any kind of lessons she could give in the safety of the house. What's left is to find work in a shop, or an office of some kind, and the thought is terrifying. But she remembers that skittish stray dog, not his sad end but the way he conquered his fear, a little bit more each day. Tells herself that she can do it like that, no reason, no good reason why not. And she tries so hard to feel her parents' anchoring hands when she stands by the tall front windows, making herself look out to all that's there.

It does become easier, in the empty house in the mornings. She stands in the cold front room a little longer each day, shifting her feet when they begin to numb. The people who pass by are dark, bundled shapes, only their glittering eyes showing through the visible breath that circles their heads, and she tries to follow them with her mind when they pass out of sight. Down to the end of Teraulay, to the grocer's on the corner with the round-bodied stove, to the snow-dusted, busier sidewalks on Yonge. Places she knows so well and nothing, she tells herself, not anything to be afraid of. She tells herself that again the morning she stands with one hand on the brass knob of the back door. Determined to open it, determined to step out, even while the thought of entering all that space is making her heart beat so hard she feels it pulsing to the tips of her fingers.

She gives the door a hard push and black birds rise, screaming, from the bare trees. They wheel through the enormous sky and she feels herself whirling with them, scattered to a thousand dark, beating wings. Every bit of her blasted and separate, like the pieces of the watch in Charlie's book, and nothing at all at the core. She doesn't remember the stairs, but she hears her own hard breathing when she burrows under the covers of her bed, curling as small, as tight as she can. Wishing she was still in that muffled white Eskimo world, still that little girl under her father's long table, his voice singing beyond the folds of black. "Little pitchers, little pitchers," he said when her mother came in with a cross voice, a jumble of wool in her hands. When her mother said, "Look at this mess, have you seen her?" Said, "That child, I love her like she was my own, but honestly . . ."

It's never really been a secret. Another thing she just knows, knowledge that seeped in from things overheard, from questions asked. Usually she didn't think about it at all but there were times when the questions of who she really was flared and she tried to work it out for herself, knowing no one would give her a proper answer. When she was small her father said the fairies brought her, and once Kez told her that they'd picked her out from a bin in a shop, carried her home along with a sack of flour. The most her mother ever said was that it was a thing to talk about when Clare was older. There were times she imagined she was a stolen princess, every squeaking cart wheel the sound of a gilded coach. Her real, royal family, come to sweep her away, the imagining followed always by a complicated shame.

As she grew older Clare asked more cunning questions, thought about the most likely answers. Ben and Charlie were too young, but not Ross, whose leaving then became banishment or flight. Or maybe she belonged to one of her so-called sisters; when she was thinking that way she followed them from room to room, stared hard at their hands, holding a duster or resting flat on the kitchen table, looking for similarities. When they were pulling on their stockings she tried to see if one had a curled-over baby toe like her own, but they both did, so that told her nothing. From time to time the question of who she really was would squat in her mind and it would matter, but then the season would change, or examinations would be just ahead, and it would disappear. Though she realizes now that it's been like a splinter that's driven in deep. You get used to picking things up, to moving a certain way, until a careless touch makes you feel it.

It's cold in the attic room, but her breath has warmed the space where Clare burrows, and her damaged heart is calmer. She thinks of the way the word *morning* floated up in her mind, all those months ago. A simple, familiar word, but once it appeared there was no going back to the timeless place she'd been. She thinks of secrets that aren't really secrets, of things that can be glimpsed but not seen. A drawing that can be two things at once, a kind of magic that can't be pinned down.

And she thinks about *time*, another simple word, used so easily and often. Yet a word you could spend your whole life thinking about, without reaching the end of the mysteries it contains. Clare thinks of her mother's cross words sliding free, like the way a solution to a problem can suddenly appear when you're thinking of other things. But she knows the remembering is not an explanation, knows that she hasn't arrived anywhere. The words are just another knot on the long string of memories that plays through her mind. Like Ben with the twitching dog's head in his lap, like her father bathing Peachey's poor bruised feet. Like the first time she heard Kez crying in the dark.

"Think of what you know," her teacher used to say. "Start from there," but maybe that's not the best way. For centuries the astronomers she read about in the small green book watched the strange tracks of the planets, and tried to make sense of their movements around the Earth. Looped, uneven paths that sometimes went forward, sometimes turned back on themselves, ever more complicated and mysterious. Until

Copernicus came along, and emptied his mind of all assumptions. Thought about those paths and imagined himself standing, not on Earth, but on the fiery Sun. The planets' tracks now simple and constant, and Earth not the centre at all but just one of them, moving forever on its own, solitary course.

She wonders then if she's been like those ancient astronomers, building everything on false assumptions. Wonders if she's really some stranger's child, not brought by the fairies but left somewhere, found somewhere. If her mother had lived until she thought Clare was old enough, is that what she would have told her? That she was a stray, taken in and cared for like Aunt Peach, but with even less reason. A kind of charity that had nothing to do, not really, with love or belonging. If so, she owes a simpler kind of debt. If that's how it was, then nothing is certain, and even her mother's ghostly presence might be nothing more than a wish.

There are voices downstairs, loud groans and laughter as Kez and Nan set their heavy bags on the scrubbed kitchen table. Clare thinks of how shakily she stood, at first, how easily her legs move now, and she's suddenly sure she can make a small, closed place for herself, thinks maybe that's all she's ever wanted. Those beating black wings still whir softly, but an idea begins to glimmer and grow. She's already memorized the diagrams and she can teach herself everything else in Charlie's book, send for the other titles that are listed in the back. Kez and Nan can tack up notices in the neighbourhood, put a small sign in the window. Watches are always losing time, clocks seizing up; it won't be a regular wage, but she'll be able to contribute, no need to force herself into the terrible world. She'll find her missing books, put them back on the shelf, and there'll be time to read and think, and it can be enough, she tells her-self, why not? A quiet little life like that.

Clare swings her feet to the floor and smooths her hair; in a moment she'll go down and tell them her plan. There will be a pause, while Kez and Nan exchange a look, but then they'll get caught up in it, they'll see that it's the only solution. And she knows there are things she could ask them now, knows that they might actually tell her; perhaps that's what holds her back. Questions and answers that can't be unsaid, half secrets maybe kept out of nothing more than kindness.

August

Clare wakes with the answer clear in her mind; sometimes it happens like that. Or sometimes when she's emptying a bucket out the back, or smoothing a newspaper to read. When she opens the door to her workroom off the kitchen, sunlight is falling on the table and she sees that she's right, knows exactly what to do. One part of the escape wheel is just slightly out of true, an easy thing to remedy, and then she can move on to the mantel clock that apparently loses so much time that it's been used as a paperweight for years.

At first she worked with the books propped open, Charlie's and the more detailed one she sent for. She copied out some of the diagrams, making them larger, and practised with her father's watch, taking it apart again and again, until her fingers knew what to do by themselves. Then she hung it on a nail above her work table, where she can always hear it ticking. Kez and Nan still think she should use the front parlour; they fret about her eyesight, but she tells them that the morning light is fine in Aunt Peach's old room, that she needs a small, bare space she can keep free from dust.

It's mostly watches she works on, a few small clocks. She's found that it's usually just a matter of taking them apart and cleaning the jewels, the pivots and escapements. Carefully oiling with the proper-sized wire at each stage of the reassembly. She has a few tools, nippers and burnishers and oilers, and a small collection of springs and other pieces. If she needs to replace a cracked or missing face, Charlie finds one for her, buys it on tick, he says. Each job a little puzzle to solve, a series of small satisfactions. When she senses that the work will be beyond her ability, she simply names a ridiculous price; so far no one has persisted.

The room is cool in the afternoons, when the sun slips to the other side of the house. She doesn't miss the shady pathways in the park, the breeze that ruffles the water of the lake, when you wade through. And she wonders sometimes if Aunt Peach found the same comfort in the voices that drift in from the street, the sounds of children running wild in the laneway. The constant chatter in the kitchen that becomes a kind of underlying music, beyond the closed door. Word has been spreading slowly and she has enough work to fill several days each week, enough money to set a little aside for the books she wants to send for. Time passes easily inside the house, and she's only a little sad to think that maybe she hasn't peeled away from anything, maybe this is the life she was always meant to have.

———

December

It's probably Charlie's idea. Clare's not even sure how it happened; one moment she was thinking of the clock on her work table, the pieces laid out, clean and lightly oiled, waiting for the morning light, and then she was outside in the cold dark. Kez and Nan linking each arm, Charlie in front of her and Ben behind; like a prisoner, she thinks, but it doesn't really feel like that. In order to move ahead their steps have to be perfectly in time, and somehow that happens easily. Her niggles of unease have no time to grow when they're walking this quickly, and she feels something clean washing through her with the cold air.

They pass houses with lamp glow, but it must be late, no one else outside. The park gate is closed but not locked; it opens with a screech that follows them to the edge of the pond, where Aunt Peach used to throw crusts to the ducks and laugh at their bobbing heads. Charlie dumps the sack he's been carrying, a jumble of skates and laces, and there is some discussion about the ice as they sort them out. Nan is worried, and Ben tries to recall exactly how many freezing days there have been. Kez says, "I don't care," and she's out there first, the tails of her long red scarf working free and lifting as she goes faster and faster, until they can only hear the scrape of her blades, then Charlie's, following after.

It's cold, but soon they don't feel it, someone always holding Clare up as they follow the path of the almost-full moon, her body remembering how it's done. The push and the glide, sleeping muscles called on to work again; that's all she's thinking of. But as it gets easier, other thoughts seep in. Long cold days and the glittering skiffs of snow on the bumpy ice, her mother laughing as she thumped down on her thick skirts, and her father warming her frozen toes in his hands. The cold lips of a boy Clare barely knew, who skated her off to a place where the black branches swept low.

Out of the dark comes Ben's voice, calling, "Crack the whip!" and they join together, only five of them but the line feels longer, as if all the others have come back. Wee Alan at the centre, grown to a man, the sum of all their imaginings. Their mother and father on either side, Ross with his big fur hood thrown back, and even Aunt Peach, her filmy eyes grown clear in the night air. A weaving, jerking line, Clare at the end, holding tight to someone's fingers.

And then she just lets go. The momentum carries her off in a spin, but she doesn't fall, she holds on to her balance while the whirling inside slows down. And she tips her head back where she is, in the middle of the dark pond, far away from everyone, from the bushes and the overhanging trees. She can hear the others calling her name, and she understands then that it doesn't really matter who they are, who she might be. With her head tipped back she watches the breath leave her mouth, heading up to the sky, black as time and stretched over everything. And the pinpoints of light that are stars, so far away they might already be gone, but still sending their light for her to see.

SLEEPERS AWAKE

"Hell and damn and damn it and GOD DAMN IT!" Kez kicks at the crate and sends it into the empty street, kicks the one beside it, but it's frozen to the snowy ground, a pain in her toe that brings new tears to her eyes, and at the same time an undignified skidding and slipping. She takes deep breaths as she settles her shawl on her shoulders, tries to tamp the roaring rage, but it's no use; she kicks out again and this time goes right down, landing with a hard thump on her behind that shocks everything out of her. She'd laugh if someone was with her. What else could she do, sitting on the hard ground in the gloom, cold seeping in through her twisted skirts.

And there's that boy again, standing in the shadows by the warehouse, across the narrow street. Watching her from just beyond where the street light reaches, maybe laughing at her; certainly smiling. A smirky little smile, she's sure of it, though it's hard to see his face properly. His hair is somehow different, and she thinks he might be a little taller, but he hasn't changed much, he just doesn't. He wasn't ever a baby—well, not that she saw, but he must have been, mustn't he. Everyone was a baby once, and then a helpless child.

As she stands she sees the boy give a twitchy shiver; his jacket looks thin and his hands, balled up, don't quite fit into the shallow pockets. He must be cold, but why should she care about that, even the tiniest bit. His own fault, hanging about in the almost-dark, spying on people. She won't give him the satisfaction of looking back, no she won't, just a quick peek before she turns the corner. Maybe he's there, maybe he's not; all she can see is a hazy, far-off circle of light.

Her rage at herself keeps her warm as she walks, but the heat can't last all the way. She turns and turns again, each street smaller and darker, until she can pick out the peaked roof of their tall, narrow house. No time now to dwell on her terrible foolishness, and she gives her head a shake, as if she can flick it away. No time now because there's work to be done, cleaning and packing, the house where she was born become like a version of itself that might appear in a dream. Everything askew and a smell of damp, raw wood from the crates they've filled with bedding and carefully wrapped dishes. The idea of moving was one thing, but this is quite another. It's terrible, that's what it is, everything at sixes and sevens, outside and in. All *mixtie-maxtie*, as Aunt Peach would have said, back when she had things to say.

Kez hangs her shawl on the hook, sits down and unlaces her boots, wraps her hands around her frozen toes, and all the while the old woman invades her mind. Her vacant eyes and her lost, trembling smile, but that's not the one to be thinking about. She makes herself remember instead the earlier Peach, nasty old thing that she was. Some relation who was suddenly there, squatting in the middle of their lives.

There must have been arrangements, but the first Kez knew of her was the morning she opened the door to the little room off the kitchen. Looking for a place to hide from her brother Ross, who'd chased her down the stairs with a shoe in his hand. Inside, the blind was pulled tight, only a little bit of light leaking around the edges, and she was blinking her eyes, catching her breath, when suddenly something squawked up out of the murk. A witch or a horrible old brownie, with its cap all crooked and showing jutting big ears, the few tufts of hair on its head. Kez gave a scream, she couldn't help it, and the thing gave a louder one, and another and another, the sound of a rusty wheel lurching over a rutted track. And her mother rushed in and gave Kez a clout with the spoon she was holding, as if everything, *everything*, was her fault. The last thing she saw, as she ran from the room with her palms clapped over her own jugged ears, was an old woman huddled against the wall with her feet pulled up. Her mother kneeling, holding on to the twisted hands.

Her thawing toes begin that tingle, and she has to tense every muscle to keep from hopping about like a fool. It must be the coldest winter ever, or maybe she just feels it more in her older bones, thirty-two already—no, thirty-three. It's nearly impossible to believe she was once like the children she sees, running with their unbuttoned coats flapping, and it's been years since she's been skating on the pond. Years since she's splintered a skin of ice with her heel to hear that satisfying crackle, since a walk through the snowy streets made every bit of her feel alive. This winter there's a shiver deep in her bones, and the sleepless nights, when they come, are even more of a torment, too cold to get up and polish the silver or buff their shoes, with the stove banked in the barren kitchen.

Still, as their father used to say, things could always be worse. In one of his rare letters her brother Ross wrote of the terrible storms where he was, the howling wind and snow and how he had to tie a stout rope around his waist to take the few steps to the shed where the animals were kept. Once he had to break up the kitchen chairs to feed the fire that was all that kept them from freezing. And more than once they spent a day and a night wrapped in blankets and quilts, he and his wife telling every story they knew to keep the children occupied. She's never seen her niece, her nephews; none of them have. But when she thinks of them, she pictures the icicle children from one of Aunt Peach's stories. Pinched blue faces, and thin voices calling out from where they hang, trapped and shivering, from the eaves.

The kitchen is emptier than when she left; her sister Nan has been busy. As the last day looms closer they've packed everything they can, and the list of things they really need has grown shorter and shorter. Now down to four plates, four knives and spoons, the battered kettle, and the big cooking pot those things will be carried in when they leave. They've already moved some of the furniture, and Kez didn't want to but Nan and Clare went along to see it placed. They told her that the old settee and stuffed chairs looked shrunken and even embarrassed in their new surroundings. The brighter rooms revealed all the worn spots in their two carpets, while in what they already call the old house the bare floorboards echo with a desolate, alien sound. Kez knows the money she pilfered was nothing like enough for a new carpet, so she squashes that thought right down.

It's been going on for weeks, this move, more work than any spring cleaning, and more complicated; as they empty drawers and shift heavy furniture things keep turning up, churning up, each one a memory and a decision. After the boys dragged the brass-cornered trunk down from Clare's attic room, Kez and Nan found an old-fashioned dress that must have been their mother's, carefully folded beneath a tiny yellowed bonnet. Nothing to do but repack them, though they are things that have no real meaning for anyone still alive.

There were things that were less mysterious too, like Charlie's slingshot, discovered on top of the tall corner cupboard. Dust-covered but still working, as he proved with a wadded-up dishcloth. "Right there, all these years," Charlie said, turning it this way and that in his bigger hands. Still where their mother must have hidden it, after he startled the carter's horse; she told him she'd burned it in the stove. And then they had to picture her, tucking in her skirts and climbing up on the stool to push it out of sight. And they had to think again about her hard hand and her punishments, think about what she must have understood about being a boy, and how she maybe planned to give the slingshot back as a reward for some run of good behaviour that he never achieved.

"Where have you been?" Nan says from the doorway, and suddenly Kez feels so frail she almost tells her. Everyone thinks they're as close as two peas and they are, but once they were closer. They still never run out of things to say to each other, but there are also things they keep to themselves. And there are things they let go, as Nan does now, saying only, "I need your long arms. The good thimble's rolled under the bed and I can't reach."

"It's not your arms, it's your fat behind that's the problem," Kez says as she stands, and Nan blows out her round cheeks, and does a little shimmy with her hips.

Up in their room, their mother's sewing box is mounded with spools of thread that must have clattered and unrolled all across the boards. Nan tries to arrange them while Kez lies down on the floor and elbows her way into the farthest corner, thinking how dark it is here, how quiet. A good place to hide, though that's not a thing she's ever done. Her fingers close around the thimble and something else that is hard and round, wedged into a crack. When she wriggles out, her opening hand echoes a long-ago day and there it is, a tiny china teapot, painted with delicate blue flowers that are little more than dots.

"What was her name?" Kez says, though they both remember it. Lisbet, of course, the daughter of a man their father got talking to, likely in Armstrong's tavern. A man who had recently arrived to take over the running of a factory, with a girl just their age who was so mopey just now, and missing her friends back in Cobourg. A visit was arranged, a thing that only two fathers could have thought was a good idea. Kez and Nan knocked on the glossy door, their hair plaited so tightly their faces felt pulled and changed. Dressed in their best, and marking the twitch of scorn on the little girl's face before she said, in a syrupy voice, "Do come in."

There was tea and conversation in the parlour, questions about their school, although of course, as her mother said, Lisbet would be going back to Miss Simpson's. When the cakes were gone they were sent to the playroom, climbing the carpeted stairs behind Lisbet's flounces and frills. "You may sit there," she said, pointing to two low, painted chairs, and then she showed them all her toys and games and told them what fine quality they were, as if they wouldn't have the wit to know. She had a lot to say about the grand house she'd left behind, and its long green lawns. The white pony that was all her own, and how her father would buy her another as soon as he found one good enough. Kez crossed her fingers and said they'd also had ponies, called Star and Midnight, but of course they were too old for ponies now. "Actually," Lisbet said, "my father is going to buy me a real horse. Maybe two."

When she tired of talking Lisbet took down her china-faced dolls, one by one, from the shelf where they sat in a swirl of skirts, and told them their fancy names before she put each one back. Wilhelmina and Jocasta and Evangeline, Felicity and Charlotte. Over by the window there was a dollhouse, sitting on a table that made it taller than they were. Three floors of rooms all papered and furnished, and smaller dolls that lived in them. They played with it for a long time; Kez and Nan were the servant dolls and when Lisbet shook a little bell they had to clump up the staircase with a miniature tea service on a miniature silver tray, and pour for the Lisbet doll, who reclined on a velvet sofa. "You may curtsey and go," the Lisbet doll said, but each time they arrived back down in the kitchen, with its heavy black stove and hanging pots, the bell would ting and she would say, "More tea—I'm parched." Until the Kez doll knocked over the table as she passed it with her rocking walk, sending everything flying and making the real Lisbet stamp her foot and tell her she was horrid. Then they had to sit down on the hard, low chairs and watch as she brushed and dressed Jocasta's hair, until it was time for them to leave.

"You must come again," her mother said, already closing the door, while behind her Lisbet crossed her eyes and stuck out her tongue. When they were out of sight, around the corner, Nan opened her fist, her fingers spreading out like petals to reveal the little painted teapot, and two cups with the tiniest of handles. They ran the rest of the way home, cheeks flushed with the thrill of their wickedness, and for a long time after they took turns pouring, behind the closed door of their room.

"Will you have a cup of tea, Miss Moon?"

"Oh yes, Miss Jug, I'm terribly parched."

Kez drops the little teapot into the sewing box, just as Nan says, "Will you tell me now where you were all that time?"

"Keep your nose to yourself," she says, blinking away the picture that rises in her mind. The warm glow of the fringed lamps and the fire behind its screen, the doctor's kind face and her soft voice, so much worse than if she'd laughed aloud when she spoke of *unreasonable expectations*. There was a time Nan would have been in on everything from the start, but that's long past and how dare she ask her questions, as if she doesn't know it.

Downstairs the last of the soup is warming in the big pot, and if Clare remembers to pick up a loaf on her way home that will do them, with some left over for their breakfast. She'll be lugging her satchel of books, and her head will be spinning with ideas from the lectures she's been to, but she's more likely to remember than Charlie, who is reliable only in his unreliability, as their brother Ben likes to say.

He's still a bit of a worry, is Charlie, with his carelessness, and staying out all hours. Their mother always said he had too much charm for his own good, and said it to him every time he made her smile in spite of herself. If she was still alive she'd be fretting about his tired-looking eyes, the way money slips through his fingers. Still, he manages to pay his share, and the house is certainly more lively since he moved back.

It's often wild around the supper table, all five of them, until Ben married, slipping into the jokes and silliness of their childish selves, those bits of their characters that don't mean much, show much, until they spark off each other.

Charlie never said why Mr. Howell dismissed him from the jewellery shop, but he stepped right into a job in the new department store that suits him well, his dapper style and easy manner soon making him the top salesman of scarves and overcoats, of calfskin gloves and fine bristle brushes. He'd learned more than he thought from their tailor father, about fabrics and quality details, and he had a knack for convincing a man that those details mattered and would be noted. That this jacket might cost a little more but it was cut to the latest style in London, and sent an important message about his taste, his status.

It was even easier, Charlie said, if the man's wife came with him. The lightest of touches on her back as he guided her into a chair. The twitch of an eyebrow, from behind her husband, that told her they were in this together, that they both knew she would do the persuading, her opinion the one that mattered. Better still was when the wives came on their own, to pick up new handkerchiefs, or a gift for some occasion. *Tricks of the trade*, he called it, the way he flattered and listened. The accidental brushing of fingers as he showed the fine stitching inside a slim wallet, or the way he demonstrated how an expensive tie would look, the four-in-hand knot neat around his own smooth neck.

Just *tricks of the trade*, nothing wrong in it, and perhaps only natural that he would also become a trusted companion. He was out most evenings, escorting someone to the theatre, someone else to a concert, or a lecture. The tickets paid for,

gladly, by husbands too busy or uninterested to do it themselves. Such manners he had, he imagined the ladies saying
to each other. And a way of settling a woman's cloak on her
shoulders. A wooden box under his bed was slowly filling with
collar studs, jewelled cufflinks and other unasked-for gifts he
sometimes pawned when his wage wasn't enough to keep him.

These were things he told Kez, the night she heard crashing in the kitchen. When she crept down with the heavy
doorstop in her hand, and found him there, with his shirt mis-
buttoned and a sheepish, tipsy look that reminded her of their
father. He was trying to make a cup of tea in the moonlight that
flooded through the bare window and she did it for him, and
sat with him while he drank it, and talked and mumbled. "Ah,
the wives," Charlie said, a slow droop to his eye that was trying
to be a wink. Kez said that she didn't want to hear any more; it
wasn't true, but it didn't matter. He folded his arms on the table
and was instantly asleep, the moonlight hollowing his upturned
cheek and giving it a skull-like look that made her shiver.

The door swings open and Charlie and Clare come in from the
dark and the cold, in a flurry of talk and stamping feet. Clare
says she had to go back for the bread, but it worked out well
because she met Charlie and had company for the walk, and
was able to show him Aldebaran, and the stars in Orion's belt.
Her eyes are bright, her cheeks flushed with health as well as
the cold, proof, if someone was looking for it, that things can
change for the better. Not so many years ago that they feared
for her life and her mind, the doctor telling them the fever had
attacked her heart. She would have to live a quiet life, he said,
and take great care not to excite her body or her brain. But
when Clare heard that the University was opening a few places

for women she was determined to sit the entrance examination, and when she passed in the first rank, determined to take up her scholarship. For all their worry it's a joy to see her so happy, to hear her talk about all she's learning, even though Ben's the only one close to knowing what she's on about.

They used to tease Clare about where she came from; she didn't mind, she knew it was all in fun. Plucked from a tree like an apple or fallen off the back of a coal cart. She didn't seem to remember anything herself, and that was a blessing, so their mother said once. The state of the room they took her from, and the daft baggage who handed her over. It was the day of that terrible windstorm, all the small boats smashed in the harbour and two men blown from a high roof they were trying to patch. The windows rattling so loudly that Kez didn't hear the door open, turned from the stove to see her parents standing solemn in the doorway, holding a grubby little girl by the hands.

Ask no questions, you'll be told no lies; their father said he threw his shoe into a fairy whirlwind at the corner of Adelaide Street and chanted, *Mine is yours and yours is mine*, the way you had to, to rescue a stolen one. Since he had both shoes still on his feet they knew he didn't expect to be believed, and besides, sound carried in their little house. Even though they were sent upstairs they all heard Ross when he came home from the Works. His bluster and his silence when their father said, "Why else would anyone send word to us, when the mother went off without her?" It became a thing they knew, though no one ever said it aloud; what mattered was how it was, having a little child in the house again. Watching their mother that first day, bathing Clare with soft soap in the washtub and so carefully combing the knots from her wet hair, Kez saw a gentleness that they all must have received, even if they didn't remember it.

Their parents never said more about what had taken them out through the howling streets that day. They had their secrets too, and things they saw no reason to explain. Things that will never be known, now they're both gone, so really there's no point in wondering about them. Even the simplest, like who Aunt Peach was exactly, and why she was suddenly in their lives. Knowing wouldn't have changed the fact of her, the nastiness that oozed out all around her. "Come here and I'll tell you a story," Peach used to say, and it didn't take long for them to learn that it wasn't a kindness. All of her tales starting, *There once was a child . . .* A girl or a boy, sometimes disobedient, like the icicle children, but often just minding their business. Walking to market or tending the sheep, sent to fetch water from the stream. Their pure hearts no protection from the terrible things that unfolded, the attentions of the malicious spirit, cloaked in a harmless disguise. It tormented Kez, wondering how you could ever know which leaf to pluck, which stone to heave to break the spell. And poor Charlie woke screaming night after night, babbling about the Water Horse that carried children into the lake, their entrails all that ever washed ashore.

It was war for a time, she remembers. Secret and determined, and who knew exactly how it started. "Help me up, child," Aunt Peach used to say, from her warm chair by the stove, and they learned to brace themselves for the hidden, vicious pinch. Maybe that came first, or maybe the sharp tack on that same chair, or the clever idea to remove the paper from the hook before her clockwork visits to the privy. Kez

remembers it going on for months, even years, a series of skir-
mishes, but Nan says, "Surely not."

The space between them now is tumbled with separate memories, from the time Nan was gone, and with their separate
thoughts. But in those days they were together all day and
all night and Kez says, "How can you not remember that,
when I do?" She thinks how most of the pleasure goes out of
the remembering when there's no one to really share it with.
Something like the way that long-ago war changed when
Peach's mind began to go. Too easy then, the salt in her teacup,
her nightcap wadded up deep in the bedclothes.

In the early days, when they still thought something
might be gained by complaining, their mother scolded them
for their lack of charity. "She doesn't mean anything by it,"
she said, and told them they needed to look through to the
good heart within. When the wandering started, Kez wondered if that was what happened when you became old. If
something was sloughed off, like the cocoon they watched,
deep in the leaves of the currant bush in the yard. The thing
that would be a butterfly emerging, all folded and wet and
trembling in the air.

She and Nan talked about it; they would have, in those
days when they spoke every thought aloud to each other.
Falling about laughing as they pictured Aunt Peach flapping
bright wings and wafting away. It didn't fit at all with her
clouding eyes, the hairs poking out of her chin. The confusion maybe more like something that slowly settled from
above, blurring everything, the way a gentle and steady snow
mounded and softened the prickly holly bushes that grew by
the cemetery gate. Whatever the cause, how could you keep

hating an old woman who got lost on the front walk? Who gave the sweetest of smiles to whoever took her hand to lead her home.

Kez thinks that she could ask Ben about the war; it was his idea about the privy, after all, so he must remember. But he and Edith are still making their way back from their honeymoon, now visiting with her aunt in Chicago. According to their last telegram they won't arrive until moving day, when there'll be too many other things to do and talk and laugh about.

It's still strange to think of Ben as a married man. He's been known to dance the Racket in the kitchen, and to honk like a goose or eat a spoon of salt when he loses at Forfeits, but he's always been steady and serious, and quite matter-of-fact about what fills his mind, everything he calls *Science*, though it's more like magic. Electric sparks and wires, and words that float for miles through the air. They never really thought of him as a man who would take the time to find and court a woman, and the first they knew of Edith was when he told them he'd invited her for tea. Nan opened her eyes wide and said, "Today? You great *gauk*—today?"

"You don't need to fuss," he said, but the more he told them, the more they did. Miss Edith Patricia Anderson, daughter of the man who owned the telegraph company where Ben had always worked, and properties all over the city besides. The man who had always taken an interest in Ben, and even paid for the patent for the new relay system he'd invented. Mr. Anderson sometimes invited Ben to dine at his fine house, and when they remembered that, they realized that he had, in fact, mentioned Edith before. They'd waited up for him the first time but he didn't remember much about the food, said he tried to keep his eyes on the daughter, who sat across the table, so he would know which fork, which spoon to use.

They were expecting someone like Lisbet. Someone holding up fancy skirts as she crossed the threshold, someone looking down her nose and not caring that they knew it. But there was no side to Edith at all, no airs. By the end of that first visit they were all half in love with her, her easy conversation and the way she laughed so often. A real laugh, not one that sounded like tinkling spoons. She seemed to fill the room, even being so small, barely up to Ben's shoulder, and he not a tall boy. Tall man.

Edith knew things about them all that Ben must have told her, which meant, they understood, that they'd spent a great deal of time together. And somehow the things she knew and the things she asked about made them sound, made them *feel*, so interesting, so unique. They were still buzzing when Ben came back from walking her home, had replayed the whole visit while they filled the dishpan and brushed up crumbs from the lemon cake she had said was the best, just the best. "What did you think?" he said. "That I'd fall for some fizgig?"

Awake in her bed that night, Kez wondered what it would be like. To be a person that everyone wanted to be close to, like a magic spell cast but with nothing bad behind it. A person any hero would ride miles to rescue. When she was young, and even not so young, she used to climb to the attic, with its window that showed a view over the tumbled rooftops, of a river and far-off green. The place he would come riding from, a speck growing steadily larger and bringing the green fields with him. All the sooty brick and stone dissolved as the spell was broken, all the people revealed in their true, hideous forms, scurrying away to hide from the pounding hooves, from the clods of earth spinning in the horse's wake. And she herself revealed in all her beauty, the one he'd been searching for the whole world over, the one he was always meant to find.

Clare found her there once, after it had become her room, and Kez was glad of the clean nightdress she held in her arms, snapped that if it was privacy Clare wanted she could do her own washing and tossed it in a heap on the floor. Downstairs she rattled the poker in the stove, though it was burning just fine, and Nan said, "What now?"

Later, when Clare said she was sorry, Kez said, "That's all right then," and that meant she was sorry too.

When they've eaten, Clare settles at the table with her books and Charlie says he's off to a performance at the Opera House. "Ooh, I'm so *cultured*," Kez says, standing behind him at the little mirror and mimicking the way he smooths his eyebrows with a licked fingertip.

"Will you just *leave* it," Charlie says, his words as sudden as a slap in the face, and he bumps out through the door, still pulling on his coat.

Kez catches Clare's eye, says, "Oh pish, he knows I'm only teasing."

"You are always at him about it," Clare says. "What do you expect him to do—stay in and watch us putter around?"

"Don't be silly," Kez says, as Clare begins to gather up her things. She tells Kez she's going to read in bed, where it's warmer, which is ridiculous; surely no place is warmer than this kitchen, with the stove burning high and the kettle steaming.

Of course she was only teasing; Charlie knows that, everyone does. She doesn't mean anything by it, she's soft as butter inside, they all know that. These people who are the only ones in the world who really know her. She crashes the dishes in the basin, and the thought comes, *What if they don't?* What if she's all wrong about that as well? She feels suddenly dizzy, staring down at her red hands in the hot water as if they are strange objects belonging to someone else, but she closes her eyes for a moment, and the feeling passes.

Maybe she does ride Charlie for his gadding about, but why would that matter? Maybe she'd like to go along to the Opera House herself, would he ever think of that? Or to that play he said was so hilarious. There used to be more to *do*, that's all, they were always going somewhere for tea, or meeting up for a picnic, or to hear that soprano—what was her name? Months ago, that was. She tries to remember the time before that; before she can stop it the memory slips through the door. An evening in the Misses Simp's fussy house, with a few people from the church, little cakes and cups of tea and Mrs. Tolton, as usual, singing that German piece, while her husband played the piano. Then some games that perked things up; it was even quite fun for a while, with Hunt the Ring, and Do As I Do, and even Twenty Questions was lively, with everyone trying to guess first. Until they were narrowing down an animal, and someone said, "Are my ears big or small? Oh, sorry, are my ears enormous?" A voice shouted out "Keziah!" just as someone else said "Elephant!" and everyone laughed, and she did too; what else could she do? And her treacherous sister reached over and squeezed her hand, a thing anyone who was looking would have seen.

"One thing I won't miss is that privy," Nan says, as she comes in the back door, blowing on her hands. "The luxury of a water closet—can you believe it?" Then she says, "Oh perk up, Jug, why don't you. Just one more night of this muddle, and anyway, you were the one first keen on it." It's true that she was; swept up in Edith's enthusiasm, how could she not have been? The words tumbling so fast from her lovely mouth, and the way she clasped her hands together beneath her chin and said, "What do you think—isn't it a marvellous idea?"

They were sitting around the kitchen table after a cold supper, the windows pushed wide to catch any bit of breeze, Edith so frequent a visitor by then that they never went near the parlour. She'd been to see a house her father owned, several blocks to the east. Two houses, actually, that had at some point been joined across the front but were otherwise quite separate. Edith's idea was that they should all move there, like the one big family they would soon become. She and Ben would have one side, the rest of them the other, and when the children came, wouldn't it be grand to be living like that, so much easier for her to call on them if she needed help, and to visit back and forth.

They needed a little fixing up, these houses, but it would be so much better, didn't they think, than her father's plan to build on the lot on Grosvenor. "That will take forever," she said, "and Ben will get quite tired of me while we're waiting, and marry someone else." They knew she didn't mean that, the part about Ben, but Nan thought her father would be sure to object. "Maybe a little," Edith said, smiling her sweet smile. "But he'll come around."

They've always thought that Mr. Anderson must have had other plans for his daughter. Wondered if he regrets bringing Ben home, the favour he had always shown him, that maybe gave her ideas before they'd even met. He's been nothing but courteous to all of them, and made a nice speech at the small wedding. But it's not as if they really *know* him, though they've heard about the black, brooding moods, the ones even Edith can't jolly him from. He told Ben once that he reminded him of the boy he wished he'd been, one who didn't have everything so easy, and they wondered why anyone would wish for something like that.

"Why not?" Kez had said that day, after Ben and Edith left for the recital at the church. Visions of sunny rooms in her head, and babies bouncing on her lap. Wouldn't it be good to see the back of their landlord, the way he'd been pushing their rent up and up? And hadn't they been saying that with Ben needing to support his own household they'd have to take lodgers, and wouldn't it be better to do that in a house with more room, and more rooms? What point could there be against it, except for sentiment, and what was that worth when you really thought about it?

In the end they all agreed, and it didn't take long to be so caught up in the practicalities there was no room left for doubts. When Kez wrote out her list of tasks, Charlie gave her a mocking salute, and dodged the flat of her hand, but he's stayed in a few evenings lately to help, and tied on an old apron to go after the cobwebs in the darkest corners. "All hail the man of the house," Charlie said, as he lifted the corners of that apron and curtsied.

Kez walked by the new place once, in the fall, saw the doors all open for the painters and paperers Edith had hired, heard the sounds of hammering and sawing. But she had no wish to go inside, as the others frequently did, to check the progress and measure the many windows. She wanted to finish with the old life completely before she crossed that threshold, not trail any of it back and forth to the new. Though she hadn't been sad, she realized that she hadn't been happy for years, not like this. Nothing but plans in her head in the night, and the satisfaction of crossing things off her tacked-up list, one by one.

When she dumps the basin from the cold back step, he's peeking over the fence, that boy. A little hard to make out, with only the light of the moon and the stars, but there seems to be something red on either side of his chin, maybe mittens he's found for his cold hands. The fence is taller than he is so he must be holding himself up, which would be difficult with his skinny arms, and must be why he drops out of sight so quickly.

The boy comes and goes as he pleases; he always has. Often he's gone so long she forgets all about him, but then she'll catch a glimpse as she waits to cross a street, or takes a short-cut through the park. Maybe he's sitting on top of a loaded cart that goes by, or shinnying up the big tree by the pond. Sometimes he's standing quite still while all the people move around him; they jostle him as they pass, making him shift to catch his balance, but their minds must be flitting around their own lives, and they don't seem to notice what they've done.

There are times, like today, when he seems to be mocking her, but mostly he's just there, his expression blank as a biscuit. There's something sad about his eyes, though she's not sure why she thinks so; she can't remember him ever being close enough to see that clearly. Now that he's back she knows she'll see him everywhere for a time, and it's something like that dream she often has, the way she never knows where it starts, but somewhere in the middle she recognizes it, knows what it is and how it will go.

It's crossed her mind, of course it has, that he might be dead. Maybe one of those babies that made their mother shake her head and say, "That one will never make old bones." It's crossed her mind, but she doesn't really believe it; unlike Clare, she thinks the dead stay where they belong, no point in looking for them in the shadowed corners, or wondering if they're happy or sad. Her parents up in Heaven, and if there's any fairness, Peach gone hurtling back to wherever she came from. Besides, what difference would it make? Sometimes he's there, sometimes he's not, and she's far too cold, too tired to spend any more time thinking about it.

They hear Charlie's stumbling footsteps on the stairs as they get ready for bed. A muffled curse and the sound of him throwing himself down on top of his covers. "I hope it works out," Nan says, meaning the man with the cart who owed Charlie a favour and has promised to come in the morning, promised to move their things cheaply.

"If it doesn't," Kez says, "we'll make a parade." She pictures them marching through the streets, carrying their beds, the kitchen table, beating the big kitchen pot like a drum. Like the circus, with a bedecked elephant leading the way—no, not that. Maybe a camel, or a dancing bear.

"Didn't Mam always love a parade," Nan says, and it's true, though Kez had quite forgotten. She's been dead seven years now, their father longer, and longer still since Ross walked away. One of her stories about Wee Alan, who died, was how he marched up the ship's gangway and gave a salute, like a proper little soldier.

If anyone asked, their mother could tell them everything about Wee Alan. The colour of his eyes and the way they dipped down a little at the outside corners, the way he held his crossed hands out to catch a ball of yarn. She didn't often say, because it was rare that anyone mentioned him, but the details must have been so clear in her mind, as if they were always there, just waiting to break through. Clare said maybe that made it hard for Ross, who came right after, but Kez said, "And so? Everybody's got things that are hard for them."

Even though they turn it every spring and every fall there are hollows in the mattress from the weight of their sleeping bodies. Like an embrace, the settling in, but the years of moulding also mean that it's impossible to feel comfortable any other way. There's a sudden thump above their heads, which will be Clare's book falling from her drowsing hands, a thing that will rouse her enough to blow out the light. *I'll never hear that again*, Kez thinks. That exact sound, and knowing what it is. The room Clare has chosen in the new house is on the same floor, at the other end of the hall from theirs. The one with windows on two sides and the best view of the night sky. From what the others have described Kez pictures a very long hallway, lined with closed, properly fitting doors. There could be anyone doing anything behind them.

"Remember that game?" Nan says, and of course she is already thinking about it. The first night Clare was in the house she was put to bed between them, and she didn't make a peep, but they could feel how her whole body trembled. So they told her about the rule, how in this bed, if one person wanted to turn over, they all had to do it together. They had to say *one two three*, they had to say *one two three—whoops!* and roll over at the exact same time. "Do you hear me, Clare?" Kez said, and she had to say it again before Clare answered with a soft *yes*.

"And do you need to turn over, Clare?" Nan said, and she said *yes* again. So—*one two three whoops!*—they all rolled over, and said it and did it again, and again, until Clare had tired herself into sleep with her giggling. A thing they did night after night after night, for who knows how long.

Just talking about it makes them both need to roll, and Kez wonders why that is. Why is it that once the thought comes into your mind you can't possibly be comfortable the way you were. And that makes her think, of course it does, of the summer before Clare arrived, when Nan eloped and she had the whole bed to herself, the first and only time. She remembers tossing and stretching, and often lying flat like a corpse in a coffin, but with open eyes looking into the dark.

"I thought I saw him today," Nan says now, their minds in the same place yet again. "Just for a moment I thought it," she says. "I was looking out the front door for you and there was a man walking down the street, and just for a moment I thought it was him." Tam O'Malley, charmer and thief, cause of all kinds of destruction. Ashes in his wake that drift through the air, through the years.

He was the older cousin of a boy they knew at school, come to visit for a while. They met him by the lake on a first mild day of spring when so many people had gone down to look out at the open water. Tam had money in his pocket and a store of jokes and riddles; he bought them warm buns and walked them partway home, had them laughing until they ached. They were fourteen, they were fifteen that spring, felt itchy and dangerous, and their mother often scolded them for taking so long with any errand, not knowing how far they ranged to pass by places he'd said he might be. Tam was always glad to see them, swept off his cap with a flourish, and he always had stories to tell. "I'm not shocking you now, am I?" he said, though he would have known he was.

It wasn't clear just when he made a choice. *"All for one,"* he'd say when they were out walking. "Do you know that story?" Brandishing an imaginary sword, swishing and lunging, and laughing at the sour look from an old man who had to dodge his flailing arm. On the narrow pathways in Victoria Park, sometimes one was behind, sometimes the other, and Kez only remembers one time, when she'd tripped and twisted her ankle, that they settled her on a bench and went on for a while alone. Fool that she was, no more prepared than their parents were for the empty half of the bed, the note on the kitchen table.

"I didn't tell you so you wouldn't have to lie to anyone," is what Nan said when they were alone on the rainy day she came back. "I was thinking of you," Nan said, as they settled to sleep that night, and what could Kez do but believe her. Choose to believe her, though she has always known how her sister, with her round, kind face, can say anything at all and not be doubted. If Lisbet's mother had sent a policeman to their door, that long-ago day, it's Kez he would have come for, not Nan, who always looked like butter wouldn't melt. The same way it was Kez that Aunt Peach pointed out with her crooked finger when someone kicked her shin hard, beneath the kitchen table.

Over the years she's come to believe that it was an accomplice Tam was looking for, not a wife, and at times she's been close to saying it. She's not used to holding her tongue, but she knows that would be a step too far, that it would undo all the careful mending between them. Nan has told her some of it, but even Kez doesn't know everything she got up to, those months she was gone. "I would have followed him anywhere," she said. "Done anything. I did." Travelling from town to town, following the fairs, any spectacle. Jostling through each crowd, leaving empty pockets in their wake, and spending every cent on meals in fancy dining rooms, dressed up like dandies. "Such laughs," Nan said. Until the day she got careless and stopped to watch the rope walker dancing his little jig in the sky. A hard hand coming down on her shoulder, her panicked eyes catching the back of Tam's new brown jacket as he walked quickly away.

Exactly what came after is a thing Nan has kept to herself. At some point it involved their parents, and a fine they could ill afford, but the apologies and forgiveness stayed between the three of them. "They were softer than I thought," is all she's ever said. Kez planned a frosty silence, but it didn't last beyond the first meal, everyone else carrying on as if there'd never been an empty space at the table. She was still determined not to ask a thing, but before they slept she found herself telling Nan about the ribbon she won at the picnic on the Island, and the time just that week she saw Ross walking arm in arm with a woman, her hips sashaying like anything.

When she said that, Nan told her they'd had it all wrong, the things they'd wondered about men and women. "There's all kinds of ways," she said. "Like that," Nan whispered once in a shop, nodding toward the grocer's wife who was bent over, scooping apples from the bottom of a barrel. "Like a *dog*?" Kez whispered back, the strangest picture forming in her mind of the fat grocer with a spaniel's head. Sometimes Nan just raised an eyebrow when they walked past a kneeling housewife rubbing hard at her brass doorknob, or a man with a hosepipe spraying the dusty street. At moments like that, when their shaking shoulders bumped and they tried so hard not to look at each other, when their laughter finally spurted out—at moments like that they were as close as they ever had been.

Things work themselves out if you leave them alone; that's what their father always said. A thing that drove their mother mad, and madder still when he was proved right. A man settling a forgotten bill just before the rent was due, a neighbour gifting them with a pair of shoes her daughter had outgrown. She and Nan have found a way to go on, without ever saying, and it's been so long now that Kez wonders sometimes if she only imagines the difference, though she has no idea why she'd do that. Surely it's real, what you think and what you remember. Otherwise you'd be as scrambled as Aunt Peach was at the end, as loony as that professor of Clare's, who told them in the first class to imagine a world where nothing that they thought they knew was true.

Her prize ribbon turned up when they were going through the little room off the kitchen. Kez poked it deep into the fire, watched it twitch and shrivel. Such a silly thing to have been proud of, but it was the first time she'd won anything, hopping over the line with her ankle tied to Mabel Crichton's from school, instead of always hobbling in third with her own sister. She wore Nan's pale green dress that day; served her right for leaving it behind. And a little straw bonnet that covered her ears, and though she hadn't even wanted to go to the church picnic, on the ferry ride to the Island she felt a little buzz of excitement, as if wonderful things could happen.

After the races, as she was making her way back to where her mother had settled with their food, she stumbled over a stone, and a warm hand clasped her arm and kept her from falling. A young man a little shorter than she was, with slicked-down hair and a smooth face. When she met him again later, as it was growing dark, it was only natural that they should begin to walk together, their steps somehow taking them away from the circle of light and sound, and into the sighing trees. She thought it was going to happen, and it did; he took her hand and they stopped walking, his lips bumped into hers and stayed there, and she thought, *So this is what it's like.* Not much to make a fuss about really, this kissing, but nice to be able to say that she'd done it. She couldn't wait to tell Nan, then remembered that Nan was gone.

Well, that's enough of that, was her next thought; it was getting late and her mother would be cross if they had to go looking for her when they were ready to leave. But the young man pressed on with his wet lips, his fingers digging into her shoulders, and then, to her astonishment, she felt his foot hook around the back of her calf. She knew that move, a girl who grew up with three wrestling brothers, and she pushed hard on his chest and gave him a good crack on the nose with her sharp elbow. The sound of his curses fading to nothing behind her as she walked quickly back to the light. "There you are," her mother said. "Help me fold this blanket." Then she said, "What have you been doing? Your nice ribbon's gotten all crumpled."

That's how she remembers it, that's what happened; it must be, or why would she remember it? When she told Nan, long after, she said she'd seen him again in the ferry line, with his nose all purple and swollen. She didn't think she really had, but she might have. "Good for you, old Jug," Nan said. "Good for you."

The dream announces itself as it always does, with the sound of a horn, with far-off music and laughter. This time she's in a boat on a river and her father is rowing, his face tilted up to the sun. Ross is splashing beside them, with a streak of soot on his face, and then everything changes. She needs to wake up; there's a smell of damp earth as she struggles with her heavy eyes, and they open in the dream just before they really do. She sees the giant face and knows she's deep in the fairy knoll, where Thomas the Rhymer is rousing himself for battle, his heavy head propped on his enormous, stony arm, and she is so tiny beside him.

In their bed Nan snuffles in her sleep and Kez knows she'll be awake now for hours, at the mercy of the thoughts in her head. *Unreasonable expectations*—the phrase floats up and there's no escape from thinking about what a fool she's been. A fool, and a thief and a liar besides; she should be locked up in jail, it's what she deserves. Going along like an idiot child who believed all those stories of rescue, of transformation.

In the dark she slaps her cheek, thumps her chest, and though the clipping no longer crackles, she imagines the sound. She's been wearing it next to her skin for weeks, tucked into her chemise. The newsprint now soft as flannel with bits rubbed away, but she folded it carefully, to protect the important part. She could burn it too, but she thinks it more fitting to leave it where it is, blackening her skin as it shreds away to nothing.

You make your own luck, her mother always said, and that's what she thought she was doing. Breaking a spell that might have been cast at the moment of her birth, or later, when Peach took shape in the gloom. It was an evening like any other, with an autumn tang in the air. The rest were all in bed and she was tidying up a few last things, folding the newspaper Ben had left spread out on the table. The picture caught her eye, above the advertisement for the Electro-Therapy Institute, on Church Street. A drawing of a woman's head, in profile, who looked so serene, so happy. The smiling curve that was half her mouth, and her hair dressed to show the flattest, most delicate swirl of ear.

She might have tossed the paper in the kindling box and thought no more about it. She might have shown someone, shown Nan; no matter what, they've always been braver and better together. Instead she let the idea settle and spread, so proud of herself for recognizing the secret sign. It's Science, of course it is, as Ben always says, that will make everything better. The next day she walked down Church Street, put her hand to the gleaming door and asked the cost, as if she was someone with every right to be there. The next step, simply, to find the three dollars, which was more than Charlie made in a week, but less than Ben did, and not an impossible sum. She thought of looking for some work she could do, but how could she explain it? And how to keep the money for herself, without saying why?

Kez tosses her head in the dark, and wonders how she didn't even feel the weave of the new spell settling around her, the evil that she did, telling herself that the others would understand if they knew, all the while being so careful that they wouldn't. How could she not have heard the gurgling laugh of whatever creature was watching, so delighted to see her plotting, the pathetic excuses she made to herself. Telling herself that if she made sure to eat less, no one else would really suffer for the money she took from the housekeeping jar. "Maybe you're losing your mind," she told Nan, who was puzzled when she tipped it out to count. "Soon you'll be drooling in a chair like old Peach, but don't worry, Moon, I'll wipe your chin for you."

She kept the coins in a little cloth purse Clare had made when she was learning to sew, adding one or two at a time, and the sound they made when she hefted it was the music of her transformed life. She thought briefly of raiding the box under Charlie's bed for something to pawn, telling herself that none of it was well-gotten, that he was so careless he wouldn't even notice; a mercy that she didn't do it, but that's the smallest of comforts now. She thinks instead of how she felt this morning, the grand day finally arrived. She slipped out the door, wondering if this was how Ross had felt, how Nan had, walking toward a new life. Thinking already of the welcome she would receive when she came back changed. And somewhere up ahead, a vision of a hazy-faced husband, of children toddling across a gleaming floor. Money enough to spread around, so that everyone would know what a good and kind person she really was.

In the dark she presses her hands to her mouth. The long moan she's stifled rolls through her body instead, and she doesn't know how she'll survive it. She's always thought that the worst thing is for others to know; that the pinch could be borne, as long as you didn't let on. All wrong about that too, this is far worse. She's shamed herself, in some deep and total way. Fooled herself, caught up in a bubble of hope, as if it would float her away, when all it did was leave something too fragile between her and the malevolent world.

There's no stopping it now, the memory of that warm and quiet room. The crackle of the fire, and the soft scratch of the pen as the doctor made her notes. She looked like the drawing in the newspaper, except for the spectacles and the hair; her eyes, seen straight on, were so gentle. Beside her desk was the magic machine and it looked, with its wires and dials, like something Ben might have rigged up when he was younger.

"So you feel generally unwell," the doctor had said, and she asked Kez to tell her more; it would help determine the course of the treatment. "Well," Kez had said, trying to think. She began to answer, and before she knew it her mouth got ahead of her. She heard herself saying all kinds of things about the way she felt the cold, and the sleepless nights, about having to take charge of things and the way her brothers and sisters always teased her because of it but really, how else would anything get done? And how this move, which had started out as such a good and exciting thing, had turned everything upside down. Nothing where she expected it to be, not even her thoughts. She said that the way she felt lately, the way it really felt, was like that game they played as children. When they tied a blindfold over your eyes and spun you around, and you bumped hard into walls, and that sent you bouncing into something else, stumbling over stools and rucks in the carpet, and all you could hear was everyone laughing.

After she'd blotted her eyes she said something about her ears, asked how many treatments it would take before they lay nice and flat. The doctor's startled blink was like a mesmerist snapping his fingers; in an instant Kez was brutally awake, but with the complete knowledge of the ridiculous, shameful things she'd been saying. The doctor was speaking kindly, saying something about other benefits, about expectations, but Kez could barely make it out; the chair rocked as she stood up and the doorknob rattled in her hand until she turned it the right way. The next thing she remembers is her pounding feet, out in the snowy street, and a voice called after her, but she didn't stop.

Things could always be worse; she tries to imagine that. Worse if she'd told any of them where she was going, worse if she'd said she'd come back with a big surprise. Worse if the new house was somehow next door to the Institute, instead of so many blocks away. Worse, maybe, if there wasn't a new house, if she had to go on living between these walls that had witnessed it all. And definitely worse if she hadn't realized her idiocy until after the treatment, when she'd already handed over her sack of coins. She'll have to sneak them back into the jar, the same way she took them out; maybe working backwards will be something like an undoing. Maybe it would have been worse if she'd landed on her head, not her bottom, when she fell in the icy street. If she'd forgotten who she was and had to live out the rest of her life with people who were strangers to her. Or maybe that would have been better.

Her mother used to say that everything would look better in the morning. Kez opens her eyes to grey light so she must have slept, and slept deeply; Nan is gone, and she hears voices and clattering from the kitchen below. She folds up their sheet and quilt, ready to go, and heads down, wondering how she feels. Not calm exactly, more limp as a wrung-out rag. And relieved, somehow, to find she's still here, not vanished in a puff of black smoke.

Charlie has been up early, made tea and toasted bread, all of it on the table with a little pot of the currant jam she loves; Nan says she's been saving it for today. Charlie says, "Miss MacFarlane," as he pulls out a chair for her, and she understands that he's apologizing for his slam out the door.

"Thank you, kind sir," she says as she sits down.

"I thought I'd feel sadder," Clare says, and Nan says she thought the same. They talk about that and Kez watches them all, her brother and her sisters, their familiar faces and the familiar things they say. She thinks that she'll find a way to make it up to them, although they'll never know that's what it is.

They've barely finished packing up their dishes when they hear the cart, the man Charlie knows, with two strong boys to help him. Everything begins to move quickly; their boots thunder up and down the stairs, in and out, and they shout to each other and joke, and one sings a loud song about a maid on the shore. Two trips it will take, they decide; somehow there's always more than you think. Clare and Charlie go along on the first one, to open the door and to be there if Ben and Edith come in on an earlier train. Kez and Nan sit on two chairs in the kitchen, the table already gone, sharing the last of the tea in the old cracked mug that they'll pitch out the back door when they're done. "Here we go, then," Nan says, and Kez says, "Here we go," and they sit there, not touching, but it feels like they are, until the men return.

When everything else is loaded Kez persuades Nan to ride with the cart, while she does the final look around. It's a milder day, and she says she may even walk down. If Nan feels like it, when she's seen everything unloaded into its proper place, maybe she can walk up, and they'll meet halfway. "Why not?"

Nan says, and as the cart rolls away she calls, "Take care of yourself," as if they'll be apart for years.

It's so quiet then; it can't be possible, but Kez thinks this might be the first time, in all her years, that she's been alone in the house. Empty, it seems a small and shabby place. The bare floors, though swept and washed, are stained and gouged, the walls all crooked and cracked. The ill-fitting doors to the bedrooms creak when she pushes them open, and she thinks of the fairies and their jewelled gowns, that fade to nothing in the light of day.

In their parents' room, with the big dresser gone, she sees the bare wall where the paper ran out that day they worked together to finish it, as a surprise for their mother. Their father had them sign their names with a thick pencil and there they all are, even Ross, even Clare, though Kez thought they'd done this before she came to them. The new people will no doubt cover their signatures with paint and paper, but that doesn't matter; she'll always know they're there.

When she climbs to the attic, she sees that they've left mounds of grit in the corners. The broom is gone, and she thinks briefly of scooping it up in her bare hands, but that would be silly. She feels suddenly like a soldier, come back from a hundred-years war. Like the fiddler who walked out of the fairy mound, and found that everyone he knew was long gone, long dust. The traces they've left here are all dirt and damage, and the new family will add its own. As will the one after them, and after that, damage on damage, as long as the house keeps standing. "Oh *fiddle*," she says aloud, and feels better for it.

————

She comes out through the door for the last time, and the boy is sitting on the front steps, a few houses down. Looking sideways at her, with his cheek resting on his drawn-up knees. It's probably been longer than she thinks, and she'll have to walk quickly to meet Nan. But she stands still for a moment and there's a sound of things melting, the icicle children all dripping in the afternoon sun. "You'll come with me?" she says to the boy, and he seems to say that he will.

BELLA

You look sad entering your dream
Whose long currents yield return to none.
—EILÉAN NÍ CHUILLEANÁIN

January

In the long afternoons my daughter wants stories, but she's too old, she says, for the one about the foolish brothers. For the one about the changeling child, or the maiden in the tower, letting down her long, long hair. The winter sun sets early, staining the cold sky, and her face fades against the pillow as the room grows darker.

It should be a simple thing, telling the real stories she wants to hear. I start to talk and the words come, and carry me along until I find myself on the edge of something I must back away from, skip around. I can tell her about the clearing in the forest, about the cabin and the sound of birds in the clear air. I can tell her about the wood shavings curled in my father's beard, but not that I saw him blaze like a lightning-struck tree. Flames from his fingertips, from the top of his head. I can tell her my brothers' names and their mischief but not the way they were found, burned into each other's arms.

We have moved Edie's bed downstairs by the parlour window, although it's a quiet street and there's not much to see. Children dawdling on their way to school and later the bustling women, baskets hooked over their arms. Sometimes a scruffy black dog, skittering along with his nose close to the ground. It's a well-built house and the sounds that reach us are faint, the whisper of a buggy's wheels or runners, the jingle of harness. When the flames leapt, our old horse kicked down the loose-hinged door my father kept meaning to fix; he ran into the night, sparks flicking from his long, wild tail.

Angus is certain that Edie's getting better and I'm not saying he's wrong. Only that I can't think in those long stages of con-valescence or decline. I see him through the window, coming home at the end of the day, know the pause before he turns the handle of the door. The first words we say to each other—was it a bad day, or a better one? How much sleep, fever or not, and what was I able to tempt her to eat. So much like the way we used to greet each other when she was newly born and every detail a marvel.

Before he goes in to her, Angus pumps water to wash his hands, splashes his face and runs his wet hands through his hair. "Well, well," he says, in a voice full of cheer, and he usually has something in his pocket, a bit of hard candy or a smooth black stone, a page from a book he found lying beneath a bench at the station. Things like the small gifts he brought home years ago, and though she's just turned fourteen Edie receives them with that much delight, rubs the smooth stone between her fingers, or reads the mysterious page out loud. When she's strong enough he props her pillows higher, and she dips her own spoon into the broth. We eat our meal with her, Angus and I at the little table he moves from its place by the wall. Sometimes our knees touch beneath it, the closest we are these days.

Edie still loves to hear about the big telegraph office in the city, about the way her father and I first met. Angus raises his eyebrows when I tell her what a dandy he was, and how full of himself, like the other bonus men, their fingers a blur as they tapped the key. "Oh now," he says, when I tell her how the girls used to jostle to be the one who carried the message slips to his desk. Again and again she wants to hear about our secret language, about the time he carried Aunt Nan's shopping basket as the three of us strolled between the butcher and the grocer. His long fingers tapping on the handle: *Meet me tonight. Meet me tonight.*

"And you did," Edie says, and I say, "Yes, I did." Telling it like it was a childish prank, tiptoeing down the back stairs when the moon was high, easing open the door. I tell her we went walking through the empty streets, and once all the way down to the lake, the moonlight spreading a silver path, as if that was the point of it all. Not the secret places he led me to, the messages tapped out on my skin. How foolish I was, thinking that I was nothing like the girls who sobbed in the cloakroom. That the things he groaned in my ear were words he'd never said before.

The doctor comes every week, looking so rumpled and tired. All the sickness, in winter, and so much weeping, the muffled black processions moving past our window when I'm not quick enough to pull down the shade. I know it's not fair, the way I've taken against him. It's not his fault that there's nothing to do but wait. "She's better each time I see her," he says, but I can't let myself believe him. Angus does, and if he's home when the doctor comes they take a glass together, talking and sometimes laughing, that way men do when women are just out of earshot.

If Angus is not there I give the doctor tea at the kitchen table, and stare at his scalp between the strands of white hair, at the purplish lump of his nose. The thick fingers around the cup, that slid the stethoscope down the neck of Edie's nightgown, that pulled at her eyelid and squeezed all her painful joints. The day she slid to the floor at school, and was carried home limp with fever, I knew that all the fear, all the sorrow I'd ever felt, was only practice.

"Thank you, my dear," the doctor says as he sets down his cup, and I remember that he has his own sorrows, and a silent house he lets crumble around him. Peeling shutters and cracks in the dark, blank windows. I lift up the teapot, but he has more calls to make; he wraps his long scarf around and opens the door to a slash of cold, blinding light.

Angus is an orphan like I am; he crossed the ocean with one small trunk, and a canvas bag slung over his shoulder, and he used to say that he understood how it was for me. But he was able to pack that trunk, that bag, he was able to choose what to take and what to leave behind; it's nothing the same. All I had left was my nightdress, pitted with star-shaped holes, and the boots on my feet. My mother's boots, as it happened, that I must have mistaken in the dark. I also had the mystery of what

I was doing outside in the middle of the night, trying to walk in my mother's boots, which had formed themselves around her feet, her pathways, her thoughts.

It had happened before, the hem of my nightgown damp when I woke in my bed, twigs in my hair. Sometimes I was missed and searched for, and my brothers found me once by the creek in the dawn. They said that they spoke to me and I answered, that I took their smaller hands and let them lead me back to the cabin, where I asked my mother to sing me a song. I don't remember any of it, but I believed them. They were terrible liars, my brothers, but only to keep themselves out of trouble, and besides, I liked to think that I was like one of the mortal girls in my mother's stories, marked out and given an extra, secret life.

So I must have been sleepwalking and that must be why I was standing still in the trees. A ghostly shape found by someone rushing to the creek for more water, although it was clearly too late. The roof crashing in and the walls, and glass cracking and exploding, the windows and all the jars of preserves my mother had just finished laying down against another cold winter. I don't remember that either, not really, but I must have overheard it in the days that followed. Even now I sometimes dream the sound of that glass, the shape of a man in flames.

"Tell me about coming to the city," Edie says, and I have to think where to begin. She knows, of course she does, that I lost my family in a fire when I was about her age, and she knows that's why I still run to stamp out sparks from the hearth, why I check that the stove is damped and check again, before I turn down the lamps. It could have started one of those ways; no one knows for certain. Aunt Kez told me once that they thought maybe a lantern was knocked over, or a smudge pot left going in the shed. When she said it I remembered a man with a bushy moustache asking me about blackflies. Asking was it my brothers' job to settle the animals, would that be why they were found there. While I was thinking he patted my head and stood, and his voice far above me said, "Never mind, I don't suppose it really matters."

Things came back to me like that, in patches, and time moved as it does in a dream; I found myself in one moment or another with no link between them, no steps to trace. Opening my eyes in a strange room I wondered where and who I was. And wondered, since I knew that the room was strange to me, who I had been before. Then the door opened slowly and I saw the smooth face of Mrs. Wroth, and knew that I was in the pastor's square frame house in the centre of the village. The bed dipped when she sat on the edge and it was hard to breathe when she wrapped me in her plump arms, tried to rock me like a little child. My hands were lost in the sleeves of the large, scratchy nightgown she said was hers, my own ruined, she told me, beyond any saving. So all I had then were my mother's boots, and after she'd left me to dress in the clothes she'd brought, I took the little scissors from the dressing table and scraped at the ridges in the soles until I had a small mound of earth. The last my mother had trod on, the last I had, mixed together.

I had nothing to put the earth in so I cut a piece from the runner on that same table, tied it tightly with another thin strip so that nothing would leak through. I arranged the silver tray with the brush and comb so it didn't show, and I thought that when Mrs. Wroth discovered the damage, as she was bound to, she wouldn't say anything about it, not to me. She would maybe think I was *maddened by grief*; that phrase came into my head and rolled around there, rolled right over the leap of shame that came when I looked at the clothes she had left. The moment's delight at the stockings and petticoat, the soft patterned dress, far prettier than anything I had ever owned.

It belonged to Amy Wroth, that dress; I knew because she'd worn it in church some weeks before. The pastor's daughter, with her pink cheeks, her neat blond hair, her cruel tongue. She had spread a story about me once, or maybe I had spread one about her. Whichever way it had been she was all sweetness those days I stayed in their house, filling my water glass before it was empty and buttering my bread, as if these were things beyond me. I joined them at the table, where the talk was mostly of the weather, and when Mrs. Wroth said, "You must be tired," I thought that perhaps I was, and went back to the cool spare room, pulled up the soft covers and stared at the lacy shadows moving over the far wall, the ceiling above my head, until she came to bring me down to another meal. It was like being under an enchantment; days and nights passed and I felt nothing, not even surprise when Mrs. Wroth pinned up my hair and led me down to the parlour, where a bearded man stood to greet me, and said my name.

The story I tell Edie starts here, with my uncle Ben appearing as if by magic. Which is how it seemed to me, although later, of course, I understood that telegraph messages would have been delivered, some in the city and some to the pastor's house while I floated in the shadow-filled room upstairs. Details tapped out, decisions made, a life arranged for me. My uncle said that I was coming to live with him, or rather, beside him; I didn't understand exactly. There was a train to catch, a buggy and driver waiting to take us to the station. He was sorry, he said, but there was no time for the offered tea, though he took the cakes Mrs. Wroth wrapped up, tucking them into the small bag at his feet. I stepped up into the waiting buggy and the turning wheels rolled me away while I smoothed the flower-sprigged dress with my hand.

Edie has known the station here all her life, and even before she knew all her letters Angus taught her to tap out her name on the old key he kept on top of his desk. This past summer she and her friends met every holiday train, their wide eyes taking in all the fashionable ladies, their enormous hats and the trim on their slippery gowns, and the handsome sons and brothers who raised a hand to help them down from the carriage. Once, in town, I saw her with her friends strolling slowly past the wide veranda of the Lakeview Hotel, their arms linked and their giggly faces close together, and I thought, *Oh my.*

I'm sure that what I've told her is true, that I hadn't seen a train myself until the day my uncle came, although I must have sometimes heard them calling. We had to hurry from the buggy and across the platform, and he touched my elbow as we went, making me jump. "Well," was all my uncle said, when we were settled in our seats, and he put up a hand to fiddle with his spectacles, which sat a little crookedly on his face. He took them off and played with the metal arm, said, "I'm always bending and breaking them," and he smiled when he said it, looking at me with his bare and softer eyes.

I knew nothing about him beyond his name, and the fact that he was my father's younger brother, though he looked older than my father would ever be. There were other brothers, and sisters too, and I tried to remember how many, and if I knew what they were called, while my uncle settled his glasses and patted his lumpy pockets, took out a thin pencil and a small notebook with a blue leather cover. I noticed these things, but my mind felt small and muffled, no words I could think of saying.

"Well," Ben said again, as the train began to move with a lurch, and I turned my head to the window and watched everything I knew slip away. I stared out the window and we went faster, sometimes slower, and stopped at platforms where people stood with bags and bundles. Sometimes, as we slowed to a stop at those stations, there were people standing without any bags and through the window I watched their faces change. Watched everything about them seem to lighten as their mouths moved into smiles. The first time, it was a woman with a jaunty hat, holding a small boy by the hand, and I thought she was looking at me, smiling at me. Until a tall man stepped into my view, set down his satchel and swung the boy up through the air. His hand on the woman's cheek, in the shadow of her hat, before they all turned their backs and walked away together. I thought that here was a thing I might never have known. How many people there were, on any day at all, who were waiting for someone. And waiting for someone who would never be me.

There were many of those stops throughout our journey and I watched the waiting faces from my hiding place, and in between the countryside began to change, to soften and blur around the edges, the trees and the hills and the rocks. Even the light was changing, becoming golden and then the softest mauve, until I understood that really I was travelling through time, that the train was rolling into night as if it was a completely different country. So many thoughts I'd never had before and they tired me out, my eyes heavy and closing again and again, but each time I opened them the changes were so small that I had no idea if I'd been asleep for moments or hours. The lamp glow in the carriage and my uncle with his open notebook, drawing lines and scribbles and tapping the centre of his forehead with the chewed pencil end. "Off to *Tir na n'Og*," my mother used to say, chivvying my brothers up the steep stairs with the promise of a story about Oisin and his battles, about the Land of Youth, where three hundred years passed in the blink of an eye.

Angus is Irish, like my mother, and when he's tired it's even thicker in his voice. He was named for his father, who was named for his, and all the way back to the first gallowglass Angus, a fierce, wild fighter who crossed the Irish Sea. That first, stormy winter in this town we piled the quilts and I lay with my head on his chest while he told me stories. Most of them were very close to the ones my parents used to tell in turn, those days when the wind and snow raged around our cabin and we all huddled together, with the white words hanging in the air. Drifting into sleep with Angus, I felt just that happy, that safe.

But that time was far from the train rolling on through the night, the window that showed only my own blank face, and my uncle's eyes meeting mine. "I'm sorry, you must have questions," he said, but not one would form in my head. Instead I stared at his fingers, that were tapping on his right knee. His fingers with their broad nails like my father's, like my own. My uncle's fingers were tapping the same pattern over and over, and when he noticed me looking he said *sorry* again, and curled them into his palm. He explained that it was a habit, that tapping, that he'd had since he was young and learning to work the telegraph key; he said usually he didn't even realize he was doing it.

"Would you like to learn?" my uncle asked, and he said that he could teach me my name. Not Isabella, that was too long to be starting with, but they called me Iz, didn't they, and I wondered how he knew. Two quick taps, and then three more. "That's far too easy," he said, though he praised me for it, as if I were a tiny child. "Let's try Bella," my uncle Ben said, and that was just right, a mixture of long taps and short ones, and he gave me his notebook to rest on my knee, so I could hear it better. *Bella Bella Bella*—I tapped it out, mile after dark, rolling mile, and by the time we reached Toronto I had a new name, and a secret way to say it.

The station was overwhelming, soot and steam and noise, and more people than I'd ever seen at the same time. Outside we passed all the cabs in a line and I stumbled in my too-big boots, shook my right foot to settle the wrapped earth more securely under my instep. Soon we'd left all the bustle behind; we turned, and turned again onto a dark street, the only sound our tapping feet that could have been a message, though I hadn't learned enough to make it out. And then there was another sound, growing steadily louder, and a kind of displacement of the air. A shape growing out of the dark, a shape that was my brother Little Ross, with a grin on his face and his arms thrown wide, and I thought I might die for joy. But in the same instant I realized the boy wasn't running to me. He had a look of Little Ross, but darker, straighter hair—another child entirely. "This is your cousin Bella," my uncle said, when he'd scooped the boy up, but I couldn't even smile, knew only my thumping heart.

Light spilled from an open doorway and then we were inside, like arriving at the station all over again. Noise and light and so many people. A woman with a very round face put it close to mine and said, "You poor child." She led me through a doorway and up some stairs, into the quiet, and maybe I was already asleep; the next moment I knew was one with daylight around the edges of a patterned window shade, another soft bed in another strange room and my clothes laid neatly on a chair, where I could see them, my boots tucked underneath.

Last summer, when she was still well, Edie came down to breakfast and told us she wanted to be called Edith from now on. "I'm not a child anymore," she said, and if we forgot, she refused to answer, and wouldn't even look at Angus when he said that since Edie didn't seem to be around, he'd have to eat her pie too. That stubborn streak that I know so well, when she sets her mind on something; she's so much like my brother Alan, in that way. The time he decided to be a cowboy he spent hours in the fenced field with a coiled rope, trying to throw a loop over our horse's head. I watched him until it was so dark I could barely make out the glimmer of his shirt, the rope snaking out and falling empty to the ground.

There are days now when Edie's fractious as a teething baby. Kicks at the covers, then pulls them up again, tosses her book to the floor. She flicks away my suggestions—a coddled egg, a game of Twenty Questions, or trying new styles for her tangled hair. "I can't bear it," she says. "I'm so tired of opening my eyes and finding that I'm still *here*."

It takes me a long, cold moment to understand what she

means. "Oh Edie," I say, and she yanks the covers up over her head, her muffled voice saying, "Go away. That's not even my *name*."

She's right to be cross and I know very well how important this business of names can be. My own was for my mother's young sister and she always said that my eyes were like hers, though I couldn't know for myself. In the only photograph, now burned and gone, my aunt Isabella was already dead, those eyes fallen shut, and her cheekbones sharp in her face. On her sad days my mother stroked my hair and said how much I reminded her and I hated the thought of it, living out a dead girl's life. Wished, always, for a name all my own, one not trailing anything behind it. I understand it differently now, though, and if Edie had been a boy I would have given her both my brothers' names. A little piece of them carrying on, and maybe whenever I opened the back door and called, *Ross Alan, time for supper,* maybe all three would have come running.

No one buttered my bread for me, in my new home on Pembroke Street, and no one threw strange arms around me, hugging me until I nearly broke. Mostly they left me to find my own way to fit, gave me simple tasks, shaking out a mat or laying the table, until I learned how they did things, knew on my own when to stir up the stove, and where to put the clean dishes. Those first days it seemed that every time a door opened, someone new came through. Even the building was confusing, actually two separate houses, though it looked like one from the front. The right side was for Ben and his family and the other, where I was, for my three aunts and their new lodger, Jack, and sometimes my other uncle, Charlie, when he was having a difficulty.

The house was built by two brothers who married two sisters, or so Uncle Charlie told me. That part was probably true, but he had so many stories, and he told me that one long before my aunts explained how you could know which ones were real. "Don't let on," they said, and they told me he always smoothed his right eyebrow before he told a lie. "Everybody has a sign like that, if you look for it," my aunt Nan said, and she said Charlie's was quite obvious and that's why he was always losing at cards, another thing I hadn't known. She said that she didn't have a sign, because she never told lies, but even without Aunt Kez's snort I would have known that wasn't true. When I began to practise letters from the telegraph manual Ben gave me, they both said the code was far too complicated for them ever to have wanted to learn. But that time the new minister came to call, Aunt Kez tapped a rude word with the sugar tongs as she dropped three lumps into his cup, and Aunt Nan had to run from the parlour, coughing hard into her hand.

Uncle Charlie said he'd forgotten the names of the brothers who built the house, and he didn't remember what business they'd been in together. A successful one, it must have been, and they built their new houses side by side, and carried their sister brides through the gleaming front doors. Together they planted a white lilac bush in the middle of the shared backyard, and each year its soft scent reached farther and farther into the houses, through every open window. The sister brides were always visiting back and forth, and after the first winter, when they complained so much about having to lace up their boots every time, their husbands built a closed-in passage that joined the houses at the front. In time there were children, and first one then the other built extra rooms out the back. But they left an open space for the lilac, and when the sisters were busy inside, they could still wave to each other through its blossoms.

"But nothing lasts forever," Uncle Charlie said. "Well, you know that as well as anyone." There was a falling-out, between the brother husbands or the sister wives, and they boarded up the doors at either end of the connecting passageway. "It was just there," he said, pointing in the front hallway. "Do you see the outline, under the paper?" When I couldn't, he said that just showed what a good and permanent job they'd done, but even that wasn't enough, because they still sometimes glimpsed each other through the facing windows, especially in winter, when the lilac branches were bare. So they shuttered those windows, and the houses became so dark that they were all, even the children, in danger of losing their eyesight. "Don't look at me like that," Uncle Charlie said. "I'm just telling you what I know." He said that Aunt Edith's father, who had been a very sharp businessman before his accident on the bridge, somehow heard of the dire situation, and bought the double house for a good price. And the two families moved as far east and as far west as they could, so they'd never have to see each other again.

Edie used to love that story, and when she was younger we carried it on farther. Imagining that at some point, maybe when they were very old and hobbling along with canes, the husbands and wives would come face to face on a busy street, and all would be forgiven. Or maybe their grandchildren or great-grandchildren would meet each other, far in the future, and without knowing why, become the best of friends. After Uncle Charlie told me about it, all those years ago, I kept thinking about that boarded-up passageway and wondering why I hadn't noticed that the house from the outside didn't quite match the inside. In the front hall I ran my fingertips over every inch of the place he'd pointed to, and thought I could trace the outlines of the secret. Though I knew it would have to be completely dark, when I thought of that space I pictured filtered light, and had a sense of something waiting, a connection that could be made again.

The green manual Ben gave me was filled with his own scribbles and underlinings, and with it he set me up an old key to practise on. Maybe it wasn't a plan, but that gave a point to my days, something for my mind to draw in to; it eased my way. I spent hours at the little table in my room, shaking out my hand when it cramped, and then grasping the key again. *The fingers and thumb borrow their force from the hand and wrist, which should move directly up and down through a distance of about three-quarters of an inch;* I began to see how everything was connected, how even my muscles could learn a new way to carry on. All the sounds in the world became messages as I learned the six principles, dots and dashes and longer ones, and I couldn't believe I'd been deaf to them all my life. The tapping of a wooden spoon on the side of a pot, feet on a sidewalk, a blind pull against a windowpane. I thought of those still days in our clearing, a woodpecker somewhere close in a tree, and wondered what conversations, what warnings I might have missed. Like a child learning to read, I could soon pluck out the letters, then learned to hear them together, to understand the words, the sentences they made. But it took me longer to realize that even the spaces between words made a pattern, and could tell you something different.

The rhythm of the house was easier to learn, coffee boiled black as tar in the morning, and not a word spoken until the cups were half empty. Aunt Clare and Jack usually left in a flurry, almost late for their classes, trailing papers and long scarves and rushing back at least once for something forgotten. When they were really gone Aunt Nan pushed herself up from the table and tied on her apron, and I went with Aunt Kez to do the shopping. She named every street, told me who lived in the houses we passed and which shops they avoided, and why. Maybe that wasn't a plan either, but I began to know where I was, and the noisy city, so different from all I'd known, began to seem like something I could manage. But there were times, walking through the park, when the sudden scent of pine trees swept me back, and I almost cried out with the pain of it. Times when I woke in the morning and closed my eyes again, trying to see the rough-hewn boards, the knots and swirls that had once been just above me, trying to hear the rattle of the poker in the stove, and my parents' easy voices floating up the open stair. I pictured my little room, and the rest of the cabin, every single thing in it, as if I really thought that if I could imagine it, complete and exact, I would find myself back there.

Like it had been for the sister brides, there was constant visiting between our households, and through the last leaves the children often beckoned from their facing windows. There were already four of them when I came to live there, though it took me some days to be sure. George was the oldest, the one who had come running out of the dark, and then Daisy, and Sandy Mac. And the little one those three called Spot, because what they'd really hoped for was a dog. Fanny and Sally came later, so there was always a baby with chafed red cheeks being passed from arm to arm. A young girl came in to do the laundry, but otherwise it was all Aunt Edith, doing six things at once but hardly ever frazzled, her apron strings tied and her hair held smooth by ivory combs. "All serene," she used to say, stepping over a tumble of building blocks to reach the steaming kettle; impossible to know if it was a joke or a prayer.

My other aunts called it *Going to the wild side*, and it was exactly like that in the other house. Always someone banging on a pot or chasing around the kitchen table, crumbs ground in everywhere and a different child standing on a stool, splashing and scrubbing at the everyday dishes. Of course there was wailing and tussling and name-calling, and though it must have happened, I never saw Aunt Edith raise a hand; she had a way of saying a child's name that cut across any ruckus. What my cousins hated most was being left out of things; that was the punishment, being sent to a gloomy corner of the parlour, with the door left ajar so they could still hear, but faintly, all they were missing. More than once, hours later, someone would remember, and whichever child would be found fast asleep, curled up in the corner by the plant stand. "What a terrible mother," my uncle said then, resting his hand on Aunt Edith's shoulder, but it was clear that he didn't mean it.

I hold that double house in my mind; maybe all of us do, who lived there. Traces floating through the dreams of my cousins, so young when they left, and maybe flickering for years behind Jack's blank stare. Even my Edie has a version of it, from the stories I've told her, and from the photograph that was taken the first summer I lived there. All of us sitting on the front steps, laughing because baby Spot has just given a rolling, adult-sounding belch.

Edie always wanted me to take her to see it, when we went to the city, but my aunts said there was no point, it was so rundown, so changed. And now, of course, it's gone completely, knocked down with its neighbours to make way for the new courthouse. Aunt Clare said once that it was as if some monster were trailing them through the city, smashing along behind and destroying every place that had meant anything to them. The narrow house where they'd all been born was gone too, along with most of that block, replaced by the expansion of the department store where Uncle Charlie still works, strolling the floor with his measuring tape draped around his neck. He told us once that when the new part first opened he used to try to work out where the old house had been. Their kitchen floor hovering, as near as he could tell, just about at chin height in the Notions section. He said that sometimes, when he climbed the stairs, he expected to see the door to his old room instead of the display of toy guitars and bugles and drums. That was just cruel, he said, but he got used to it.

Weeks passed on Pembroke Street; the leaves flared and dropped from the trees while I did my tasks and tapped my letters, and then slow, fat flakes of snow fell through the grey air. Once we dragged two sleds to the park with all the children and went down the hill in different combinations. Aunt Nan fell off in a tumble of skirts and when George and Daisy tried to help her they all ended up rolling on the ground, right to the bottom, and Aunt Edith laughed so hard she almost dropped the baby. Long evenings came, and I held a skein of red wool between my spread hands while Aunt Kez rolled it up. She'd decided to make hats for Daisy and Sandy Mac, a pair of warm mittens for George, and while we worked she told me a story about Uncle Charlie and a slingshot. When it was done I said, "What about Uncle Alan, where does he live?" and the red ball dropped and unrolled across the floor. "Well, that's two shocks you've given me," Aunt Kez said, as she began to roll it up again.

Wee Alan, she told me, was the first-born, but he'd died on the ship, just days after leaving the Old Country. So long ago that my father was a baby himself, and now no one living would have seen the white shroud or heard the splash, would remember the way the ocean stretched all around, under the chilly sky. Which meant that I couldn't have remembered, as I thought I did, my father telling stories about him, the way he sometimes did about Ben and Charlie, who were clearly very much alive. That was a puzzle, but even stranger was the second thing Kez said—that these were the first words I'd spoken since the fire. At first I thought she was teasing, the way I'd learned she often did, but Aunt Nan put her soft hand on my shoulder, and said that it was so. And the red wool scratched as it wound again from my fingers.

I had to look at everything differently then, every outing, every conversation; I had to understand that I was somehow not the person I thought I was. I thought about how quickly I'd come to know the house and its people, the sounds of the city and the different look to the light. How little time it had taken before I could walk without even noticing the lump of hard-packed earth still tucked in my shoe. That night, before I slept, I thought about how everything was starting again, and I vowed to be good and kind, as if I always had been.

February

In the mornings the children call out to each other, as they make their way to the school, and it's really not that long ago that Edie was one of them, linking arms with her friends with no thought at all that there might be someone trapped behind a window. Not long since my aunts' last visit, when we hired a buggy for a drive in the countryside and Edie fell asleep with her cheeks flushed with health, not fever, while over her bobbing head Nan whispered about Charlie's latest trouble. It's been months, not years, yet that day seems as distant as a story, and I suppose that's the only way to bear it. People get used to all kinds of things, don't they? They move house, lose limbs, lose their sight, and if the time before was just as clear, I don't suppose they could go on. Each time a new building rises in the city, raw and strange, it quickly becomes familiar, and when people walk by they may still have the idea, but only the idea, of what was there. The tall trees or the row of houses with painted front doors.

It's like that when I think of the time before Edie got sick, and it's hard to imagine our days back then, the routine of shopping, of cleaning and cooking. I do the minimum now, needing to be within earshot, and the grocer's boy brings what I've ordered, speaking into our new telephone that's meant to be only for station business. I don't know what Angus is doing about all his paperwork, but he's home now in the evenings, and sits and talks with Edie, or reads to her, while I clear up what's left from our meal. I sleep quite comfortably on the parlour sofa, that we moved into the kitchen to make space for Edie's bed; when I climb the stairs now it's only to run the duster quickly around or to fetch something that I need, and it's like another world. So empty and still, so abandoned.

"Tell me again about my name," Edie says. "How it jumped right into your head when you saw me." And it's true, I knew right away I would name her for Aunt Edith, so sunny and strong, the best charm I could imagine. When she was six months old we rode the train to the city for Easter, and everyone made such a fuss over her chuffie cheeks, her two sharp teeth. Aunt Edith had a little cough she was afraid of passing on, and just watched while my aunts took turns holding her, watched Uncle Charlie dance her around, waving her wooden rattle. My cousins clapped her hands and bounced her on their bony knees, pulling faces to hear her gurgling laugh and tiring her out so she slept right through the night. In the morning Angus touched my cheek and said, "Maybe that's the secret, maybe we need to have a whole houseful of children."

I can hardly bear to think of that giddy time, when we still thought everything was possible. As foolish as the boastful tailor, sewing his magic coat and not hearing the Elfin Queen's laughter, her plan unfolding with every stitch. We had two sons in the years that followed, but they didn't survive. The first I held and wept over, touched the smooth blue eyelids that never opened. With the second I heard a thin mewl and the midwives' shocked whispers, as I sank into a dark place of pain and fever. When I came back to myself I understood that no other child of mine would be allowed to live, and even without the doctor's warning to Angus, everything between us would have changed. And it torments me still, that the charm I intended was really a curse.

Aunt Edith's cough got worse and it wore her out; she could barely leave her bed by the time our Edie let go of our fingers and began to walk on her own. When the latest doctors told Ben that the only hope was a warmer climate, he found a new position in California, and everything changed so quickly. It was an expensive business to move them all, and my aunts convinced him that the only thing was to sell the double house, and most of the heavy old furniture that they wouldn't need. With Clare married and settled in Washington there was just more empty space in the old house, and Charlie could squeeze in anywhere if he needed to. So really, they told Ben, their new small place was just right, and only a trolley ride away from everything.

At first it seemed that the doctors had been right. Aunt Edith wrote that she was a bit tired still but so much better, and the children were running wild and sounding like little Yankees already. Kez and Nan began to talk about taking a trip out there to see the white house on the hillside, dip their toes in the ocean. But then there was a telegram from Ben, followed by a long letter describing how Edith had slipped away. They buried her, as he said she'd wanted, under that strange, bright sun.

My aunts assumed that they'd all come back, that something close to the old life would start again. *Perhaps,* Ben wrote, but there'd been so much upheaval for the children already. *Perhaps,* but first there were projects he had to see through. He talked about coming to visit, or sending Daisy and George for the summer, though it was such a long way for them to travel on their own. There were notes from the children inside every letter, that of course became shorter and shorter. One from Sandy was just a scribbled drawing of their new dog; "Looks more like a donkey," Kez said, when she took it from her bag to show me.

"Look who I found," Angus says, kicking snow off his boots as he comes through the door with Ida and Becky right behind him, unwinding their long scarves to reveal their healthy pink faces.

"We made a cake," they say together, holding it out, still warm through the white cloth that wraps it. Much too rich for an invalid's diet, but no one hears me say that. Angus rubs and claps his hands as he leads the way to the parlour, where Edie squeals and the giggling starts; I know those girls, they can keep it up for hours.

"What?" Angus says, back in the kitchen, and I turn away with the cake knife. "They'll cheer her up."

When I say that they'll wear her out, he makes a little *tch* through his teeth and says that then she'll rest, as if it was that easy. "I don't want to argue," he says, touching my cheek with his still-cold hand, and he drapes the dishtowel over his arm and carries the cake into the parlour. He pretends to stumble in the doorway, the plate waving wildly and the little forks rattling, and the girls all laugh and Edie says, "Oh, *Daddy*."

Something eases in me then, and I remember what a revelation it was, when she was born, to watch him pacing the floor with her, bending to whisper in her tiny ear. The two of them in their own magic circle, with the songs and jokes and rituals that still aren't for anyone else. When Edie was two or three they played a game they called *Schedule*, that started with Angus reading out the names of places from the list tacked up by the back door. "Where are you going today, madam?" he'd say. "Hamilton? Yp-si-lan-ti? Pough-keep-sie?" Adding outlandish names until she could barely breathe for laughing. Then he dropped to his hands and knees, saying, "Last call for Schenec-tady. All aboard for Kalamazoo!" and that was the signal for Edie to fling herself on his broad back, and they went round and round the kitchen and the parlour like that, until he chuffed them into a heap on the Turkey carpet. His own laughter as free as hers and his face, when he looked up at me, wide open like the boy I never knew.

I'd like to believe that I somehow discerned that boy from the start, and recognized an essential goodness beneath his confident look, his practised, flirting talk. But I know that I was besotted, and not capable of any kind of sober thought like that. I would have followed him anywhere, borne anything; I would have clung to his feet as he tried to shake me off, if that was the way it had been. That hunger is gone and I don't exactly miss it, though I miss feeling anything so strongly that isn't dread. It's hard not to think of her as another person, the girl I was, clinging to each glance, each smile. Our hands so close to touching, when I laid the message slips down on his desk, that I could feel the leaping spark.

I was seventeen that spring, and time played tricks. The new buds on the trees seemed to hold forever, unopened, as I walked through the soft light to the office on Wellington, and through different light, home again. In between was a strange world, with its own language to learn, new faces and names, and the other girls like cruel sisters, letting me make errors and. be chastised for them, while they watched with their sly little eyes. I told myself that it was because I was the manager's niece that they left space around me in the tiny room where we ate our dinner, and there was so much going on in our house on Pembroke Street that I didn't need to be included in their talk, or in their Sunday outings.

Then one day I met Angus by chance, on King Street, surprised that he knew who I was. The next day, in the park, he said that he liked that I wasn't a chatterbox, and I realized that everything had been transformed once again, that I was living a new, charmed life where even my tongue-tied state was a choice, and something in my favour. His strong fingers worked the pins from my hair and combed it out; before long he was saying that he adored everything about me and I became that girl, the one that Angus adored. The one who wasn't anything like the others. Away from him the hours dragged, but the hands on his pocket watch raced when we met on Sundays, making our way to the deepest thickets in the park, or following the sandy stream back from the place where it spilled into the lake. All the secret places he led me to, and sometimes, at the office, he would whisper, *Tonight*, when we passed in the stairway, and that was the slowest time of all. The long way home and the longer evening, listening to the settling house until it was safe to make my silent way down the back stairs.

I was right about the girls' visit, all that whispering and laughter. Edie fell asleep not long after they'd gone, and though her forehead stayed cool, she didn't wake properly until the next afternoon. She said that she'd dreamt she was in California, though she didn't know how she knew that's where it was. But the streets were narrow and all the houses were white and then a dream-thing happened and she was up above, looking down, and California became an island with a collar of sand; she could see the white waves breaking all around. Then everything changed again and it became a painting she was looking at, in a sunny room. "Because we were talking about it, I suppose," she says. She wants to see the postcards and the pictures of her American cousins, and I tell her I'll fetch the album and her keepsake box, if she promises to eat the broth I've heated.

It might have been a year after Aunt Edith died, or not even that long, when Ben wrote that he'd decided to marry again, a widow they'd both known, with a young son of her own. Her name was Robina, a thing that made Kez sniff and say she and Nan had best go out there after all, and see for themselves how things were. They sent postcards from the station stops along the way. Buffalo and Chicago, Omaha. On the back of one, Nan drew a stick figure saying *Ow!* to show how she kept falling from her berth.

Our first son was not long in his grave when they went away and I was distracted, settling into our bigger house and keeping track of Edie, who was of an age where everything was a danger. But still it shames me to realize how little thought I gave to their journey, to how difficult it would have been, in all kinds of ways. "Didn't we have a time," they said when they were back, giving Edie a beautiful big shell, and showing the photographs they'd taken, which, they said, didn't give you any idea of the *heat*.

One photograph was of the new house, taken from far away to fit it all in. One was of Robina with her son, who was, they said, a sturdy, *frowning* little fellow. Robina wore a large hat and it was difficult to make out her face, but she was quite *pleasant*, Nan said, and the children seemed easy enough with her. They were settled enough, happy enough, each with his own room, and the yard so long you'd need one of Clare's telescopes to see the end of it. Of course the older ones were long past coddling and fussing over, and they seemed to be always coming and going, to school or to parties or lessons of some kind. In fact, my aunts said, everyone was very *busy* in California; they saw the ocean and they saw mountains, but they hardly saw Ben at all, and when they did he didn't seem like himself, somehow. Though one night when Robina was too tired they sat up late, telling old stories that made them all laugh and teasing him about the way he talked now, like some kind of *mongrel*.

Kez and Nan came back, with their photographs and souvenirs and stories; *Didn't we have a time,* they said. And I looked and I listened, but I wish I'd spared a thought for how overwhelmed they must have been there, how out of place. I'd lived in their household for years, after all; I knew how they talked, all the meaning that hummed just beneath what was actually said. I should have thought about how it was for them, to find that the younger children didn't remember them at all, that the older ones were polite but not very interested, caught up in their new lives, new friends. In California, Kez said, there wasn't even time for stories. Robina didn't want the little ones frightened, and the others preferred to run around in the yard, or hit a ball with a stick.

I wish I had thought about that, and acknowledged it in some way, though if I'd actually said, Kez wouldn't have thanked me for it. *Spilt milk,* she would have said, in her matter-of-fact way, as if it had never been important to her. As if she never thought about those grey afternoons on Pembroke Street when the children piled onto her bed, and she took off her shoes and stockings and let the smallest ones play with her crooked, bony toes.

She told them stories in the rainy light, about fiddlers and enchanted rivers and trees, about magic shoes, and instead of ending the usual way, the clever children in Kez's stories always outsmarted everyone who had wished them harm. One of their favourites was the one about the boy who had been stolen by the Water Horse, how his father smacked his own face, while his mother sank to her knees and keened on the shore of the loch. Kez had the children keen with their loud little voices, and when they fell silent she said, *Then* ... Then a ripple, spreading wider and wider, and they emerged, the gentled horse with the boy on his back, high-stepping out of the water. And the water sparkled as it flowed from their bodies, and the sun cast colours through the droplets flung wide when they shook their sleek, wet heads.

Maybe it's because I have too much time to think, these past months, or maybe the stories I've been telling have stirred things up. The things I leave out, with Edie, that have poked through from wherever they've been lurking, the things that torment me. From the time I began to speak again on Pembroke Street there were things I could have said, things I could have told them about my father, about our life, which I knew they wondered about. One of those nights around the kitchen table, when they were remembering the tree house he had once tried to build, I could have told them how he'd described it to my brothers, a grand structure all the neighbourhood children admired, and they would have laughed, but it would have brought him closer. And they would have thought better of him if I'd told about the saplings he planted and tended so carefully, one for their father and one for their mother.

The good and kind girl I had vowed to be would have shared those things, and she wouldn't have said that she didn't remember when Charlie asked about the fiddle. That girl would have told him that from the day my father opened the package it sat on a shelf with our Bible and the picture of Isabella. No one else was allowed to touch it, but every so often he would take it down and press in different places, pluck each string. Once my mother said why on earth didn't he ride over to Talbots' and ask Linc to show him; how hard could it be, if a fool like that could play. "I just might," my father said, but he never did.

I didn't tell them any of that, and I lied to them, too, when I'd been with Angus, made up stories to explain the grass stain on my blouse, the trail of sand when I took off my shoe in the kitchen. The worst thing, I see now, was not that I fooled them, or thought I did, but that my mind somehow turned them into people who deserved to be fooled. How ridiculous they became then, with their penny-pinching and their silly jokes. Aunt Clare lost in her reading while the supper burned on the stove, and the annoying way her glasses slid down her nose. Aunt Kez poking her nose into everyone's business, but not caring enough to notice mine, and how she tried to make an adventure out of her dull life, telling every little detail of her walk to the butcher. I even felt scorn for poor Jack, his clumsiness, and when Aunt Nan said, "Be careful, Bella," as I left the house, I saw nothing but a silly old woman, one with no idea what it was to burn like I did. How little time it really took, in my new life, for me to become again the selfish and deceitful girl I had been before.

March

"I can do it myself," Edie says, so I leave the basin and cloth, and wait in the kitchen in case she gets dizzy and falls. The house is quiet except for the soft trickle as she dips and squeezes, and the falling water reminds me quite suddenly of the little creek not far from our clearing. The sound of clear water moving over mossy stones, and how often I stole away from my chores to sit there, dreaming about a grown-up life, far away.

Edie has been fretting about the school work she's missing, and these past weeks her teacher stops by on Thursdays to catch her up. I know that she really does care about the missed lessons, but I also know that it's his expected visit that has her asking for the basin, for a brush and a ribbon to tidy her hair. He's a good-looking boy, is Robbie, and a credit to his mother, no matter what people whisper. Angus has always rated him, and gave him work at the station and taught him the wire, paid him one summer to knock down an old shed and tidy up our yard. I felt such a pang when I saw the two of them out back, looking over what was to be done. Young Robbie standing close beside Angus, copying his stance and crossing his arms in just the same way.

He's not really a teacher, of course, though when he takes off his overcoat there's chalk dust on his cuffs, a sprinkling in his curly hair that I first took for snow. When Miss Tunstall had her trouble at Christmastime he agreed to step in, and he seems to know what he's about, though he's not long out of school himself. I've explained that Edie mustn't overtax herself and he keeps his visits short, and never leaves her too much work to do. A few problems to work on or a poem to memorize; I thought at first she was raving again, when I heard her whispering: *beside the ravelled seas, beside the ravelled seas.*

Today, Robbie says that the trustees have asked him to stay on until the end of the school year. "You'll be back by then," he tells Edie, as if he's quite certain. When she asks if Miss Tunstall is still unwell he says he believes that's so, though I'm sure he knows, as even I do, that no one has heard a thing since her brother came and took her away on the night train. After she'd started singing in her room, and staggered down the main street with a frozen clod of horse dung in each hand. It happens like that, sometimes; the winters are terrible here, and people break. When the first breeze comes and melting snow trickles down the sides of all the roads, we step carefully out of our houses, blinking and looking around to see who is missing. There are always a few, besides the old and sickly. A few who have chosen a rope, a knife, a gun. Sometimes they just walk out onto the frozen lake, until the ice gives way.

While Edie and Robbie go over her work at the kitchen table I change her bedding, bundling the old sheets into a basket for later. Remembering, as I do, her wide eyes when Charlie used to tell her how much deeper the snow was when he was a boy, and how much colder the winters. So cold, he said, that sheets on the line froze solid, and the wind snapped them to pieces that blew through the air like a blizzard. *I swear*, Charlie said, as he always did, and he told her he could hardly make out the shape of his own mother in the yard, standing in a swirl of white, with a clothes peg in her hand.

How funny he used to be, my uncle Charlie. Everything was lively when he was around, with his easy charm and way of carrying you along. These last years he's grown terribly fat, his face stretched and shiny, and the winks, the jokes and the flirting are grotesque now, when even a short flight of steps makes him puff and wipe his damp forehead. He didn't come with my aunts when they visited this past summer; they said he was unwell and perhaps he was, but I also knew that something had happened at the hotel the last time he'd come, and Robbie's mother had a quiet word with Angus. That day we rode out in the buggy, Nan whispered about the drink and all the trouble it caused. And she said that for all that, he was still her wee brother, and there were times when, just for a moment, she saw his little-boy eyes looking out from his round, red face. Not the mischievous ones, but the look he used to have when he was frightened the *powries* would come and gobble him up. I could barely hear her, over the sound of the turning wheels, when she said that sometimes she wondered if that's what had happened.

Edie tries to get up for a little while each day, as the doctor has said she should, though even a walk to the front door tires her out, and she sinks back into her bed with a sigh. She won't let me pull the shade until the sun has completely vanished behind Mrs. Leary's cottage across the way, and she writes down the time it happens, proof that the days are getting longer, but the only way you would know. She asks me questions, while the room grows darker, and I answer as best I can, thinking how much easier it was when she was small and wanted the same stories every night, every day. The same stories with the same words; she knew every detail and I suppose it was as soothing to tell them that way as it was to hear them. The one about Angus and his friend Liam climbing the church tower, back in their village, and ringing the bells in the middle of the night. Or the one about Aunt Kez trying to ride poor Jack's bicycle in the laneway, how she shot out into the street and startled a horse, ended in a tangle on the ground, with her skirts up over her head.

She wants to hear different things now. Did Aunt Nan really marry a scoundrel, like she said that time? Did Kez ever have a beau, and would Charlie stay a bachelor, and did I think Aunt Clare really *loved* the Professor? Did I know from the moment I saw him that I would marry her father, and what was it like when he asked me? Sometimes when I say I don't know, I really don't, but Edie says, crossly, "I'm not a child anymore."

How quickly it seemed to happen; one day she woke up too old to play with her dolls, and then hugs and kisses were for babies. Another day she fussed with her hair, and walked with her friends past the city boys, lounging on the veranda of the Lakeview Hotel. *Be careful what you wish for,* people say, and long ago I learned the truth of that. But when she was first born we seemed as close as thought, and somehow I always knew when her covers were too heavy, when her toes needed warming; when she began to speak I knew every thought in her head. There are things I don't tell her now, that have nothing to do with her age. But sometimes I feel the tug of it, the need to have her know me through and through, because no one else can ever be so close.

Angus and I were married in the parlour on Pembroke Street, just family there, which made quite a crowd, and two friends from work who were going to the West and teased Angus about changing his mind. Edie likes to hear the details, what I wore and the cake Nan made, how baby Fanny spit up, sour gouts sliding down the minister's shiny sleeve. She thinks her father looks so handsome in the photograph where I stand with my hand on his arm, and today she wants to know exactly how I *felt*. "Happy," I tell her, and I must have been, though that day is just a string of small moments in my mind. But I do remember how solid his arm was, how steady in the flash of that camera. I remember that as clearly as I remember all the whispering in the office, and the girls who didn't care if I heard, when they told each other it was the oldest trick in the world.

But it wasn't a trick, unless it was one my body played on us both. It was perhaps too early to be certain I was with child, I know that now, but I told Angus I was, and for all he knew about persuasion and loving, he must have been just as ignorant about the rest. Ben got him the post here as station master and we were married in the parlour; they all came to see us off, waving and calling as the train moved out of the station. Snow appeared on the fields as we left the city behind, more and more of it; we both fell asleep and opened our eyes to see white banks piled high on either side, like a passageway leading to some separate, enchanted world.

We stepped down from that train in a swirl of white, and my bleeding started not long after; perhaps there never was a child, but it didn't seem to matter. We were so happy and full of each other, with the blankets heaped and the old stove roaring, snow piled up to the windowsills of our little rented house. Everything suddenly allowed and we laughed at what Angus called our outdoor romance. The twigs that dug in and the times we lay in our thicket, still as statues, while people passed by so close, arguing about the stranger who had tipped his hat, or whether that fish had been off.

There were days so cold that it hurt to breathe, days the reflected sun dazzled. And there were storms as fierce as any I'd ever seen, the wires down and no trains running; we only left our bed to fetch more wood, to grab bits of food that we ate under the covers, like mischievous children. By the time spring came my stomach was round with Edie; that summer we walked in the evenings to watch the sun slip into the lake and nothing else mattered. Not the girls in their white dresses, not the sound of the train whistle calling people away from the too-short streets of the town.

The notebook where Edie records the setting sun is actually her old diary, that she hasn't bothered with for years. When she came across it in the keepsake box she turned the pages and said, "All I did was write about the weather—what a silly." After I lit the lamps today she read bits out to me: *So much snow . . . A little warmer . . . No rain today.* On the first of May it seems I made an apple cake, but Angus was too late home to eat it. On June 12 she got a star for penmanship, and on July 15 *Ida T was horrid*; "I wonder why?" Edie said. And then she said, "It's all so dull, it might as well have burned up like yours did," a thing I must have told her once, though it's not exactly true. Maybe I looked sad, thinking about that; Edie said she was sorry she'd mentioned the diary, sorry to remind me. I told her it was fine, and it was, but now that she and Angus are asleep and the house is dark and quiet, I lie awake on the sofa in my wrap of blankets and remember that last long summer in our clearing, filled with biting flies, and filled with my rage. When everything seemed to bother me more, the sun and the bites and the old hoe that drove splinters into my palms, and I longed to be living in town, in a house where the floors were level and there were things to see through the windows; when I thought I knew what it was to be unhappy.

We met along the way, was all my parents ever said about how they came together, and when I was younger I'd imagined them as star-crossed lovers, forced to hide deep in the forest from their wealthy, feuding families. But mostly, that summer, they seemed to me two fools who'd stumbled across each other. My mother's feet heavy on the stairs, those days when she moved like a person underwater, and the way she fussed and wound her hair three different ways before we headed off to church. And my father, who would spend hours working out the theory of a thing, but always end up with a door that hung crookedly from its frame, a cow that would never calve. He fussed around the trees he'd planted, watering and snipping and sometimes dragging out a kitchen chair and just sitting, as if he could watch them growing. Quite forgetting, no matter how many times I reminded him, to fix a lock to my bedroom door, and making silly jokes and teasing as if I were still a little girl.

My brothers were worst of all, allowed to roam the bush to snare birds and rabbits, and praised for each scrawny thing they brought home. Smug looks when they walked out the door, leaving me piling dishes in the basin, or dragging out the heavy washtub. They pretended to break their teeth on the biscuits I made, complained about my lumpy darning, waving their stinking stockings under my nose. "Oh Iz, they're just boys," my mother said. "They're just trying to get a rise out of you, and maybe they'd stop if it didn't always work so well." As if it was somehow my own fault. I knew that she didn't understand a thing, and I sneered at the dress that she said she'd make over for me, nothing at all like Amy Wroth's that I'd pointed out in church.

I filled page after page in the diary that had been my present for Christmas. Things I'd always helped my mother with had become unbearable chores and even her voice scratched at me as she explained about what to use instead, when the flour was low, or how to keep a seam running straight. When she talked about Isabella, about the quarantine station on the rocky island, I closed my ears and sent my mind away, and whenever I could

I slipped off to my place by the creek, though even it was not the same, not much more than a trickle that dry summer.

My brothers were her spies, sent to fetch me back to do more work, and they were spies on their own, always prowling through my tiny room. Sniggering as they recited sentences from my diary, and they were never punished enough to keep them from searching and finding it again. So I tucked it back under my straw mattress, after I had written: *My brothers are terrible snoops. I'm going to hide this in the cowshed, where they'll never think to look. Way back in the darkest corner, under a mound of hay.*

I was so proud of my trick, my cleverness. Proud of the real hiding place I'd made, in a hole I'd scooped out at the base of a tree near the path to the stream. I wrapped it in a piece I cut from the new oilcloth my mother had set aside, and for all I know it's still there. I was proud of my cleverness, and I may even have smiled to think of my brothers sneaking into the dark shed when everyone was asleep. Burrowing deep into the hay, with a lantern to give them light.

April

"Why is it always *poor* Jack?" Edie says, looking up from Aunt Clare's letter. It's a clear, cold morning and her colour is better, I think, even in the bright sunlight that reaches every corner of the room. Since she's been ill Clare writes her every week with all the news from Washington, and tells her not to be discouraged, tells her that it will seem like forever but she'll recover, just like Clare herself did. *Everyone will fuss about your heart,* she wrote once. *But don't worry, you can still do anything you want to in your life.*

This time Clare writes about the new telescope at the Observatory, what a marvel it is, and how it would have fascinated poor Jack. "Well," I say, and when I say that he was a friend of Aunt Clare's, from the University, that he boarded with us on Pembroke Street, Edie rolls her eyes, the way only a young girl can; "I know *that*," she says. "And I know he could do magic with numbers, and that he fell off the roof one time. But why do they always say *poor* Jack? Did Aunt Clare break his heart?"

I tell her that they weren't friends like that, and while I'm thinking of what else I can say, I suddenly see Jack's long face. His brown eyes and the curving lashes that made him look, when he was still, like some gentle and noble horse, one that would dip its head and take food from your flat hand, if you were patient enough. Though he was only really still when he was reading, and even then his right foot tapped and his thin fingers combed through his hair. Most of the time, now I'm thinking about horses, I would say Jack was more like a rough-coated colt, not yet used to its long, spindly legs. The way he could trip over the edge of the carpet, or over nothing at all, forever banging his knees and his head, and knocking things with a wildly gesturing arm.

Remembering that, I realize that there are all kinds of things I can tell Edie about Jack, that have nothing to do with how it was at the end. The numbers and symbols scrawled over his walls, the ragged fingernails that gouged skin from his own pale cheeks. It strikes me now as a terrible betrayal, the way I rarely think of him. The way I remember that part as if it's the most important thing about him, as if it cancels out all the rest. Jack deserves to be remembered as he once was, the clever boy Aunt Clare sometimes called BG, for Boy Genius. So many strange and wonderful ideas in his head, and so well-meaning that even Aunt Kez forgave the disasters, like the time he thought to surprise them by mending the kitchen pump with a rubber band and a lump of glue. "So nice to have a man around the house," she said in her sharp way, but she was almost smiling as she swished the mop through the water that had pooled all over the floor.

My aunts used to say it was a good thing Jack and Clare were just pals, both of them so scattered they'd forget to eat, and so intent on their books that the house could fall down around them. He slept in what they called the peach room, though it was papered blue, but his things spilled out all over the kitchen and parlour, folders and papers and the special inks he liked, the cameras he was obsessed with one summer, and often parts of the bicycle he'd bought himself, that he was always taking apart, to see if he could make the wheels turn faster. One spring he and Clare borrowed a telescope from Professor Whitrow, and climbed through her window onto the low back roof. Jack slipped and rolled off, of course, landing flat on his back on the hawthorn bush below. Unbroken and grinning up at Clare, who was still standing above, surrounded by stars. "He gave his life for Science," he said, when he caught his breath, and how they laughed.

These are the things I can tell Edie, and I tell her again about the magic shows, when Aunt Nan found pennies in the children's hair, and slipped messages in and out of people's pockets. Jack predicting the numbers we had whispered to each other by making us add and subtract, divide. I can tell her how much delight he took in everything, from one of his long, worked-out equations to the slow, steady opening of the lilac clusters. The smooth heft of the old darning egg, when he took it from Aunt Clare's hand. There are so many things I should have been remembering, instead of the way he began to sleep crammed underneath his bed, to keep his brain safe in the night. So much that was Jack, before the black eyes of birds began to glitter. Before the notes of their songs became threats, and the wind whispered warnings in his ears.

"What happened then?" Edie asks, and I tell her enough of the rest to make him *poor Jack* forever, even without the details I keep to myself. I tell her that he was taken away, but I don't mention the spittle that flew from his mouth, the streak of blood left on the door frame, when the strong men dragged him through. I tell her that after some years he was well enough to go back to his father's dark house; I tell her that he stayed there until he died, but I don't say anything about the heavy chain, about the river.

The doctor says there's a point where rest does more harm than good, and he tells Edie that she must do more, and stay up a little longer each day. He shakes his finger at her, in a way that tells her that he's serious but not cross, and he calls her *young lady*, as he always has, but I'm struck by how it fits her now. Angus bought her an album to mount the loose photographs from her keepsake box, and she sits at the kitchen table with a shawl around her shoulders, a blanket over her knees, and shows me the things that had settled to the bottom. The twist of wire she'd practised with after Nan showed her how to pick a locked drawer. Two buttons and a small, pearly shell, a piece cut from an outgrown dress, and three brittle leaves, their significance lost, that she crumbles to dust between her hands.

I tell her that I had a collection like that, though I'd forgotten until I said the words. Not the notes or the photographs, but an old biscuit tin filled with feathers that had drifted from the sky and green river pebbles, a curved tooth my father said came from a bear. Long gone now, all of it, and nothing I'd have had any reason to keep, except for the notion that those things had once meant something to me. Like the plug of earth I walked on for so long, the cloth that wrapped it turned grubby and rank. It's still tucked inside my mother's battered boots, that I haven't worn for years, but keep at the back of the wardrobe. Every time I see them I think of the story my father said his old aunt liked to tell, about Katie Crackernuts and the danced-out shoes. It terrified him, he said, the thought that his own feet could be made to do something he didn't want at all.

Edie wants to try, so for the first time in months we eat together at the kitchen table. Potatoes that she has peeled, a bit of liver, though she hates it, to help her blood. She goes to sleep not long after, and I heat up the iron to press Angus a shirt for tomorrow, while he settles with the newspaper, reading out bits he thinks might interest me. Redcurrant bushes are on sale already, and there's talk of a general strike in Toronto. Frank Ogilvie has had a letter from his brother, Ferd, about the bad wreck at Dryden. He was in one of the train cars that tumbled down the embankment, but not much hurt. *Have a roll? I'll thay we did!* Angus says, reading out the last part in Ferd's lisping voice.

We're both tired too, and when I set the iron to cool he folds and smooths the paper. Stands and stretches, hooking his thumbs under his braces while he does it, and pulling them smoothly off his shoulders. It's a thing I've seen him do so often, but I'm always struck by the smoothness of that motion, the ease of his body, and I think again of our early time together and how we knew each other, something that only the two of us shared, that will always bind us.

In the quiet kitchen I check that the stove is well damped and fetch the blanket, unfold it to make my nest on the sofa. Angus says surely it's time I moved back upstairs, but Edie's still ill, might call out, and I can't be that far away. He says, "Do you think I don't worry too? Do you think I'd suggest it, if I wasn't sure everything will be fine?" And suddenly we're in an argument, the way that can happen, and I try to explain that I know it's all I can do. That it's my fault, only mine, and mine the debt that's owed. We're still speaking quietly, but our words come faster. "What fault," he says, "what debt?" And I say something I didn't intend to, about all he doesn't know. About the black heart within me, the ugliness that squats inside.

Angus shakes his head and he sounds so tired when he asks if that's how little I think of him. If I really think he's a man so easily fooled. "Don't you think I know you, know all of you?" he says, and though quietly spoken, his words are a smack that leaves me dizzy. It's too much for me and I remember Pembroke Street, and the red wool unrolling. Another time when I had to question everything I thought I knew, everything I was. I come into his arms and in the dim light of our cooling kitchen he holds me up, and I feel his beating heart. Angus comforts me, like a mother would do, as if I'm someone who deserves it.

The days really are growing longer; forty-two minutes, Edie tells me today, from when she began to keep track. I wouldn't have known the number, but there's a different quality to the afternoon light, and when Angus comes up our front walk he's no longer surrounded by darkness. But it's still very cold, the snow piled high, and that leaves me a little off balance, in a way I try to explain to Edie. Something to do with the seasons and how they struggle, the way the old one holds on against the new, not yet ready to let go. The uneasy way they exist together, for a time.

"Hmm, I'll have to think about that," Edie says, sounding just like Aunt Clare. Her forehead puckers, and with the way the shadows fall, she suddenly looks like an old woman and I'm swept by such a wave of sadness, not because she'll one day be that old, but because I'll never see it, will be gone long before. I blink hard and she's my girl again. "Maybe it's because the weather's harder here," she says. "If we lived in California, say, you wouldn't have to be sad like that."

"Maybe not," I say, "though I imagine there are other things to be sad about, in California."

When the letter came about Ben it was a shock, but my aunts said that in a strange way it was as if he'd died already. Robina wrote that there was no warning, that he was found at his desk, his forehead resting on an unfinished drawing. Neat, numbered wires and circuits, a solution to a problem that would remain incomplete. She wrote that of course the children would stay with her, that she loved them like her own, and that's what they wanted; she said we were all welcome to visit any time, but somehow that never happened. Every year, around Christmastime, she sends a photograph, and we have watched the cousins grow, like strangers.

I don't think of Ben very often, but sometimes, in the autumn, I remember the train, and all the things he taught me.

And I remember a time, when Kez was bashing on about my father, that Ben told her to shush. Then he asked had she never thought that maybe Ross was walking *toward* something that just happened to be away from all of them.

Edie is tired today, but she says it's nothing like the way she felt, even a week ago. That's a good thing, I know it is, but I'm afraid to let myself think too much about it. "Do you remember that day?" I say, looking at one of the pictures in her album, and she says, "Wasn't it wonderful?" The first summer of the new century, when the big circus came, along with the wire walker called Jerome The Magnificent. He was going to cross high over the river, where it empties into the harbour, and there were still some in town who remembered when Harry Leslie did the same thing, so long ago. Angus told me that the old men who sat on the bench outside the station were in their glory, chins resting on their folded hands on top of their canes, as they watched the excursion trains roll in and relived their old excitement.

The photograph is one Robbie's mother took; Angus said she gave it to him, because she thought I might like to have it. She must have been near us that day with her tripod and camera, taking photographs like she did at every town occasion, such a familiar sight I doubt I even noticed her, but I'm glad she thought to give Angus the picture. It's taken close, just his head and Edie's, tilted back as they stare up, with the same rapt look on their faces.

"I remember the ice cream too," Edie says now. "And how much you laughed at the clowns, with their big flappy shoes." That's a thing I've completely forgotten; we talk about what else she remembers, and what I do, and I'm reminded of that game we often played on Pembroke Street. A tray of uncon-nected objects—a thimble, a pressed flower, three buttons. Maybe a little mound of sugar, and a brass key. All kinds of things gathered and placed until the tray was almost covered. We could look at it for a minute, ticked out on one of Aunt Clare's watches, and then a cloth was laid over it and we all wrote down how many items we could recall. It was always such a surprise, when the cloth was whisked away, to realize the obvious things you'd not remembered at all.

Jack would have always won, of course, because of the way his mind took pictures, so he was usually the one who set up the tray. And then, more often than not, it was Aunt Clare, who said that the trick was to make it into a story. Say a man with a crumpled flower in his lapel was distracted, and tried to put sugar in his cup with a key; the sugar spilled and trickled down the front of his three-button vest, and his wife noticed that one of those buttons was loose and said if he would just fetch her thimble she would fix it. "You can make anything into a story," Aunt Clare used to say. "Everything is connected, or at least you can find a way to make it so."

It's getting late when the telephone rings, a thing so rare that for a moment I think I'm back at Pembroke Street, where the sound of the fire wagons always made me shake. When I lift the earpiece Aunt Kez is already bellowing, and my voice echoes back to me, saying, "Yes, it's me, it's Bella, yes it is. Kez, are you there?"

"Of course I am," she says, "I'm calling you, aren't I?" Though that's always been her objection to the telephone, how anyone can say they're anyone, and you can never be sure who you're really talking to.

My heart is already thumping as my slow brain begins to ask what has happened, to ask who. "What about Edie?" Kez roars, and for a cold second I stupidly think that's the bad news. Meanwhile Kez says that she has to talk quickly since she's calling from the grocer's and the old biddy wants to close up. I can picture her, bent over with her lips close to the mouthpiece, thinking no one else hears a thing, as she tells me they're all coming to visit next week. Well, maybe not Charlie, but she is, and Nan, and Clare has free time for Easter, so she'll come from Washington, and they'll take the train together. "The Professor will just have to comb his own eyebrows for a while," she says, her old joke about why he asked Clare to marry him.

Kez says they'll stay at the hotel, like always, and when I tell her it's mostly shut up for the winter she says everything's been arranged, which explains why Angus hasn't been down to see what all the noise is about. I tell her I'm not sure it's a good idea, tell her the house is in disarray, that the weather might be bad, that I'm not in any state for company. "Oh, get over yourself, Bella," Kez says as she hangs up with a click, and it's so like her.

There's a story I used to tell myself, on the edge of sleep, where I thought it would do no harm. A story where something wakes me; maybe a sound, maybe the sound of hooves on a loose stable door. In this story I'm a good girl, I'm a brave girl, and I know just what to do, though the cabin still burns, sparks spiralling up to the moon. The glass still cracks and shatters, the horse still bolts, but we are all outside, safe at the edge of the clearing. In this story I've saved everyone, and we are all alive and together.

And sometimes I think, why shouldn't it be true? I think of the strange way time moves, think of how it feels as if Edie went to bed one night, prattling in her little cot, and woke up nearly my height, with her own secret thoughts and dreams. I think of the fiddlers in the fairy mound, I think of *Tir na n'Og*, and wonder if this life is the enchantment, if it's the place I came to when I walked in my sleep, a thing I don't remember having done since. I think of the first months after the fire, the closed and silent world I lived in, though I had no idea, and anything seems possible. I get myself in such a muddle when I start thinking this way, tell myself of course this life is real, but even if that's so, it could easily have gone a different way. "You're lucky they were there," Edie says, when I talk about how I came to Pembroke Street. And it's true, I was; they could easily have turned their backs, the way they believed my father had done to all of them.

If that had happened, I would have had a very differ-ent life. With the Wroths, perhaps, a despised almost-sister to Amy, who would have stopped filling my water glass soon enough. Our evenings spent in prayer, until they could marry me off, maybe to some earnest young preacher, and then a life of more prayer and endless good works. If there was no one to marry I might have stood behind the counter in the dry goods store, boarded in the village and spent the rest of my days with other people's furniture. Or perhaps I'd have become a teacher, ended up in a tiny school somewhere even more remote, where the winters were even darker. My aunts and uncles and cousins living out their overflowing lives on a busy, bonus wire, while mine was the separate, quiet one, meant for those who didn't know or want anything more.

I tell myself that I wouldn't have known what I was missing, that I wouldn't even have known to think that way, but I've brought myself to a terrible place, one where there would be no Angus, no Edie. Or perhaps they'd still exist, but somehow altered, two people with no connection to me at all. People I might see, passing through a lighted room, while I stand outside in the dark, close to the cold glass. *Oh, for goodness' sake,* Aunt Kez says then, in my mind, saving me again.

If there wasn't so much to do I'd be angry about the visit arranged behind my back, but there's no time to think about that, or wonder how Angus managed it. With Robbie's help he's moved Edie's bed back upstairs, and though I heard her tossing and turning through the night she claims to have slept very well. The larder is filled with things for our Easter dinner, and I've mixed up the dough for the crescent biscuits Aunt Nan likes so much. I leave Edie to shape them while I sweep out the empty parlour, and when Angus comes home we'll put everything back as it should be. The floor is streaked with sunlight that shows up the dust and grit in the corners, and the room is so bare that I keep turning my head to remind myself that she's not gone, no matter how much it feels that way.

As I sweep and wipe down the walls I find I'm thinking of all the dark afternoons, the stories Edie wanted and how carefully I told them, how lightly. Uncle Charlie, and the "wild side," all that was Pembroke Street. And our cabin in the clearing, farther back, things I'd forgotten coming to me, more and more of them. The way my father could change his rumbling voice to an old woman's quaver, a little boy's squeak, and how he could make my mother laugh so hard. I remembered the foul poultices when we were ill, and the feel of her chapped hand on my forehead. The way my brothers' hair smelled, when they were small enough to be carried about, and how for so long Little Ross called everything *blue*. Even the sun, even our horse and the floppy-combed rooster. I remembered times, when we were at peace, that I helped them with their school work, or untangled a knotted shoelace, and I remembered their smiles, how they looked at me like someone so clever, someone who would always be there. In the empty parlour I think of the stories I picked out to tell Edie and wonder why they should be any less true, less real, than the dark threads I kept to myself.

I look again through the open doorway and see Edie's bent head, hear the quiet tune she hums, as she often does when she concentrates, and it almost overwhelms me, the thought of how I know her. The tune she hums and the way her hair falls, all the things that make her laugh, and her sometimes unreasonable temper. There's nothing I wouldn't forgive her, no need even to call it forgiveness, and I wonder, suddenly, if my own mother felt the same. If she knew more than I thought, understood more, if there was never any question.

When I open the back door to shake out the mats there's something in the air. Maybe a scent, or something softer in the way it feels, and there's warmth in the sun. The ice along the eaves is melting a little, drops of water tapping on the wooden railing, and I catch myself in my old habit of trying to make that sound a pattern, a message. I've lived here long enough to know that there are still weeks of winter left, but also to remember that a thaw like this can come like a gift, making it easier to survive the rest.

Behind me, in the house, Edie is now washing the bowls, and behind me farther than that, my aunts will be pulling down the shades and getting ready to make their way to the station, prodding Clare, who still always believes there's time for another cup of coffee. In a few hours they'll board the train in a flurry of coats and scarves and bags, bumping into each other and tussling, in a good-natured way, over the window seats. Talking and dozing as the train makes its slow way from small station to station, and nodding to the strangers who board, bringing cold air that rises from their clothes.

There on the back porch I tip my face to the sun, and the movement reminds me of that photograph of Edie and Angus, how I would have seen them exactly like that, if only I'd looked. But like everyone else in the crowd that day, I was staring up. Squinting into the sun while the rope walker stepped out; he had a red sash tied around his waist, and the ends fluttered in a breeze that didn't touch us, so far below. He started slowly, one foot in front of the other, with the long pole held across his chest, and I remember how he shifted that pole, just a little, to find his balance. The tiniest movements, they seemed from below, but I remember thinking how enormous they would have been, from the high, lonely place where he was.

II

1916–1968

BURNING BOY

Someone was saying his name, but not his real name. Someone was saying what his mother called his *paper* name; he could hear it quite clearly when the other noise stopped. Someone was saying his paper name, and that's how he knew he was dead.

The other noise was somewhere between a bellow and a roar, and he thought it might be important to work out what it was. It made him think of summer when he was small and of the circus, the animals. Not the sleepy-looking lion with its sores and bald patches but the elephant, that was it. The noise was like the elephant when it unfurled its long trunk from between its stubby tusks and trumpeted. His mother had taken a photograph of that elephant and tacked it to the wall by his bed. He could picture it, he was picturing it, but then the noise rolled through again, taking over. Filling up everything, not even the tiniest space left for a thought.

A different voice was saying his paper name, saying, "Francis, Francis." Not a voice he knew, although he knew a lot of people who were dead. The elephant began to trumpet again but not quite as loudly, as if it was not right beside him anymore but maybe shambling away. When he thought that, it occurred to him that maybe he wasn't dead, maybe he was small again and at the circus. Though if he was small again, how would he know it was *again*, and how would he be thinking these thoughts?

He'd lost track, didn't know if it was the same voice or a different one, but it was saying, "Francis, Frank, can you open your eyes?" He thought he probably could, but not yet; first he had to think about the circus, and he held on to that word until the noise subsided. Then he thought that it didn't smell like the circus so maybe he wasn't small, maybe he was dead after all. The circus smelled like hot canvas and sweat and dung, and this was different. Something rotten, underneath a stronger, sharp smell. Clean, but not the clean of a white shirt snapping on a line. "Open your eyes, Frank," the voice said again, and it was so *annoying*; he wasn't ready yet. He kept his eyes closed tight and said, "Robbie. My name is Robbie."

The walleyed nurse wrote the letters for him, and helped him work out what to say. Her name was Janet, but she said all her friends called her Fizz, because of the hair he'd never properly seen, tucked neatly under her cap. She chattered about things like that while she straightened his sheets and changed his dressings and he supposed they were trained to do that, to distract from the pain and keep things civil, but he was still grateful for it. She had a way with a razor too, gentle but not timid, gliding it over his cheeks and chin, and when he heard one of the other nurses making her way down the line of cots he feigned sleep, a thing he told her once. "Well, I don't know when I'll have time to shave you," Janet said, but he could tell she was pleased, knew that she would find the time, as she did.

He'd tried to write those letters himself, thinking how hard could it be, but he soon found out. The wavering lines were like something traced by a blind man and then the writing tablet slipped and he made an unthinking lunge to stop it, sending fierce howls through his body. Janet *tsked* and dragged the screens around the bed, the way she did when she came to share one of his cigarettes in the middle of the night. She said, "You don't have to say much, and anyway, they'll be so happy to know you're alive and coming home. Shall I just write that there's a problem with your arm?"

"You mean the fact that it's not there?" he said, and they fell into helpless, stifled laughter, like children in church.

"Something like that," Janet said, when she could speak, and that set them off again. "My goose is cooked if anyone complains," she said, but they knew that no one would.

The other nurses were all kind and some were beautiful, but he felt a connection with Janet that had something to do with the glint in her eye when she tapped the end of a cigarette on the tin before putting it in her mouth, the small sound clear in the darkened ward. It had something to do with the sharp things she said about the village she hoped she'd never go back to, and the way every joke she told was on herself. She wasn't there when the porter delivered his kit, finally sorted from the splintered wreckage of the train he'd been on, but she came hurrying as soon as she heard. Looked at the banjo on top of his battered bag and sat down beside his bed, held his only hand between hers.

Later that night, when the ward was quiet except for the usual coughs and moans, she told him a thing she was ashamed of, looking right at him with her straight-ahead eye. She said that she couldn't help thinking, with so many not coming back, that the men who did would have their pick, and what chance did someone like her have?

Once he was past the indignities of the bedpan he made his slow way to the toilets on his own, getting used to the fact that even the way he pissed had changed. The journey tired him out and in the daytime he barely made it back to his cot before he tumbled into sleep, but the nights were different. He knew that this hospital on the coast was really someone's grand house and when he wandered the night-lit hallways he wondered if they were still there. The lord and the lady now living a smaller life behind one of the *Private* doors. There was a stone staircase near his ward and a small window that was usually left open, and though he couldn't see it he could hear the restless sea, a sound that soothed him back to being a boy in his own small bed on the other side of the world. Shuffling through the dim corridors he sometimes passed other night-roamers, their faded blues glowing against the shadows. There might be a tiny nod but mostly they ignored each other, making their silent way like ghosts from layers of time.

One of those nights, as he moved down the ward, he heard Janet's loud whisper from somewhere near the screens that surrounded the burned boy's bed. "Then what chance does someone like me have?" she was saying, and Robbie almost laughed. As he closed his eyes, back on his cot, he realized that there had been a hazy idea in his head, pushing aside the thoughts he should have been having. Thoughts of his wife, Edie, and thoughts of the son he hadn't yet seen, who'd been made by a different, whole man.

Things were not quite the same between them, after that, and he thought Janet knew it, though she didn't let on. He knew it wasn't fair to begrudge her, and he knew he was no better, not really. Letting her wrap him in her sympathetic hands, letting her think what she thought about the banjo. "No, no—you won it fair and square," Duggan had said, throwing his cards down. But he hadn't, of course. When he was a boy, helping out at the hotel, he got to know Edie's great-aunts when they visited every summer. Her aunt Nan was a bit of a devil, hiding behind an old lady's soft pink face. She taught him all kinds of shuffles, and how to deal from the bottom of the deck without being spotted, and she was always opening her wrinkled hand to show the coin or the shiny new marble he'd had tucked deep in his pocket. "Don't *torment* the poor boy," her sister Kez said, giving her a swat on the shoulder, but they all knew he didn't mind.

When he did his finger exercises now, trying to train his neglected left hand, he always thought of how Duggan was, after that game on the ship. The restless movements on the table in the mess, twitching and tapping his fingers and toes to all the music, trapped now in his head. Robbie remembered what Nan used to say on the wide hotel veranda, when they piled up their matchsticks, or smooth pebbles from the beach. She said, "Never bet a thing you'll mind giving up," so really there was no reason to feel badly about Duggan, who should have thought it through. Against the banjo Duggan had asked him to bet the picture of Edie, with her hair falling loose around her face, and that was the uncomfortable

thought. How easily he'd agreed to it, even if he'd been sure
he wouldn't lose.

They came from different places, but they were all missing
something. One wag made a sign that said *Lumberjack Ward*,
but spoiled it by saying, "Because of the stumps, see?" Everyone
made black jokes like that, and they didn't need spelling out.
He did it himself, but there were times he got so tired of the
need to always be wisecracking. So tired of saying, "Oh, it
could be worse, I'm better off than so-and-so." That was true,
he supposed, there was always something worse, though he
wondered what it was for the burned boy, in his raw yet crispy
shell. The minister, when he visited, told them to remember
that the Lord never sends more than we can bear, and Robbie
felt his missing fist clench with the need to punch him, for the
terrible trick that was.

He knew he was not so bad, compared with some; he could
play that game all day. The two brothers from Newfoundland,
for example, who'd been blown up together and between them
lost three legs, two arms and an eye. They talked sometimes
about what they wouldn't miss. The raw, freezing hands and
the sheer slog of hauling in nets, muscles screaming no matter
how many times you'd done it. And the terror when the boat
was storm-tossed, at the mercy of the wind and the raging sea.
Though he knew that on the far side of that terror was a feeling of such power, such absolute joy, and they'd be missing that
too, for the rest of their days.

The fisher-boys still had powerful voices, and sometimes
they sang in what was called the lounge. Judging by the paper
on the walls it had once been a lady's bedroom, and there were
jokes about that too. One brother tried to play two spoons

on the other's leg, while it tapped up and down, and Robbie's favourite was the song about the maid on the shore, rollicking yet lonely-sounding, that reminded him of his mother. Reminded him of running ahead of her on the pebbled beach in the early morning, with the wind blowing hard through their hair.

Before the *Erebus* he hadn't had much to do with boats, and that had surprised the girl in the bed in Liverpool. He'd just finished telling her about the town on the shores of Lake Huron, the big ships lining the horizon. "Whatever'd you join the navy for then?" she had said, kneeling to push aside the curtain, the dubious blanket still pooled around her legs. She had a splotched mark on her shoulder blade and he reached to run his fingertips around it, trying to think what the shape reminded him of. Too ragged for a teardrop, but maybe a far-away island he'd seen on a map. "Still pissing down rain," she said, letting the curtain slither back, and she said that she didn't mind staying longer, only she'd need more money, she had bills to pay, same as anyone.

Her name was Caroline, or so she told him, and she didn't mind what he did. In the end she stayed through the after-noon, though he had to open his wallet from time to time. "No offence," she always said, and each time he made a little bow and said, "None taken, miss," just to hear her giggly laugh. He told her that for some reason it was not boats but trains that had always drawn him, and he told her that one of his first memories was being held in his mother's arms, that's how small he was, while a big, gleaming engine huffed to a stop. Panting and grunting like a living thing, belches of steam swirling around them. He'd shrieked and his mother thought he was frightened, but it was a cry of pure delight.

He told her too that when he was eight or nine he played a sort of game, standing on the rail, out of sight of the station, until he felt the vibration through the soles of his feet. The game was to stand as long as he could, with the train coming at him around the long bend, to wait as long as he could before throwing himself sideways and rolling, the world spinning along with the angry blast of the whistle. He did it for days before the station master caught him, dragged him home with a hard hand clamped on his neck. "Poor little Robbie," Caroline said, leaning closer with her smudged mouth.

Later she held on to his hand in the dark and glistening street. He felt hollowed out, and completely at peace, walking her to the pub on the corner. She told him he could find her there, if he ever came back on leave. "Ta-ra then," Caroline had said, and just for a moment he wrapped both his arms around her.

He had other, lesser injuries, including a bad knock on the head. One of the beautiful nurses, Elizabeth, told him that was probably why everything was scrambled. Apparently he'd been on his way to Liverpool again and he remembered the train station, remembered mothers and children, suitcases and shopping baskets; he remembered feeling strangely like an intruder in the normal world. He remembered the slam of the closing door and the conductor's whistle, the old woman in his compartment who was knitting something grey, but nothing at all about the crash. "Think of that as a good thing," Elizabeth said, as she tucked and smoothed his blanket.

In his other life things had always brushed by him, though sometimes close enough he felt their breath. A fall from a tree, cushioned by lower branches, or the time he and his friend Stevie went through the ice but somehow managed to crash their way to shore. They had sidled through the blacksmith's doorway and he let them steam by the fire until they were dry enough to avoid a fuss at home; the dim air rang, and sparks flew and sizzled. "Hellfire and Damnation," Stevie said, thumping his chest like Whiskey Ted did when he shouted in the street, and it was the funniest thing ever.

Another time a fever clamped hot jaws on him, shook him around and then dropped him, spent and gasping. It had lasted for days and those days were also lost to him, as if he'd stepped out of the regular flow of time. The fever dreams, if they were dreams, were almost too vivid to bear. Once he was suddenly fishing from a rowboat on a hot, still day, the lake a sheet of dull green glass. Someone was with him in the boat and he knew it was his father, though the man was bent over baiting a hook, his face hidden. In the dream, if it was a dream, Robbie toppled over the side while he was leaning to see what his father looked like, the glass lake turned to thick liquid around him. He was soaking wet when he opened his eyes, and in the early morning light his mother was whispering, *Please please please*, as if it was a thing she would say forever.

Even the war brushed past him, in a way, shut up as he was in the ship's wireless office at the bottom of the steep staircase, the steeper ladder. The knobs and bars and switches all within reach, his tiny desk hard by the cage that surrounded the root of the great communications cable. His whole focus was on what passed between his ears and his fingertips, on getting it right, passing it on; no time, and anyway not his job, to think about what it meant. Mostly they were on convoy duty out of

Gib, and at first it was like some strange holiday, with the sun and the sparkling Mediterranean. He tried to describe it in his letters to Edie, along with the routine of the ship, the men he was with. In the margins he sketched pictures—tall Beadle with his headset and his knees crammed up to his chin, and the gunner, Duggan, with his huge buckteeth.

Sometimes they steamed through chains of small islands, barren-looking mounds rising separate from the empty water. Once he borrowed a pair of binoculars and saw that what he'd taken for a puzzling play of light was a herd of brown goats, trotting in a mass that flowed. Wild ones, he supposed, but then he caught a glint of brass and knew that there were people, at least one person, who had fastened bells around their warm necks; the engines were too loud, but he knew just how they would sound, that particular clatter. *Shall we do that*, he wrote to Edie, *when all this is done? Shall we come back here and be goatherds?* It would be as though they were courting again and they'd lie in the sand, different sand, and look up at the stars in another sky.

When the season changed there were storms, and even the solid *Erebus* pitched and rolled. And when it changed back there were days when the cabin was a furnace, his fingers slippery with sweat, and even breathing was work. They only had to fire their guns once, at a sub that completed its dive untouched, but sometimes there were flames on the horizon, and there were times they sailed through days-old debris fields that stretched as far as they could see. He had thought then that if he learned more about tides and currents he would have some idea where all that wreckage would end up. Empty life jackets and crates and splintered wood, shredded cloth, things much more mysterious than the coloured bottles, the floats and torn nets that had washed up on the shore of his childhood. He imagined it all floating into the future, so slowly and gently, the dull knock as a bobbing table leg nudged the side of a fisherman's skiff. He imagined a small boy, one who'd never had to know any wars, wading into the surf that foamed around his shins and dragging his treasure to safety.

The closest call he had came in the hot middle of a quiet day. He was on deck with a man named Jury, both of them trying to put an exact name to the colour of the water they were moving so serenely through. Looking down they saw something dark streak by below them, just under the surface, and part of his brain knew that was just how Death would come, dark and blurred and when you least expected. But nothing happened, no alarm bells, no sudden yaw, and for whatever reason, no second torpedo. He remembered that they just looked at each other, and then Jury shrugged his shoulders and said, "Aquamarine?"

His paper name was Francis James Robert Sears. He remembered learning it when he first went to school, remembered how fitting it had seemed, as if he were becoming a whole new boy. The first two names were for his mother's lost brothers, the last, she said, for his father, who'd been dead all along. Robbie didn't know much about him, and there were times when that had mattered. He knew that he'd done something brave, and that he was an orphan as his mother was, and Edie's parents too. He'd never really thought about that before, how rare it must have been to keep a family whole, in the old, harder times they'd come through.

He didn't know much about his mother's life either, though he remembered her telling a story about being chased by a bear, and another about a ship with white sails. When he was small he'd had the idea that she'd fallen off, while the rest sailed on without her. Or that maybe there'd been a wreck and they'd been marooned, still hoping someone would find them; he'd thought about that on the ship that steamed up the St. Lawrence, realized he was looking for flickering fires all along the shore.

Every form he'd had to fill in had all his names, but in the war itself he was mostly *Sears*, and he wondered if, along with the bang on the head, it might be this business of names that had him so confused about just who he was, about his life. Janet told him more than once how lucky he was that things happened as they did. That he'd gone first to a regular hospital, the amputation done cleanly, by a good surgeon, instead of in some field hospital, seething with infection. She said she could tell him stories that would curl his hair even more.

He knew what she meant, but he also knew what *lucky* felt like, and it wasn't this. Lucky was lying in his own bed in his own house, with his arms crossed beneath his head. It was watching Edie, with his blue shirt draped over her shoulders, as she bit hungrily into a pear. Lucky was watching Edie laughing as she cupped her hand over her chin to catch the juice falling from her lovely mouth, but that wasn't a thing he could tell Janet. Instead he said there was another word he was thinking of, and that word was *irony*, and she rolled her mismatched eyes, and blew out a hard jet of smoke.

There were things to be sorted out, and apparently the fact that he'd been on leave, and on a civilian train, made them complicated. Not impossible, but it took time, though he didn't care. He knew he should be chafing to get home and he put on a show of disappointment every time the limping clerk arrived with yet another form to sign with his shaky, wrong-handed scrawl. But really he was quite content where he was, with the rhythm of the ward, the food not bad. He could close his eyes and sleep when he wanted, even without the prick of the needle, now that the pain was easier.

He was healing beautifully, they told him, and he'd found a new balance when he walked. When he shuffled, rather; he still moved carefully, as if he were carrying the most precious, delicate thing. Sometimes he made his way outside to the bench that was surrounded by roses, and the misty light made the green lawns glow where they rolled toward the sea. There was a high fence there, at the cliff's edge, that was said to be against invasion, but he was certain it was really in case anyone had the urge to leap over.

When Janet asked he told her his son was called Robert Angus, named for his father and Edie's, and she thought it had a nice, solid ring to it. He didn't tell her about the photographs he had, good ones, that his mother had taken. On the back of one she had written, *He's the spit of you at his age,* as if she knew about the crazy thoughts in his head. She'd sent other photographs, of Edie standing sideways, with her hands on the growing shelf of her stomach, but a different picture had slithered in. Edie lying with someone else, the two of them laughing at how easy he'd been to fool. He knew it wasn't true, but the thought was hard to shake. That time Beadle tore his letter in two and went mad in the mess, throwing plates and anything that would smash, Robbie knew what that rage would feel like.

———

Every so often people came to look at the burned boy. Sailors and soldiers of different ranks, and wives and parents, once an elderly couple all the way from Dundee. No one recognized him, though as Janet said, they'd be lying if they said they could. The story was that he'd been plucked from the smouldering sea after a battle, though no one could explain how he'd ended up here, nor why he was lying in *Lumberjack Ward*, surrounded by screens near one of the tall windows that lined whatever grand room it had once been. There was no chance at all that he'd live, and the doctors were baffled he'd survived this long. His hair had burned away, his nose and fingers, his toes. His uniform, of course, but even if he was a Hun, if his moaning was German moaning, you couldn't feel anything but pity.

There wasn't really anywhere you could touch him, the nurses said, and they all hated the sound of the morphine-filled needle going in. Some of them thought it would be a kindness to give him too much, and some thought he should be moved to some far-off, private corner, to spare the rest of them, but the men all said to leave him be. Robbie wondered how many shared with him the small, mean thought, beneath the genuine, comradely sentiment, that as long as the burned boy was there, there would always be something worse.

The nurses had a lot to do, and women from the nearby town, all ages, came to read and visit and help out with the craftwork that was supposed to be good for them, grown men weaving baskets from thin, pliant strips, and clumsily poking thread through canvas. They'd been told, he was sure, to be cheerful and matter-of-fact, and he wondered if that was how it would be for the rest of his life, people speaking to him in that bright tone that forced him to answer the same way.

One of those volunteers asked what his work was, back home, and she said that once she'd broken her arm and had to do everything with her other hand, and it was strange, wasn't it, as if you had to change your whole brain around. She got flustered, in case he thought she was saying it was anything the same, and he felt sorry for her, with her prim dress and shoes and her pale hair so carefully brushed. He told her that he'd been a schoolteacher for a little while, that maybe he could do that again, and she beamed as if he'd said the cleverest thing, and threaded his needle for him.

Another day a different woman told him about an article she'd read, the amazing work they were doing on artificial limbs, and he just nodded. Everyone said the legs were not bad but the arms were shite, and if he'd still had doubts, watching Kirkwood's struggles would have convinced him. He'd tried so hard, Kirkwood had, but developed a ring of sores from the straps, a bad infection on the stump from all the chafing, and the arm was put in store with the rest of his things. Elizabeth carried it away, trying to work out how to hold it. In the end she braced it on her shoulder, the way you might carry a rifle, or a baby that wanted to look around, and the hand bobbed along the length of the ward, waving goodbye.

Kirkwood had been a bus driver before, and he grinned with the others when they ribbed him. When they said, "What did you think? Did you think you could stick a glove on it and no one would notice?" *Irony* was the word, all right; it was everywhere. The best was Gillis, when he wheeled himself into the lounge, where the man from the Ministry was asking his questions. "Step dancer," Gillis said, and everyone laughed till it hurt.

Janet asked, quite hesitantly for her, if he wanted to give away the banjo, but he said no. Remembering how he'd imagined himself, on their little front porch back home, the dark, soft air and the sound of summer insects. He'd be holding that battered banjo, having magically learned to play it. Edie somewhere in the house behind him, maybe rocking his son to sleep and he was helping, plucking out a slow, restful tune. His son could hear it and it soothed him, the sound threading through his dreams, and in some way he would remember it, and would always feel safe, and cared for. Robbie tried to make that a reason, a pure and important reason for why he'd wanted the banjo and the way he had set about getting it, the sneaky shuffle, the tricks.

Duggan had been someone who'd got to him from the start. Got to many of them, for some reason, the butt of all jokes, a foot stuck out or a stool moved at the last second, grown men laughing like bullies in a schoolyard. He seemed like someone who'd grown up in a sack, so little did he know about the world around him, even the names of the countries that were fighting this war. Straw hair and bucked-out teeth and a snorting laugh. But something wondrous happened when he took out the banjo he toted wherever he could. The way his fingers flew over those strings, over the frets with the mother-of-pearl glinting between them, and no one could keep from clapping along, from stamping their feet and whooping. Sometimes he looked up with his quick goof's grin, but mostly he was lost, transported, hunching over and rocking back, and he didn't sing but sometimes he gave a little *yip*, and sometimes an eerie, low crooning, as if just for a moment the voice of whatever was possessing him had burst out. Until he stopped playing, and then he was Duggan again, with his hideous teeth and his big, clown's feet; just Duggan, stupid as mud.

Robbie knew that Janet had the wrong idea about what kind of reminder the banjo was, and before he'd realized that her confidences were spread all over the ward he might have tried to explain. His new, lopsided self understood that his war had released something ravenous in him, something he didn't recognize, but didn't resist. There were things he wanted, all kinds of things, and no reason why he shouldn't have them. *I want that*, he'd thought in the pub in Liverpool, when he saw Caroline sit down on a drunken man's lap. And on the ship, when Duggan played and the men stomped and whistled, he thought, *I deserve it more.*

Eventually the proper papers were signed in the proper places, and he said his goodbyes. Janet came to share a last cigarette and told him she'd decided to marry that butcher's son. The one with thick glasses that she'd joked about, who'd been asking for years. "Is that irony too?" she said, and he supposed it was something close.

He'd thought he'd have trouble on the train and he did, a little. His heart beating faster, his palms and forehead damp, but he closed his eyes and imagined himself in a boat in the middle of a lake, no land in sight. Not the *Erebus*, nothing like that, but a small boat, rocking gently. The sun picking out bands of colour in the water, and just enough breeze. He might have slept; when he opened his eyes they were still rocketing through the countryside, but he was calm, removed. That feeling stayed with him all the way to the docks, to his berth on the ship that would carry him back across the ocean; that feeling stayed.

On board he kept to himself, as most of them did. There was none of the bravado and hijinks that had marked the voyage over. He thought of the distance unfurling behind him like something that was slipping through his fingers, becoming as hazy as what was ahead, though it had seemed so real at the time. He remembered how it was at first, teaching his left hand to take over. How aware he was of his brain saying *squeeze*, saying *lift*, saying *move this way* or *that*. And he thought that maybe that scrambled feeling had nothing to do with the knock on his head. Maybe it was just a snarled phase before things untangled, reordered, and he really was coming home with a different mind too.

The ship docked and there were trains and more trains, but that calm feeling stayed. There was so much bustle in the stations that he couldn't hear his own footsteps, and he always seemed to be moving against a flow of young faces, fresh uniforms; he thought how much easier it was to get into the war, swept along on a wave of cheers and brass bands, and fluttering handkerchiefs. The journey felt as though it could go on forever, but finally he was on the last, shorter train, and the people getting on and off at its frequent stops were familiar, although he didn't actually know any of them. He must have looked very fierce or sad because no one sat with him or tried to start a conversation, though a few times someone asked if he was getting off, if he needed help with his bags. "No, thank you," he said. "I sent them on ahead."

Those bags would have already arrived, would be sitting somewhere in his house, like the effects of a dead man, and he wondered how large they would seem, in his son's small world. He tried to imagine himself walking through his own front door, but another picture formed in his head and he saw himself slumping down, heavy in his seat as they drew into his station. He saw himself staying on the train and riding farther, riding north to the end of the line. There was a ferry there, he knew that, and he could sail with it across the neck of the lake. He saw himself walking down the short ramp on the other side, walking on and on until he reached the start of the dense bush that would seal itself behind him, after he'd passed through.

That would be right, that would be better, and it would be a better thing, a braver thing, to leave his son with the story he would make for himself, from the things unpacked from the battered bags. From the banjo with its snapped strings and the jacket with polished buttons, from everything else he'd be told. They would tell him the only things he should know, Edie and Robbie's mother. The funny stories and the scrapes he got into when he was a boy, the facts of the rest of his life. And that way his son would grow up knowing the best of him.

It had nothing to do with his missing arm, although that's what everyone thought. Would think. Back at the hospital Elizabeth sometimes sat with him on that bench by the roses, her cool hands folded in her lap. She told him once about her fiancé, Patrick, who was somewhere in muddy France, and she asked him to believe her when she said that nothing would matter, *nothing*, as long as Patrick came home alive.

He had let her believe that she'd helped him, because she was kind, and it was kindly meant; he knew that Edie would say the same, but he also knew that he didn't deserve it. He'd seen something in himself, he'd *been* something, that left him shamed and grim. The smooth skin of decency had shredded so easily, leaving something raw and puckered and angry. He had no memory of the racing speed of that other train, no memory of the crash, or the broken bodies flung wide. But he remembered the old woman with her smoky grey ball of wool, and he knew that he was a man who would have kicked her aside to save himself.

The train carried on through the scruffy countryside and he began to recognize each tree, each weathered barn, and each place where the lake glinted briefly before vanishing again. Time seemed to have speeded up, and suddenly he wasn't sure of anything. What was courage, and what the worst kind of cowardice. He remembered the burned boy, holding on for all of them long after he should have let go, and wondered if it was really that, wondered if he even knew that he was alive.

Splinters of thought were piercing the calm that had wrapped him; he tried to imagine himself in that boat on the empty water but he couldn't do it and then, too soon, they were into the last, long curve before the station. There was a point in that bend where he could see the track ahead, and he looked for the boy who had balanced on the rail like a rope walker, both arms held out at his sides. He looked for the boy who was trying so hard to be brave, staring straight at everything that was rushing toward him.

THE MAID ON THE SHORE

She used to stand on the shore with the boy, looking out at the vast ruffled lake and imagining that it was the ocean, that at any moment a ship could appear, bringing her lost ones back to her. Just for a little while; the boy was always hungry for his breakfast and when he tugged at her hand she let him draw her on to the wooden steps, counting with him as they climbed. One two three four. The wind and the sound of the waves falling away, replaced by the sound of their own harder breathing, until—seventy-three, seventy-four—they were back on the bluff near the bandshell, back in the town.

Every night before he slept, when Robbie was small, he liked me to talk about all we'd done that day. "Tell it like a story," he used to say, and I did: *It was a cold, windy morning and the woman walked with the boy. She made him wear his new warm sweater even though it itched him, and the lake was all ruffly, and he found a black stone with a hole right through.* "And the woman is you," Robbie said. "And the boy is me, I found it." And I said, "Indeed you did."

Sometimes I told him about the ship the woman watched for, that was bringing her family back. The snapping sails and brother Frank at the big wheel, with a peaked cap on his head, brass buttons on his jacket. Millie and Jim high in the rigging, holding on with one hand as they lean out, waving, and our mother standing in the prow with the baby in her arms, both of them dressed in the cleanest white. She points to the shore, showing the baby, and they are smiling so wide, maybe laughing, as if they would never be anything but happy. "And that's why you're Francis James Robert," I always told him, and it was mostly true. Though Robert was my own father's name, or so my mother once said.

How can it be, that all that time has vanished? All the days and years we walked through together, my same hand turning down the lantern, night after night. A silly question to be asking myself, no point in wondering, no answer. Like the rules of light and shadow, some things just are as they are, and the only way is to start from there and carry on. Robbie was a boy and now he's a man, he's been to war and come back changed, has children of his own. Like a seedling growing, like a bud that opens to flower, you can be there every day and still not see exactly how and when it happens. Though when I think of that, I know it was the boy who was wide open, a bright flower. His growing up somehow a process of folding away.

Those old steps from the beach are not much used now, except by children, or by people who don't want to be seen. But I climbed them this morning, pleased that I still could, though I needed to stop and rest along the way. And each time I lowered myself onto a step, looking west out over the lake, I marvelled at the changes that had happened while my back was turned.

Curls of pure white breaking everywhere farther out, and the band of pinkish-mauve along the horizon slowly expanding, pushing up the lowering clouds. The scrub on the hillside turning from grey to green, and then different shades of it. By the time I reached the top and turned to look out again the sun had cleared the trees, cleared the town behind me and poured out over the lake. The gulls that had wheeled by the score from wherever they slept, high flashes of silver and bronze, had settled on the rocking water. I thought about where I had started and where I was now, about the way everything is transformed by time, by light.

I've never been much of a churchgoer, except in the Home we were taken to when I was young, that was supposed to give us a better life; between scrubbing and praying we spent most of our time there on our knees. It would be comforting, I'm sure, to be able to believe that everything happens for a reason. To believe there's a plan, God's plan, and you only need to surrender. There are rules in the world, I know, things that clever people understand. The path of the sun, the stars and the tides and currents, and gravity that lets some things rise up and keeps others firmly on the ground. But it's always seemed to me that the rest is all chance: the people you meet, the places you end up, which way you turn at a corner. That all you can do is make the best of where you are, no point in dwelling on what might have happened if you'd gone another way.

It was just chance, I know, that brought me to Inverhaven, when Robbie was still curled safe inside me. I had an advertisement for a housekeeper folded in my bag, and if the connecting train hadn't been so late I would have carried on to that other town and had a different life. Chance too that the sun was shining that April day, and the station master—not Angus, but the one before—gave me directions to a hotel with a dining room that was reasonably priced. The town was like all the others I'd ever been in, a short main street, still frozen and rutted, a grocer, hardware store, pharmacy. But the sun was actually warm, and a man who was stretching in a door-way wished me *Good day*. I passed a school just as the children tumbled out; a young boy running with his jacket unbuttoned called back *Sorry missus* after he bumped me, and I was struck by his grin, by his healthy pink cheeks.

I must have missed the street I was meant to take, and found myself following a cleared path that led past a band-shell to where a snow-covered bench looked out on the sudden expanse of lake, a strange landscape of frozen mounds and fur-rows, and the enormous sky. It should have reminded me of the boat from Liverpool all those years before, the terror of so much open water, but perhaps because of the ice, I didn't think of that. Instead a great calm settled on me, even my hunger gone. I brushed off the bench and sat looking out until the sun had lost its warmth, until I heard a distant train whistle and knew that it would go on without me.

Robbie's house is in the opposite direction, but this morning I followed the sound of hammer blows to the place where the new inn, huge and modern, is rising from the ashes of the Lakeview Hotel. The old Lakeview burned to the ground one January night, burned so fiercely that even if the lines hadn't been frozen, people doubt that much could have been saved. A bitter smell lingered all winter, the blackened mess softened by falling snow. Everyone knows what happened and who was behind it; cheaper to rebuild than repair, especially with the insurance money. There was an investigation of sorts, but of course nothing could be proved.

Maybe it wouldn't have happened, if I'd done what Robbie and Edie thought I should and tried to fight the will. Or maybe I'd have burned up with it, maybe it was lucky that I didn't have the heart. I know they were right about the principle, and there were others in town who made a point of saying the same, which was maybe kind of them. Whatever they've thought and said about me, it seems they count me as belonging, compared to some slicker from the city. Though I'm sure there would have been muttering too, if the hotel had come to me. That's just how people are, and I'm sure not only here.

This morning I found it hard to remember the old hotel, looking at the high, new walls, the workmen moving in and out of the spaces where doors and windows will be. I tried to picture the dove-grey paint, the shady wraparound veranda, but the sun was bright, daubs of colour everywhere. A splash of yellow on a ladder, the back of a man at a sawhorse, his blue shirt criss-crossed by bright red suspenders, and I thought of a double exposure in a photograph, that can happen by accident or design. A ghostly image that doesn't belong, mixed up with the one that does, past and present together in a way, and hard to tell which is which. I thought of how it is with a child you've watched grow, or a person you haven't seen for years, how you still know them, and they seem to trail all their ages with them.

Once thoughts like that get going they roll like waves and can be just as impossible to stop. This morning, by the spot where the Lakeview once was, those thoughts led me to Angus, and I remembered a time when we sat together near those old beach steps, in the late summer dark. We were talking about similar things, I suppose, about changes and the way the edges of the town were spreading out, new houses where there'd been nothing but bush and open fields. Angus said lately he'd noticed that when he gave directions from the station, they were based on where things used to be. Turn right where the big maple was, go past the corner where MacArthur had his store, left before the old iron footbridge. He said maybe he had a ghost town in his head, an ideal one, and if he could put together all the places that came into his mind, from their different times, he could imagine himself walking down its streets, maybe we both could. Remembering that, how I missed him. I never had the right, but I always did.

It was luck or chance that brought me to Inverhaven all those years ago, and the same that I walked through the door of the Lakeview Hotel when I did, with my story about hard times, a husband lost to a fever. I'm sure Maggie didn't believe a word, but the sun and melting snow that day had her in a panic. A reminder that spring was near, that she'd fired the last two women for miles around who were willing to work for her and now had no one to help get the place ready for the coming season, to take care of the rooms, serve the meals. I said that if she had a bed I would start at first light, and I made myself useful enough in the coming weeks that when the pains came she sent for the midwife, and there was never any question but that Robbie and I would stay.

Maggie was difficult, with her moods and her rages, but I'd known much worse, and once I understood that there was no point in trying to please her we went along all right. She said a crying baby would disturb the guests, so Robbie and I lived in the two-room cottage she owned nearby, and that suited me very well. Her husband, Reuben, was as sweet as she was sour, just tilting his head and smiling when she called him an old fool, and worse. That only made her wilder, which I came to see he knew very well. People said that deep down they were devoted, the complaining and name-calling just their way, but I think that says more about what people need to believe. It's harder, after all, to accept that things can be exactly as they seem, that there's nothing gentle beneath harsh words, beneath cruelty.

Reuben, I learned, was a man of sudden enthusiasms, and he always plunged right in. Perhaps that's what happened when he met Maggie, one October when his ship was storm-stayed, or perhaps it was as she often said, that he took advantage, that all he wanted was an easier life. *Fool's Folly* is what she called the shed out back that was filled with things he'd moved on from. Curling rocks and bicycle wheels, a white-painted board covered with pinned butterflies, their proper names written crookedly beneath. In one corner there was a heavy wooden easel, a floppy kind of hat draped over the top, and stacks of paintings. Strange, wobbly portraits of Maggie, of the fat orange cat that slept in the doorway, and others with streaks and blobs of colour that were meant to be sunsets over the lake. They were dreadful, Maggie was right about that, like something a blind person might do. I used to think it would be hard to be like Reuben, with the desire to do so many things, but no knack at all. But perhaps he didn't think like that, just set his failures aside and moved on to something new.

The year before Robbie started school it was photography Reuben was keen on, and he bought a copy of Bayley's book and read about plates and lenses, focal lengths and development processes, things I'd learned from watching Sam years before, and learned for myself by trying them out, without ever knowing there were rules all written down. Reuben made a list from the book and cleared out the Folly to use as a darkroom, and I told him I could help him with that. It surprised me, how quickly it came back, once I stopped trying to understand the long sentences he was reading out, and surrendered to the movements my body remembered. The gentle tipping of the bath and the mixing and pouring, and along with it the feeling of the moment when the image began to appear, the rhyme I used to say to myself, so I would know exactly when to pluck it out.

Reuben had a passing idea, and it was a good one, that we would take photographs of the summer guests, and views of the lake and the town, and offer them for sale at the front desk. His pictures never turned out well, for all his strict measuring and timing, and he'd soon decided that photography wasn't really for him either. By the end of the season he'd bought himself a new banjo, and grown the fingernails on his right hand long, strange crooning and plucking sounds slipping under the kitchen door, when all the guests were asleep. He gave me everything, his camera and chemicals, all the tools and the darkroom to use; I carried on and it filled a space I'd been too busy to know was there.

What Reuben could do was cook, though he didn't see that as anything special. He said he'd learned when he worked the lake boats. Being in his kitchen was like watching some kind of dance, a nudge here and a shake there, cracked eggs falling golden into a mound of flour. Sauces and pastries and stews, all made up out of his head. Robbie became his taster, sitting on top of the table, with a too-big apron wrapped around; *More salt,* may have been the first sentence he said. Even when rooms were empty, because of the weather or the season, people came from all over to the dining room, and once a lawyer from the city tried to persuade Reuben to come and be his chef, but Reuben said he was fine where he was. Said he knew he was right where he belonged.

The other thing left over from those lake boats was the drinking, of course; he stayed sober at the hotel, but every so often he'd be gone for hours or days, coming back with rumpled clothes and his face still sloppy and loose. One of those times he stepped off the sidewalk and into the path of Hump Waller, who was driving too fast through town, showing off his new Ford. "Old fool," was all Maggie said when they told her. But she gave him a good funeral and wake, with fiddling and special cakes brought in that everyone said weren't a patch on his. Maybe that was the beginning; in the months and years that came after, Maggie seemed to lose herself in food, dreaming up dishes and menus, and prowling the kitchen in the middle of the night, leaving crumb-strewn plates for the new cook to find. She'd never been a small woman, but she became enormous, rarely moving from her chair behind the front desk.

Things had already been changing, but they began to slide faster, and new places that opened with their arranged picnics and entertainments, their private baths, drew away more and more of the summer guests. The yearly lick of paint couldn't hide the way the Lakeview was crumbling, and though the running of it now fell mostly to me I was getting not much more than my keep. "Don't fret, it will all be yours when I go," Maggie said, closing her mouth over a custard-filled spoon, her eyes shut and a look of pure bliss on her face. And though

I didn't wish her ill, not really, there were plans in my head when I lay down to sleep those nights, back in a room on the second floor, because we'd had to sell the cottage I'd come to think of as mine.

When she did go, Maggie dropped to the floor with a crash that made the room keys rattle on their hooks. "Dead as a doornail," the cook said, when he came running, but we sent for the doctor anyway. It took the three of us to roll her over; I closed her eyes and wiped the smear of jam from her cheek. When the undertaker's men came they had to tie her to an old door and push and slide her out and down the top steps, to where the wagon was pulled up close, and she was laughing somewhere, I know, watching those strong men strain.

I don't think she'd be laughing at me, though, for all her temper and meanness; I don't think she lied, or dangled owning the Lakeview as a way to take advantage. But I think that when it came to putting it on paper, she couldn't do it. In the end I think she realized that family is family, even if it meant a great-nephew she'd never met. I would have understood that if she'd told me, and I wonder if she was planning to; she was grumpier than usual near the end and maybe that was why. The last photograph I took of her was on the veranda and it's a good one, though I never would have shown her. Just her head, half turned, and all her chins rolling, her mouth open in a giant O as she shouts through the open door at the poor kitchen girl, who has just dropped a tray of clean cutlery with a terrible clatter and clang.

I've walked the shore with Robbie and I've walked it more often by myself, and I don't know if it takes something from me or gives, that changing water, that sky, but it leaves me soothed, and feeling able to meet anything that might come. This morning, though, I was restless and jagged-edged; I left the Lakeview behind and kept walking down one street and another, and I had the strangest feeling that I was passing pieces of myself, that they were all falling into step behind me, trailing along, and if I turned and opened my arms, we'd all stutter and shift together. Thinking about that I came close to bumping into a lamppost at the end of the main street, and I tried to remember to keep turning my head as I walked, the way the doctor had told me.

It was Edie who first noticed the way I knocked the side of the doorway, walking through, kept banging my hip on table corners. She thought it was something more than not paying attention and brought me to Dr. Jarrow's office, stayed in the room while he shone a light in my eyes, his own big and close. He made some kind of measurements and had me follow his moving finger, held up like someone saying *Wait*, saying *No*. I'd thought I might come away with some tablets or a pair of spectacles, but instead it was an appointment with a surgeon in the city and strange exercises to do in the meantime, three times a day sitting straight in a chair, my fingers making slow circles on my closed eyelids.

I said I would go on my own to the surgeon, but Edie came with me; she can be a little bossy but I was glad of it in the end, the way she knew where to go, and guided me across streets filled with cars and trams and people in such a hurry. Edie was the first married woman in Inverhaven to bob her hair, to wear her skirts shorter, and she fit right in on those city streets, while I felt like someone who belonged to another time. She'd planned to be a doctor, before the war and all that came with it, and as we walked by the University she pointed out buildings where she'd taken her classes, the boarding house where she'd stayed, and the tailor shop on the corner that had once been a tea room where students gathered and argued and laughed. A map in her head, too, of parts of her life, and places where it might have veered in a different direction.

The surgeon said I was lucky, that I'd lost quite a bit at the edges but the centre of my vision was still fairly good; he said some people have the opposite, and imagine how strange that would be. Trying to move through a world with a big smudge at the centre, wherever you look, guessing at what you're seeing by the edges around it. He told me it comes with age, this glaucoma, something to do with pressures and fluids; he said that it runs in families and he asked about my mother, but of course I had no idea. She was young when I last saw her, though I don't know how young. Whatever came after I'm sure she never sat on a stool in a white room, while a man with clean hands touched her face.

I needed an operation, the surgeon said, but apparently it was quite a simple one, involving some cutting that would produce a scar. He said that although it might seem odd, making that deliberate scar somehow made things better. While he explained it to Edie I thought about that; it did seem odd, and I've never noticed that the scars I already have do anything like. Edie and the doctor talked about the details of the operation, how long it would take—not long—and the care I'd need after. "She lives with us," Edie said, "so that won't be a problem." Then he took out his calendar and when I said, "What happens if I don't have the operation?" they both looked startled, as if I'd vanished at the edge of their vision too. "You'll go blind, is what," the surgeon said, and he said it again when we left. Said it would only get worse, so I'd best make my mind up soon. And I said that I would, and we went back to the shouting streets.

People say that if one sense goes, another becomes stronger to replace it, but I don't think it's just that; I'm certain the world is noisier than it ever has been. There must have been a time, long ago, when the new sound of a train whistle made people start and complain, but now everything makes a racket. Typewriters clatter from offices along the main street and telephone bells ring out, even from quieter ones. Motor cars sputter and cough and roar, and I'm sure voices are louder too, because of it. When I say things like that, Robbie says I sound like a grumpy old woman. He says progress is progress, that I can't pick and choose, and reminds me how pleased I am with my new hand cameras; even if I still prefer plates I have to admit that rolled films are so much lighter to carry around, the tank so much easier for developing.

Robbie had other plans before the war, two-handed plans to be an operator in the city or a train engineer. But people say he's a very good teacher, and the boys in the Science Club he started are always stopping him on the street to talk about waves and antennas. He says what can be wrong with *discoveries*, and who cares about giving up a little silence, and I pretend to give him a swat. "You and your spaceships," I say, remembering the books he read when he got too old for tucking in. Mechanical monsters and strange beings that lived on Mars and the moon, machines that moved like men and could almost think. "It will happen," he used to say, as if it was something to be welcomed. So like his father, who wasn't afraid of anything changing except, of course, his easy life.

It never happened but I used to think about it sometimes, especially in summer when there were visitors in all the hotels, strolling and eating ice cream and splashing in the lake. Sam might have come to Inverhaven, with the wife I'd heard he'd married, and he and Robbie might have passed each other on the busy main street, or even in the doorway of the hotel, and Robbie had such a look of him that if that had happened they would have had to recognize each other. My son would have known me for a liar, even about his father's name, and who knows what Sam might have done, face to face with a living boy, instead of the idea of one. Something it seemed he had thought of as another mess for me to take care of, the way I used to wash his soiled shirts and sweep up the crumbs he scattered.

Times I fretted about that, I reminded myself of how often I've heard people say that their photograph doesn't look anything like them; perhaps it's not so easy, after all, to recognize yourself, let alone in other people. The shutter falls and captures one exact moment instead of the one just before or after, and I suppose that a photograph traps a person, as surely as a body frozen in ice. Chance imprisons them, in a way, and someone who didn't know them would think they always smiled just like that, wore their hair that way, had that mark, whatever it was, on their chin.

Perhaps it's something to do with that, the reason people were so drawn to moving pictures. In the beginning, I mean, before they were made-up stories. The idea that you were seeing something that was more real, a train chugging in or people leaving a factory, even though they were things you hadn't given a thought to, all the times you'd seen them in life. I wasn't curious enough to make the trip to the city, but I paid my ten cents and joined the queue when a cinematograph was set up here, during the celebrations for the new century. Real people doing real things but disappearing so quickly, their jerky movements carrying them away to one side or another. Glimpses, but no one to recognize, and when we came out, blinking, into the day, I knew what the little girl in front of me meant when she said, "Why wouldn't it *slow down?*"

With what we see now it's funny to think how fascinated people were by those first shows. Robbie and Edie are mad for the movies, like most people here, and my grandsons, of course, who have never known a world without them. I do go sometimes, especially when there are real things to see, a trip through Japan, or Princess Mary's wedding. But I don't have much interest in the ones that are all pie-in-the-face, or the love stories with penniless girls and wealthy lords. Besides, the way Robbie explained it, it's all a trick, and I don't mean just the miniature castles and painted scenery, things Edie reads about in her magazines. Even with the fastest of shutters there are still gaps, still lost moments, and there's a name for it, though I forget what it is. The way our minds fool our eyes and we don't notice those gaps, the way we see what we expect or want to see. Like the audience that gasps at an illusionist floating in the air, like an old woman looking in a mirror. Like the people who complain about their photographs, forgetting or ignoring the fact that in that instant they did look exactly like that, and that instant is part of them too.

Inverhaven is a town like any other, though perhaps a little more tolerant, because of the strangers who flood in every summer. Different faces, different clothes, different ways of talking and carrying on. There's a certain banding together because of that, busy times and money to be made, and relief when the cool mornings come, and we're left to ourselves again. But people here talk and they judge, like everywhere else, and I never minded for myself but I worried for Robbie, though he was not the only fatherless boy in town. Now that I've seen how it is with Young Rob and Stevie, the things they ask their parents, the things they know, I wonder that Robbie didn't ask me more. That the bits and pieces I told him seemed to be enough. I told him that his father's hair was curly too, and how handsome he was, and clever, how we met in a different town, not here. To my shame I once said that yes, his father was brave, had rescued a woman and a dog from a burning building, a story I'd read in the newspaper the day before, about another man entirely.

I couldn't say much more about my own life, but he liked to hear about the big ship that crossed the ocean, and the time I had learning how to milk a cow. And I told him about walking in the woods with my friend Lucy, how we thought we heard a bear and ran splashing across the shallow river, our wet boots collecting mud and twigs and moss until they were so heavy we could barely walk. I made it into a funny story, left out all the things it would do him no good to know. How I was alone in the woods that day, long before I met Lucy, and running from the farm where I'd been placed. How I was caught, how I was punished. My grandsons sometimes ask about the ship, about the burning building and the bear, and I've realized that the bits and pieces I told Robbie, over the years, made some kind of picture for him of where he came from, a version of the family we might have been. I always knew that when he was older there were other things I should tell him, about how we came to be in Inverhaven, but the longer I waited the more clearly I understood the uselessness of a truth that comes too late, when it can do nothing but harm.

I'd always thought I would be too damaged inside from things that had been done to me when I was a girl. The farmer's thick hands and the hatchet handle, all the rest of the things I closed my mind against when I came to a new place, and my life got better. My bleeding had never been anything like Lucy's, so regular she knew to the day, and when I was sick in the morning I blamed the oysters, then the milk from O'Hare; Sam said he hadn't noticed that it didn't smell quite right. The possibility of a child wasn't anything that entered my mind, but when I felt a sudden flutter inside, as light as the touch of a small bird's wing, then somehow I knew it at once.

Well as I knew him, some foolish part of me thought that Sam might surprise me. Thought he might place his hand on my stomach, his long fingers spread, and we wouldn't say a word, just smile. Instead I saw the quick flicking away of his eyes, heard the sound of him exhaling a curse, the door closing hard, in anger or just haste to be gone. I lay in our bed as the no-colour winter light turned to dark, and everything in me that had become careless and easy lifted away, like a magician's bright cloth. What was revealed was not a treasure, but the hard, dull stone that had always been there.

Lucy would have said, "What did I tell you?" She would have sighed, would have tutted, and then helped me any way she could. But Lucy was far away, married to a widower who had advertised. She wrote once about the drafty house, filled with the dead wife's runners and samplers. The three sly children who rummaged through her things and shook salt in the soup when her back was turned. The widower himself was a little man with a big voice; *He shouts Save Me Lord— you know when I mean,* she wrote, and I could hear her voice, could imagine her giving me that Lucy-look. *None of it matters,* she wrote, *I'm just waiting,* and I knew she meant for Heaven, where her real husband was, and her own little girl. I'm not sure about Heaven, but I know the comfort it gave her to believe she knew exactly where they were, the ones she would always miss.

I've known terrible nights, but maybe that was the longest. Sometimes I thought I heard the click of the latch, a creak that was Sam, trying to move quietly, like those times he came home from the tavern and rolled me awake, his breath sweet with ale and his hands so gentle. As it came close to morning the room began to appear, filled with things that belonged to the day before. A pair of my stockings crumpled with Sam's shirt on the chair, and the blue dish on the dresser that held the lucky river stone with a few loose buttons and coins, the combs that he'd taken from my hair. Everything was quiet except for the thin sound of the river, as it struggled to find a way through the hard-forming ice. All I knew was that I had to be away.

There was never much money in the cash box but I took what was there, nothing else except a leather bag to hold my few things. Not his father's gold watch, that would have kept me for months, not either of his new cameras, or the old one he'd given to me. Not the picture of the two of us with our heads close together that we'd tacked up where only we would see it. I stood at the end of the station platform and boarded the first train that came, and when I overheard a man say they were hiring at the factory in Wilton, I got off there. The next months were like that; I wound thread in the factory in Wilton, served drinks in Coldwell, helped a laundress in Stour. There's always work to find if you don't mind what you do, and I didn't. My mind was fierce but restless, until the day the train was late in Inverhaven, and I came upon that cold bench looking over the ice-tossed lake.

I don't often think about that time, but this morning it unspooled in my mind as I walked down the main street, and I was slow to notice the sound of something behind me, a whir in my ear as a boy on a bicycle raced by on the new, smooth sidewalk. Head down and elbows up, he clipped my shoulder as he passed, a strange, rude echo of that earlier boy, and skidded to a stop up ahead, in front of the Verity picture house. Nothing more important to him, apparently, than checking what the new shows would be. Robbie would say I sound like an old grump again, but it's true that something's happened to manners.

He teases me about things like that at the supper table, tells little Stevie to fetch me a pen so I can write one of those letters to the paper. He asks did I know that the grumbling old men are saving me a place on the bench outside the station, and I play along. He'll never be the same, but it's so good to hear him joking, to see him full of ideas and plans. When he first came back from the war he was like a bad actor, the rest of us giving him cues so he could recite the lines he knew he was supposed to say. I thought Edie harsh sometimes, the way she carried on as if nothing had changed. Paid no attention when he wrestled with his laces, or left him to scoop up a struggling Young Rob, who was making a fuss for candy from the grocer's glass jar. But I see now that without her certainty he might just have drifted away.

Robbie took a camera to the war, a little Kodak, and in the beginning he sent pictures he'd had developed, city streets and the places they'd trained, and ships and open water, the Rock of Gibraltar. *Would you ever have thought*, he wrote, *that your boy would be sailing on the Mediterranean Sea?* He tried to describe the colour for me, wrote, *It's just like the lake, on those certain days when the sky is very blue and the sun picks it out on the water. There's a particular colour that shows in bands on those days and it's exactly that, do you know what I mean?* And I did.

I sent him pictures too, of Edie and of Young Rob when he was born, of their little house that would be all fixed up by the time he came home. Pictures to tell him he *was* coming home. And though I knew the direction was wrong, and the time, when I looked out from the shore I imagined that at just that moment he was looking back at me, from wherever he was. I even fancied one day he'd come sailing in, though I knew he'd return to the station, as he did, looking so rumpled and tired. Looking like someone who was missing more than an arm. It could have happened differently, and he could have become one of the ruined ones. The twitchers and shouters, the drinkers and layabouts; years on they're still around, and we're not as generous in our thoughts as we were at first, when we thought they'd get over it, when we thought that we understood. But instead he found a way to go on and he's a good husband to Edie, a good father to his sons. They still play ball in the yard most evenings, and with his left hand he can throw and catch well enough. "I could hit that with one hand tied behind my back," he shouts, and when the boys were smaller that made them laugh so hard.

How easy it was, even if I didn't know it, when Robbie was small, and the two of us were enough. He learned his numbers from the brass ones on the hotel doors, his colours from the boats in the harbour. Most mornings we walked a little time on the beach, and I was happy just to listen to his chatter, to feel his weight in my arms when he said that his legs were too tired, though before long he'd wriggled away again. When he was old enough he helped me lay the tables and turn out the rooms, and older still he buffed all the boots before he came home to bed, and carried bags and ran errands for the guests, who sometimes tousled his hair, and tossed coins he snatched from the air. The ones like Edie's great-aunts, who returned year after year, always made a great fuss about how he'd grown. Away from the hotel he lived a boy's life, sledding down the steep harbour hill and climbing on roofs and tall, swaying trees, walking far from shore on the winter ice, and other things, I'm sure, I never knew about.

It was easy until it wasn't, until I had to drag him from his bed in the mornings, until he began to leave tasks half done and vanish, never where he should have been. Once he stole a bicycle so he could ride around with his friends, whooping and charging and causing all kinds of trouble, and more than once he came home from school with a split lip, a torn shirt, and shook me away when I asked what happened. A proper mother, I was sure, would have known what to do or say, but I had no idea. And then one day I opened my door to find him standing with Angus, who had a firm hand on his shoulder and told me Robbie had been staring down trains on the tracks, putting more than his own life in danger.

Angus said that his first thought was that the boy needed a good hiding, but on their walk through town he'd changed his mind. Instead he had Robbie come sweep out the station before school and after, found other jobs that needed to be done, and before long I knew that if I couldn't find him, that's where he'd be. He learned the whole schedule and Angus taught him the wire, sometimes left him in charge of the key when things were quiet. A few times an engineer would let him ride in the cab to the next town, and another would bring him back again. Angus gave him a book filled with maps and he used to sit, tracing his finger over the rail lines. His talk was full of things Angus had said or done and he held his shoulders a little differently, tried to make the same parting in his tangled hair. And one evening, during that time, I opened the back door of our cottage and Angus ducked his head a little, to meet my eyes. "Robbie's not here," I said, and he said, "I know," and that was that.

We were together for years, in our way, hours that could be counted. It was never right but that's how it felt, as if there was a magic circle around us, and what happened within it a completely separate thing that had nothing to do with his wife and child, with mine. Angus knew me better than anyone had or would, because I let him. When he touched my scars I told him a little, and more over time, about the worst things and about what came before, Miss Weir and the Home, and how my family was scattered and lost. If Robbie remembers it at all it will be as a story about the white-sailed ship I imagined them on, all together. But Angus knew how real it was, the watching, and he knew what I was looking for those times I took my camera into crowds, and later pored over the prints, not yet dry from the developer. Once he lifted his head from my lap and said, "But Abby, how would you even know them?" And I felt something loosen, understood that maybe I wouldn't. I could keep looking forever but maybe it had already happened, maybe we'd walked past each other and carried on with no idea at all, and that wouldn't be anyone's fault.

I know it was chance that Angus found Robbie on the tracks that day, that we stood in a doorway and spoke the first words we ever said to each other. If that hadn't happened we would have lived our separate lives, and maybe never known the lack. The things we told each other would have stayed inside, but we would have been different, I think. The first time we lay together he asked me about the photographs tacked up by my bed, and though I don't think he understood, he listened while I tried to explain that they were ones I took for myself, not for money. Faces, mostly, like that last one of Maggie, that capture some essence, that somehow satisfy, even if I can't say why or how. I told Angus so many things I'd never said aloud, and things that hadn't ever been actual words in my head, and when his heart exploded and he was gone, really gone, I understood how much that had meant. That for a little while there had been someone in the world who carried my secrets. A good man, who guarded them like a treasure.

This morning I walked restless through town, down one street and another, and it was maybe because of my eyes, but I felt as if things were going on, just out of sight. As if maybe I was walking through that ghost town, different times all jumbled together. And I suppose all along I knew that I would end up at the beginning of Centre Street, looking at the square brick house where Stinson from the newspaper now lives, with all his wild children. The front yard is a mess and one of the windows is boarded up—they must have broken it with a ball—but other than that it looks just the same, the house where Angus lived, and Bella and Edie. After the summer that Edie fell so sick I didn't see him again, not properly, and I understood that, though from time to time I walked down Centre Street at an hour when I thought he might be leaving for the station. Taking care not to loiter, a basket over my arm as I walked quickly enough that it would seem I was on my way into a busy day.

Angus used to say that he came to me wrapped in a cloak of invisibility, and once, when the fog rolled in from the lake, he told me about the magic mist that could be called up to surround all of Ireland, keep it hidden from those looking to cause harm. He'd lived in Inverhaven almost as long as I had, but maybe he really didn't know how it is, the way someone always sees something, and passes it on. A sign, I suppose, of how well he was regarded, that talk never made its way back to Bella. Or maybe it was more to do with how people didn't quite know what to make of her. A kind of paying back for what they assumed was thinking herself better, the way she held herself apart.

They didn't know what to make of me either, until Reuben gave me his camera and I started carrying it with me. I took pictures of circus parades, the Dominion Day races, the wire walker high above the river. Sometimes people asked to buy them, and they started coming to me when they were putting together souvenir booklets for the Old Boys and other reunions and events. People got used to seeing me with my equipment, and it gave them something to latch on to, when they thought of me, and that brought with it a kind of acceptance, though maybe no more than a stray dog would have when its habits become predictable. And I followed the rules; when Angus died, before the war, I knew that his funeral was a place for people with a right to grieve. Most of the town turned out, it seemed, and sang the hymns so loudly I could hear them tumbling over the bluff, passing over my head where I sat on the damp sand, near the place where we sometimes met, growing fainter, those words, as they moved out over the lake.

I didn't know her well, of course, but there was something I recognized in Bella, some darkness she was folded around. It showed in the way she held herself, always, the way she seemed to slip away, without ever leaving a room where other people were talking. Everyone thought she'd fall apart after Angus died, but she surprised them, at first. She kept the house but went back and forth to the city, where Edie was studying, where her aunts and uncle lived together in a main-floor apartment, the people above them always rapping with a broom handle when the piano playing got too loud. Robbie told me how jolly it was there, with music and singing and all the tricks they played. Like a second childhood, he said; their minds were all right, except maybe Charlie's, but it seemed they'd decided to do whatever they wanted, and not care who minded. And I could imagine it, knowing them all from those years they came to stay at the Lakeview. I noticed other families, of course, but those MacFarlanes always made me think what it could have been like, growing up, growing old with my own sisters and brothers.

Then the war came and Robbie was gone. Edie came home again and Young Rob was born, Bella and I two grandmothers, spending time with each other because of that, and sometimes pushing the baby's pram around town when Edie needed a rest. Once we rounded a sunny corner and the youngest Connell girl was skipping ahead of us, her hair aglow, flipping up and down, her thin arms and legs, her thin voice singing a bubbly song. And it may have been my fancy, but it seemed that for a moment we both had the same thought. That it could have been each of us, skipping along in a life we might have had, with the sun warm on our shoulders, the tops of our heads, and the green leaves shifting high in the trees.

I've known this place for more than thirty years, and I don't exactly have friends here, but I have a place. I've known people who've died and people who've been born, jokers and liars and gossips, as well as the kindest you could ever find. Buildings and businesses have come and gone, the storefronts painted a different colour each time, fresh at first and glowing in the light. So many changes, in thirty years, and now a criss-crossing web of wires everywhere, carrying light, carrying voices and the whole modern world, right into people's homes. There have been fires and catastrophes, there's been sickness, and that time so many ships sank in the November storm I went down to the shore with all the others, bringing our own sheets and blankets to cover the dead as they washed up. We rolled bandages and packed boxes in the war, and held our breath when the telegraph boy appeared in the distance; whatever I sensed that first day has proved right, that this is a place to stay.

And always there's the changing water, the sky in all its seasons. Lives overlapping through years and years, and we're part of it for our own brief time, but comforted, or at least I am, by knowing it will go on and on. Even the young ones, who couldn't wait to leave, come back from wherever they've ended up, take off their shoes and walk through the sand, sometimes holding their own children by the hand. On the train home from our appointment in the city, Edie said that she'd realized she no longer missed it. The bustle and the entertainments, the crowds of people who didn't know the first thing about you. She said that maybe a place like Inverhaven was better, like a family in the way everyone knew everything about everyone else and you could be whoever you were, and know that you still belonged.

There are so many things that bind us, and I couldn't have known that first day, but I soon learned what it meant to feel the first warm sun, after a hard winter. How giddy people become, when the snow begins its trickling melt, doors thrown open and scarves and layers shed, turning their faces up to the pale sky. There's still a party in the town hall every April, all kinds of wildness and laughter, not just for the promise of warmer weather, or so I think, but relief at coming through once again. All winters are hard here, and everything more difficult, from leaving the warm nest of your bed to making your way home again, with the setting sun blood-red on the snow. The dark comes sooner and sooner, months when the whole world is a dead and gloomy place, and those clear blue days that make your skin tingle are too rare to be more than a cruel reminder. I've known that from other places but not *felt* it the same way. Here there are also the storms that blow up, days on end with the wind beating and howling, the woodpile dwindling, and people driven deeper into their own dark thoughts.

I suppose it's there in all of us, that darkness, though in some it's buried deeper. Like those circus parades I used to photograph, all glitter and big smiles, but when you look harder, stand closer, you see the cracks in the thick face paint, the tears and the soil on those flowing capes. There can be a desperate need to keep busy, to fill our days and our minds with lists and entertainments, with errands and news of any kind, about anyone. A need to be in company, to seal up any crack with talk and tasks, with feuds and jokes, anything to muffle the call of the long white field, to keep from seeing every rafter, every bare tree limb, as a place to sling a rope. Maybe that's what happened with Bella in the end; much as she wanted to, I don't think even Edie believed that the sleeping draft was an accident.

This morning I climbed the old steps, and I walked to the place where the Lakeview once stood; I walked down the main street, along Centre Street and all the others, out to the station and back again. I walked until my feet were sore, my legs so tired, and then I went back to Robbie's house, climbed the stairs and closed the door to the room where I stay. It was meant to be for a short time, when my plans for the Lakeview were gone, but it was harder than I thought to work out what to do next, and took longer. Things happened last winter, I know, but when I try to remember it seems like all I did was look out through the new window while the snow fell, unfamiliar mounded shapes in the yard and I had no idea what would be revealed when the spring thaw came.

Last week Maggie's great-nephew wrote, and offered me work at the new hotel, getting things prepared and running smoothly for the opening next spring. "What a nerve," Edie said, but I've been thinking about it, principles and pride being luxuries I've rarely been able to afford. Robbie and Edie have done everything to make me comfortable here, make me welcome, and I know I am, but I don't think they understand how it feels, living at the edges of other people's lives. Not a thing I know how to explain without seeming ungrateful, but I've had my eye on a narrow storefront on the main street, where Lily Trimble has her hat shop. People say she can't hold on much longer, can't keep up with the changing styles and the way it's so easy now for people to do their shopping in bigger places.

If I had a wage from the hotel, along with what I've been able to put aside over the years, it would be enough to cover the lease and set it up as a little studio, with space for me to sleep and cook at the back. I know everyone owns a camera these days, but there are still special occasions to mark, and events, and I'm sure Stinson will take prints for the newspaper. I'll feel better there, I know I will, on my own and with all my things, my equipment unpacked from the boxes now piled in a corner of Robbie's parlour. I'll put up all my pictures again, and maybe enlarge one or two to go in the window. Though I would never have thought it, lately I've been wishing that I had that photograph of Sam and me, the one where we're laughing, with our heads close together. For a long time I couldn't remember, but there was a time we were exactly like that.

I haven't mentioned my plan for the studio to Robbie, or to Edie. They'd think it too difficult, too uncertain, not understand why I might want it, a woman my age sleeping on a cot behind a curtain. They'd point out, carefully and kindly, that I'm going to need more help, not less, that they'd worry. They mean well, I know they do, and I've always found it hardest to deal with people who have good intentions. It's different because they're family, but I learned long ago that people who think they know what's best for you usually don't. Sometimes they march you up a gangway, and set you loose in a vast, empty sea.

Edie tapped on my door at lunchtime, but I said I was resting; before she went away she reminded me that we needed to let the surgeon know, as if I might have forgotten. It's not the thought of a knife in my eye, though it's not surprising that's what she thinks, and Robbie too. And it's not the small chance the operation won't work, or even make things worse; there's nothing I can do about that. I know I'll do it in the end, but I'm not quite ready. When the surgeon explained about my vision like a tunnel, what I thought of was looking through the lens of a camera, the way everything else disappears and you see so clearly the small, perfect view that's left. The thing that's exactly what you want it to be.

I heard my grandsons come raucous through the door downstairs, their voices smashing together as they argued about one pushing the other, and unfairly winning the race up the front steps, until Edie rapped hard on the stove. In some ways I feel I knew them better before I moved into the middle of their lives. Not that they behaved better, I don't mean that, but we used to take long walks together, and they asked me all kinds of questions, as small boys do, and listened to my answers. Little Stevie wondered once if seagulls recognized each other, if they looked as different to each other as people did, and then we talked about how people have two eyes, a nose and a mouth, but don't look anything the same. "And two arms and two legs," Stevie said, and his brother said, "Not everyone, stupid," and they called each other *stupid* for a while, as they sometimes did. Edie says if they have another child she hopes it will be a girl;

she asked me once if I'd been just a little disappointed when Robbie was born, but I told her that instead I'd been so relieved.

All through the afternoon I kept thinking that I should get up, that I should splash water on my face and tidy my hair, go down and eat the meal I knew Edie would have set aside for me. She's a good girl, is Edie, and a caring one, and there's not much, except spiders, that frightens her. When she sets her mind on something it's not often she can be knocked off course. With a decision to make she sits down with a piece of paper, columns for plus and for minus; that's a thing Robbie teases her about and she can laugh at herself too. Edie's known sorrow and hardship, like everyone, but I've always admired the way she gets on with things. People like to say that suffering makes you stronger, as if that's a reason for it, but I don't believe there's a reason and no point in looking for one. Things happen, and they can bowl you right over, but what can you do but go on? It's harder for some, though I didn't always understand that. Hard not to cling to it, the wrong or the loss, as if letting go would be some kind of betrayal. As if that would make it a trivial thing, make you someone who didn't matter at all.

I meant to get up, but instead I drifted through thoughts that turned into dreams and back again, different light when I opened my eyes, changing shadows. Still aware of the noises, slamming doors and the boys home again from school, Robbie's deep voice, the scrape of a spoon in a pot. The sounds of lives going on but at a remove and muffled by my closed door. Then I opened my eyes into silence, the shadows reaching farther on the ceiling, and knew that I'd slept deeply but had no idea how long. Downstairs the dishes stood clean in the rack, no one there, and I thought maybe they'd taken the boys to the early show, thought I'd half heard talk about that. There was no plate warming but I wasn't a bit hungry, so I carried on out the door.

Outside it was earlier than it had seemed, but the only people about were just shapes turning the corner far down the street; I tried to remember what picture had been advertised on the stand outside the Verity that must have drawn so many to see it. And though it was a different season, I was reminded of the walks I used to take in the weeks before Robbie was born, at the hour when everyone was making their way home. The streets lined with solid brick houses, lamplight glowing in the windows, and how lucky I felt to have found this place, where people stayed warm and together.

I'd intended to walk to the bluff, but I found myself on the winding harbour road, moving faster as I went down but my legs weren't too tired, my feet barely touching the ground. I carried on along the beach, wrapping my shawl a little tighter against the breeze coming off the lake, and there was a faint sound of music that must have been the town band practising in the bandshell near the top of the rickety stairs. The autumn sky was a tumble of clouds, all shades of purple, of grey, with a glow near the horizon where the sun must have been. A great peace settled on me, and I remembered the girl who had felt the same thing, on the bench near the edge of the bluff up above me. The girl who couldn't have known, no matter what she told herself, that things would turn out all right.

The music would be louder, up there where she was, and I thought maybe she could see the waves crashing, but only imagine the sound they were making. I'm the same person, I know that, but it was as if she was hovering at the edge of my vision, where I couldn't quite see her. I thought of all the things that had happened, and all she remembered. I thought of all the times she imagined a flicker of white sail, far out where the water is a clean line at the sky, and suddenly there were no gaps, everything flowed, and the ship was right there, or we were. Blue sky and the sound of a sharp prow, swishing through calm water, and the sun shining down on the spray that seemed to hang in separate droplets in the air. Nothing but light, and then we're skimming along too, with that spray in our hair, we're sailing away.

AFTERMATH

Children are planting their shoots
that will become the forest
they'll get lost in, terribly, when they grow up.

— YEHUDA AMICHAI

That summer she sometimes came home in the long dusk, with her fingers stained green from pulling weeds in other people's gardens. A small trowel held loosely in one hand and limp bits clinging to her shoes, threaded through her grey hair. "There you are, Edie," Uncle Robbie said, "just in time for *The Whistler*." As if he hadn't been pacing, and peering out the screen door. As if he hadn't just finished saying, "Another ten minutes, son, and we'll go find her." *I'm not your son,* Alan thought, though it didn't matter. Uncle Robbie wasn't even his uncle, Aunt Edie not his aunt, but some kind of cousin on his father's side. His mother had explained it when she drove him to the station, but he'd been too angry to listen.

I am the Whistler and I know many things, for I walk by night. He sat on the floor, close to the radio, and it was a good story, nothing quite as it seemed. The Whistler knew everything, he always did, but he revealed it slowly and in the end no one was blameless, everyone got what they deserved. When it was over Alan said good night and they smiled up at him from their chairs, the batty old woman and the one-armed man, and he didn't know how he'd survive it; the war was over but he was a prisoner in a town so small he could walk down every street in less time than it took to go around a city block, trapped in a strange house with people he'd never heard of, who didn't know a thing about him either. He climbed the stairs into stuffier air and his hands hung heavy at his sides, as thick and clumsy as his father's were, his brain just as empty.

There were fathers who had come back with medals and fathers who hadn't come back at all, and then there was Alan's father, sometimes sleeping in his hospital bed and sometimes sitting in a chair in the noisy room at the end of the dull green hallway. He was still a big man, his knees bumping the underside of a muddy brown table, the top of it scraped and scarred. His thick white fingers pushing around the oversized pieces of a jigsaw puzzle. Sometimes he said *horsey* and sometimes *yup yup yup*, but mostly he said nothing at all. Most times he didn't even look at them, not even when Alan's mother said his name, touched his cheek with the palm of her hand.

Once a week, for as long as Alan could remember, his mother painted on a bright red smile and backed the big humped car out of the garage while he stood behind, directing her right and left. Sometimes he thought about doing it wrong, thought about the screaming scrape of metal on brick, but his mother was counting on him; she told him so all the time. On those days the hard knot in his stomach was there when he first opened his eyes and clenched tighter and tighter as they crept through the streets, his mother hunched, peering through her thick glasses with her chin almost touching the steering wheel. His job to call out the street signs, although she had to know the way by now. "Here we are already," she always said, when the hospital came into view, dark brick and creaking trees and sometimes people outside, nodding and drooling in their chairs. That was the only good thing about being sent away, Alan thought, not having to go through those Sunday visits.

What happened first was a fight in the schoolyard, a boy with crooked teeth who questioned Alan's story about the charge on the Nazi machine gun, his father the last one standing, with enemy bodies thick on the ground. That boy had whimpered like a girl when the principal rolled up his sleeves, and if it had been one of those sappy stories their teacher made them read, the strapping would have been a bond between them. But it wasn't like that. The other boy whimpered but Alan stood straight while his palms burned white-hot, not able to make a fist for a week. Stood straight like a proper soldier, not one who fell from the back of a truck and hit his head on a rock in the road. One who didn't even make it out of the country.

Other things happened after that, and when summer came he woke up angry every long day. He mowed their tiny lawn and drank lemonade while his mother answered telephones in an office downtown, threw himself on the bed in his stuffy room, the plaid blanket scratchy beneath his legs. "What did you and your pals get up to today?" she always said, when they sat down at the dinner table, and he shrugged and said, "Just stuff." He started sneaking money from her wallet, just enough for the bus and a movie, and stood in line with the oldies with their sticks and canes, their money folded into small squares in little zippered purses. Even the best shows had mushy parts and he made quiet retching noises in the dark, like he would have done louder if he'd had a friend who was sitting beside him.

One Saturday morning he stuffed two comics under his shirt, and tried to saunter out the door of the shop on the corner; the owner marched him home with a tight grip on the scruff of his neck and his mother cried and said she didn't understand, said it wasn't like him at all. When the man left she said didn't she have enough to worry about, couldn't he think about someone else for a change, and Alan slammed the kitchen door so hard that things rattled on the shelves. He slammed his feet down too, walking around the block, but that didn't change anything and in the end he threw himself down in the coarse, dusty grass in the vacant lot two streets over, rolled and stared up at the sun in the hard blue sky until he had to close his eyes. When he opened them again he felt weak as a flutter of cloth, walking back past long-shadowed cars in all the driveways. All the fathers home and sitting at the heads of all the tables and mumbling words, maybe prayers, that floated out through the open windows. He would say he was sorry and he *was* sorry, would have said it, but his mother had already made arrangements. She said it would be good for him, a summer by the lake, and they were *family*, these people, not strangers, and happy to have him. The pieces of a fallen teacup were lying on a soft cloth on the table, beside a jar of glue and a little pile of toothpicks, and his bag was already half packed on his bed.

The next day he sprawled in his seat on the train, swearing to himself that he wouldn't touch the lunch she'd made, but once they'd left the city, clanking between the back sides of

182 · MARY SWAN

houses, all the mess and clutter, once they'd picked up speed through empty countryside he was terribly hungry and he took out the sandwiches wrapped in waxed paper, wrapped in that special way of hers, folded and neat and no chance for anything to spill out. He had a hard time swallowing at first, but it got easier. The trip took several hours, nothing to see but fields and trees and sometimes a dusty truck, waiting at a crossing as they blasted through. Once two boys and a girl leaning on a fence and waving, as if anyone would wave back. The train slowed for every small station, shuddering along the length of the platform before it stopped, and he saw the people who were waiting for someone, the way their faces changed from nothing at all to spreading smiles, as if a switch had been flicked. The first time his own lips moved, stupidly thinking they were smiling at him.

Every morning now he opened his eyes in a dead boy's room, though the bed he slept in had belonged to the dead boy's brother, now a grown man with a family of his own, who lived out on the coast. Mrs. P., who came to clean, told him all about it, swishing a bleach-soaked rag over the countertops while he tried to eat a sandwich at the still-damp table. "Such a tragedy," she said. "Those four young boys, such good friends. Far out on the ice when they fell through, and only one of them made it back to shore. Patch Coulter, who has the butcher shop, you'll have seen him."

"I guess," Alan said, trying to chew faster, trying not to see the way her fat behind wobbled as she scrubbed at a stubborn spot. The story made him uneasy, reminded him of the nightmare he sometimes had. His arms and legs bound tightly, and cold water flooding into his mouth.

Mrs. P. said what happened to Alan's father was a tragedy too, and she said she thought she remembered him, from when they were children. Aunt Edie had told him the day he arrived that his father used to come for the summer, and she brought out some old photo albums to find him a picture, turning pages filled with people in old-fashioned clothes. "Now here's one," she said, "let's see if I can remember." A larger photograph, a group of people laughing on the steps of some building, and Alan didn't say but he thought they had one just like it, hanging up in a fancy frame. "There's my mother," Edie said, "oh, she looks so happy. And Aunt Kez and Uncle Charlie; my great-aunt Kez, I mean. You never knew any of them, of course. And this one's Aunt Nan—you know, I always had the idea she once ran away to the circus, but that doesn't sound very likely, does it."

From his armchair across the room Uncle Robbie gave Alan a wink, as though he knew what he was thinking, and said, "You'll be getting the whole family tree, son."

"Hush you," Aunt Edie said. "There's nothing wrong with knowing where you come from. Now this one's Aunt Clare—such a shame she never had children, she was so good at *understanding*." Then she pointed to another woman who was holding a fat-cheeked baby, and said, "That's Edith, I was named for her, but she died young. And Ben beside her, that one with the beard, now he'd be your—what? Great-grandfather, I suppose. And one of these girls is your grandmother, though I guess you never knew her either. Fanny, she was, I think she's this one."

Alan looked where she pointed and tried to listen but they were too distant, all these people with their similar hairdos, their long skirts and too-tight jackets. They had to go through another whole album before Edie found what she'd been looking for, a snapshot of three boys squinting into the sun, with their arms slung around each other's shoulders. "That's your father in the middle," she said. "He was such a nice boy, such a live wire, and the fun they had together."

On the facing page the same three boys stood beside a contraption that was taller than they were, made out of lengths of wood. "Oh, I'd forgotten that," Edie said, and she told him it was a catapult that Uncle Robbie had helped them build, that they fired a watermelon clear across the street and made such a mess of Mrs. Todd's front walk. "They tried to convince her that it was *Science*, but oh my," Edie said, "wasn't she cross."

When he had unpacked his bag that first night there was an envelope with his name on it, tucked underneath his socks, and he thought it would be a note from his mother, telling him she didn't mean it. Telling him she'd be there in a day or two, and they'd drive back home and everything would be fine. *I'll be good*, he'd say, and he would be, and things would go back to how they were, when he was a normal boy with normal thoughts, a boy you'd want to have around. But it wasn't a note, instead it was another picture, the one of his father holding him, a baby, on his knee.

He remembered that photo, from when she used to bring out their own album. He could picture the empty black corners left behind, and the smaller snap below it on the page. He's not a baby in that one but he's small, wearing a scarf over his mouth and a snowsuit so puffy that his arms stand out from his sides. "Your father was such a joker," his mother always said, wanting him to laugh at the rest of the picture. Small pine trees dusted with snow and his father beside him, a mighty axe poised just above little Alan's unsuspecting head.

The first week he was in Inverhaven some kids had come around; maybe Aunt Edie had set it up. Two freckled brothers, both younger than he was but bigger, and another boy with a twisted foot who was called Gimp. There was a scrappy girl named Bet, and once or twice her sister, Pammy, who had rolling blind eyes and had to walk with her hand on someone's shoulder. They mooched around for a few days, and one afternoon Uncle Robbie gave them all money for the show, *Phantom of the Plains*, and they sat in a row with their feet up on the seats in front. The others took turns whispering to Pammy about what was going on, not that she would understand it, even if she could see.

For some reason they never went to the lake, but instead waded in the scummy river near the place where it emptied, swatting at bugs and feeling the silt squish creepily between their toes. Once they hiked out of town to the place where there had been a bad train wreck, years before. The freckled boys said they'd find bones, but there was nothing to see except a spot where the bush was sparser and lower, marking the place where three cars had tumbled from the tracks. They told him that sometimes in town you would hear a long whistle, at the exact time, and they told him that once a man who was out near the tracks after midnight had seen a ghost train, all dark, hurtling by at this very spot. On the way back to town Gimp took a few pennies and a nickel from his pocket, and they laid them on the rails for the express to flatten. After it had blasted past they plucked them off, shrieking and shaking their fingers as if they were hot to the touch.

He tried to tell them things about the city, how tough his gang was and how tall the buildings, but they weren't much interested. Bet asked if he knew any movie stars and he told her he once saw Ginger Rogers getting into a taxi. "Really," she said, her voice hushed and her eyes big, but she held on to it too long and he could tell she was mocking him. Later that day they locked him into an old shed during a game of spies and soldiers, a stick dropped into the hasp, and it took far too long for him to stop calling, to understand that they weren't coming back. The Man Called X had been in a similar spot once and blasted the lock with his revolver, but all Alan could do was bang into the door over and over until the rusty screws gave way.

His shoulder was sore for days, a reminder of his stupidity, and when they came calling the next morning as usual he told Aunt Edie that he had a stomach ache, and the next day that he'd rather hang about on his own. After that it didn't matter, because they all went away to a church camp. All except blind Pammy, who he sometimes saw walking down the main street, one finger hooked into the belt on her mother's dress. Or sitting on her front porch at a little table, sorting buttons by size and the number of holes, a thing she liked to do. Bet had told him that when they were all sorted their mother dumped the buttons back into a big tin, and the next day told Pammy they were a new batch. When he said he thought that was cruel, she gave him a shove and said he was the stupidest boy ever.

Mrs. P. was a nosy old bat; Robbie and Edie called her The Hoover for the way she sucked up information, and then dumped it all on you like greasy, clinging dust. They said it in a laughing way, not a mean one, one of the jokes they had together, like the way they always said, "It's another case for Nick Carter, Master Detective!" whenever someone knocked on the door. Not that anyone knocked much in this town, they walked right in, even ones who didn't belong. Like the smelly old tramp Alan found in the kitchen one morning, sitting straight in a chair with his hands folded in front of him on the table.

Alan had no idea what to do, but Aunt Edie was right behind him. She touched his shoulder as she moved past and said, "I'll make you a sandwich, Rolly, but you'll have to take it with you," her voice sounding firmer, like a teacher's. "The war," she said, after the man had shuffled out, already cramming the bread into his nasty mouth. "The first one, I mean, poor thing. He used to be so dapper, and such a good dancer." Even with all the windows open the whiff of him lasted for hours. "Did he sit?" Mrs. P. asked, when she came, and she gave the chair a good scrub.

That day she didn't have much to report, just a girl who'd run off to be married, leaving a note on her pillow. She and Aunt Edie agreed that the tighter the leash, the harder the pulling to break free. Outside a steady, steamy rain was falling. There was nothing he felt like doing, and he was glad when they sent him up to the attic to fetch a box of old books for the church sale. It was stuffy up there and the light was dim when he pulled the chain, nothing to see through the dusty, small window but more rain, hissing through green leaves.

He poked around for a bit, after he'd dragged the books to the centre of the floor. There was a stained duffle bag in a corner where the roof sloped down, old letters inside and a jacket with dull brass buttons. He put it on, even though it smelled, and tried to imagine Uncle Robbie wearing it, sailing off to the war with two arms in its sleeves. Behind the bag was something wrapped in a grey blanket that he thought might be a rifle, but it turned out to be an old banjo, with curls of broken strings. Everything else was just attic stuff, skis and poles with brittle bindings and boring board games in a pile, a set of dumbbells. Boxes labelled *Curtains* and two labelled *Christmas*, that he didn't bother opening. He'd be long gone by then, back home, back at school, and with any luck there'd be a big storm or the car would break down and they wouldn't have to go to the party at the hospital, with the pathetic tree and the streamers and tinsel, the horrible singing along to the banging piano. Sometimes, when Robbie and Edie were out, Alan opened the photo album and stared hard at the old pictures of the boy who was his father, when he was still a live wire, a joker. He had the same big ears, but otherwise he was as much of a stranger as those long-dead grandfathers and aunts, as the dead boy at the bottom of the cold lake.

His mother called on Tuesdays after supper; she said she knew it was an extravagance, but she needed to hear his voice. "It's sweltering here," she usually said. "You're so lucky to be by the lake." But after that there wasn't much to talk about. She asked if he'd been swimming and what else he'd been doing and he said, "Not much." Once she told him about a funny noise the car was making, and asked him what he thought it was. "Don't know," he said, "you should ask Uncle Robbie," but she didn't want to right then. He'd almost forgotten the annoying way she did that, asking him about the car or if he thought the furnace would make it through another winter, whether they should get a new armchair while the sales were on. As if he really was the man of the house, as she liked to say, as if he had any idea about any of it.

The calls never lasted long; "Well, it's almost time for *Nick Carter*," she said, and he knew she must have timed it like that.

They used to listen together, although she often dozed off and woke with a start, asking what she'd missed and then he missed things too, trying to explain quickly. He could picture her, suddenly, settling down in the chair that had the lacy thing draped over the hole in the arm. Her heavy glasses on the little table beside her and the sore-looking marks by the bridge of her nose. "We miss you," she always said, just before she hung up, and he wished she'd make up her mind. One minute he was supposed to be the man of the house, the next a little kid who believed his father could actually form a thought. "It's not easy for your mother," Aunt Edie said, as if she knew anything about it. He picked up the bowl of ice cream that was waiting for him, the first mouthful sliding cool and easing the burning in his throat.

The dead boy's name was Stevie and there was a framed photograph of him on the mantel. "You have a bit of the look of him," Mrs. P. said, "only he wasn't so scrawny." She said that poor Edie never got over it, well you wouldn't, would you. "Maybe that's when her trouble started," Mrs. P. said, and Alan knew she meant the weeding and the times her eyes had a blurry look, as if she were peering up through water. He thought about how things can start, if you leave a crack open, and then there's no stopping them, no matter how hard you try.

Alan didn't see anything of himself in it, but the picture was a good one; it made you feel like you knew that boy, or had seen him somewhere. He's nine or ten, just his head and shoulders, and he's laughing so hard you can almost hear it, his hair a mess, standing up all over the place, and all kinds of mischief in his eyes. Mrs. P. said Robbie's mother had taken it, as well as some others they had in the house. She'd been dead for

years, but a lot of people still remembered her, with her long
skirts and her cameras, and they remembered seeing her, in all
but the stormiest weather, a small, dark figure, walking by the
shore. The photograph of Stevie had been taken the summer
before he died, and you could tell he didn't suspect a thing.

Uncle Robbie was a teacher but he still had things to do in
the summer, and Aunt Edie went to teas and to meetings at
the church when she remembered that she was supposed to.
"I think I forgot that one on purpose," she said to Alan, after
someone had called to see where she'd been. They left him
little jobs to do, cutting the grass and snicking the edges neat
with the big shears, scraping the back porch ready for painting
or washing the old car that got so dusty on the gravel roads
around town. "We used to be quite a double act, didn't we,
Robbie," she said, and she told Alan that when they had their
first car, after the war, Robbie could steer just fine but she had
to shift the gears for him. "People dove for cover when we were
about," she said, "and once we got stuck on the courthouse
lawn." They were both like that, telling him things about their
younger days, what they thought of as adventures. He paid
more attention after he'd been there for a while and knew the
places they were talking about, had seen older versions of some
of the people.

He was allowed to do what he liked, and in the hot afternoons he usually went down the winding path to the lake and
walked the length of the crowded beach, spurts of fine sand
flying out when he jammed his crooked stick down with each
step. No one seemed to notice and he thought of the invisibility potion Aunt Edie had told him about, a story of her father's
that she'd really believed when she was small. Women lay on

patterned towels with their eyes closed, others stood down by the water with their children, holding hands and laughing as they ran backwards from the waves rolling in. The sun beat down and sparked off the pins in their hair and he felt it on his own head, the same heat, and the shrieking voices sliced through him.

Most days he walked on farther, right to the end and around the little point, and then it was better. A narrow curve of empty sand and all kinds of things washed up, fishing floats and water-smoothed glass, and tree trunks bleached pale and smooth, with huge tangles of roots washed clean. Aunt Edie had also told him that when she was a little girl she had the idea to put a message in a bottle and her father threw it far out in the lake, almost to the horizon, it seemed to her. Her father said that maybe it would come back and sure enough, a few days later a bottle was there, bobbing right near shore; she held up her skirts and fetched it, used a thin stick to fish out the roll of paper inside, and he read her the message. It was from a girl named Amy Jane, who lived deep in the forest on the other side of the lake, and she wanted to know what Edie's favourite colour was. Aunt Edie told Alan that she never wondered how her bottle had ended up in the middle of a forest, and that in her memory she and Amy Jane sent messages back and forth all summer; she didn't seem to mind a bit that it was all her parents playing a trick. Though it was just a silly story he kept his eyes open, on the shore, in case a real secret message came rolling in.

Uncle Robbie was going to teach him how to swim but he hadn't yet, and Aunt Edie made Alan promise to just wade near the shallow shore. That was all right, and when the water was calm he took his crooked stick, sharpened with Robbie's penknife, and tried to spear the minnows that flashed around his feet. A castaway on the empty beach, maybe a pirate captain, set adrift by a mutinous crew. He made a shelter, a scooped hole surrounded by bigger pieces of driftwood, and watched for the sails of a ship that could be friend or foe. Once he tried to start a signal fire, using matches he'd taken from the kitchen shelf, but the wood was sandy and water-logged and the breeze off the lake sent the trails of smoke right into his eyes, made tears run down his face. Sometimes he wondered how far he could walk out, before the bottom fell away and the water closed over his head.

Alan understood the joke about the Hoover, but Mrs. P. always reminded him more of a leaky tap. Sometimes trickling, sometimes gushing, but never completely shut off, making him think of the way dripping water could wear a hole in the hardest stone. She was always asking about his mother and father, where they met and when they'd married, and was it true what she'd heard, that they'd run off together and their families had disowned them. So hard it must be for his poor mother, Mrs. P. said, and did she ever talk about—well, she was still a young woman, wasn't she, and it would be easier for her, wouldn't it, if she could marry again.

Alan kept his mouth shut, like a POW would have, and though she kept on sneaking in her questions he knew that soon enough she'd get caught up in the flow of her own voice and move on. Mrs. P. knew everything about everyone, it seemed, and it was hard to keep things straight, the way she wandered off into the backgrounds of brothers and grandfathers and cousins. She wandered through time too, one minute talking about the unhappy English brides, with their accents and pale skin, then something about Uncle Robbie's mother and a hotel.

What she'd read about Lana Turner that very morning, then back to dead Stevie and his brother, Rob, who was so wild for a time, and how Robbie and Edie hoped to travel out to meet their grandchildren before school started up again. She told him about Hook, the grocer, with his fat thumb on the scale unless you kept your eyes on him, a thing everyone knew. "Like his father before him," she said, and that reminded her of another old scandal, Hook's mother caught laying down poisoned meat, after dogs had been dying for years.

Mrs. P. had other stories that were more interesting, about spirits and hauntings, about curses that followed families for generations. She told Alan about the ghost train, of course, and about people who made nooses or blew their heads off. The ones who jumped from boats, or walked away into the snowy bush, and were later heard scratching at windows in the winter dark. The whole town full of suicides, it seemed, who had changed their minds and wanted to come back. "You'll give the boy nightmares," Aunt Edie said in a sharpish tone, if she overheard that kind of talk, or the old stories about the *brollachan* and the *doonies*, the *sluagh*. It was true that he thought about them, if he woke in the night. The shape-shifters and the unforgiven dead, always looking for a living body to slither into, and the stories about the changeling babies left by the fairies, who never belonged, never thrived. Mrs. P. said she didn't believe it herself but some of the old people thought blind Pammy was one; how else to explain it, how different she looked, how she was.

Mostly, though, he didn't wake in the night, and the dreams he used to have had gone quiet, along with the rage that left him limp in its wake, with an image of his father's white fist as it pounded a thick puzzle piece that would never fit. He was still changing, he knew that, but it seemed to be in a good way. After the first sunburns, which Aunt Edie soothed with a cool spread of Noxzema, his skin had turned brown and the soles of his bare feet had hardened; even his eyes looked diffcrent in his tanned face, when he stared into the mirror. Every night now, before he got into bed, he lifted the dumbbells he'd brought down from the attic and did push-ups on the floor Mrs. P. kept gleaming, and every other day he measured his biceps with the cloth tape he snuck from the sewing basket; a quarter of an inch already, he was sure. He thought of those pasty boys in the schoolyard back home, how they'd not dare mess with him now, and if they did he could knock them over with one hand tied behind his back. Uncle Robbie said that about things, though at first Alan didn't know it was a joke.

Even without the measuring tape he would have known that he was stronger, no burning in his legs when he climbed the secret steps near the place where he'd made his beach shelter. Climbed in a half crouch, a grenade in his hand, waiting for the right moment to pull the pin with his teeth and lob it into the machine gun nest at the top of the bluff. Once, in the dusk, he surprised a couple in the bushes up there; the man yelled and tried to chase him, tripped up by his trousers sagging around his knees, and as Alan slowed to a walk at the edge of the little park he thought how much funnier it would be if there was someone he could tell. *I am the Whistler and I know the secrets, hidden in the hearts of men and women who have stepped into the shadows*; he said it out loud, but quietly, and whistled the tune all the way home.

It wasn't that he liked it, exactly, but he'd got used to it. The town and the shops and the lake, the house that was always clean but cluttered in a way his mother would never have stood for. He was used to Aunt Edie and Uncle Robbie and the way they were together, the shorthand talk and the jokes between them, that had at first seemed designed to keep him out. Once he climbed on a tall stool to reach the big glass jug for lemonade; when Aunt Edie said, "Be careful," he twisted his mouth and said, in a hard-boiled voice, "I *deal* in danger," and they all laughed as if it was even funnier than it actually was.

When he finished painting the back porch they ate supper out there to christen it, and sat until the bats began to swoop, listening to the music from the band people danced to on the deck of a boat far out on the lake. "Remember those dances?" Aunt Edie said, and Robbie tapped his pipe on the sole of his shoe, and said, "Of course I do." Alan could picture them, young and dressed up in fine clothes, spinning and dipping beneath the strings of coloured lights, so far from land. Before he fell asleep that night he wondered what it would be like, if he could travel through time and become a boy who closed his eyes in this room every night of his life. If he'd been a fourth boy hammering that catapult together, whooping at the splat on the pavement. He wondered how different it would be, if all the people he knew hadn't already had things happen to them, how much he would matter.

It had been very still that night and by the next day a dome of stifling heat had settled on the town, not a whisper of a breeze. With the windows closed the house stayed cool at first, but as the days passed there was a point where that tipped, and Alan helped drag the mattresses down so they could sleep in the living room, where it was a little better at night. Aunt Edie said they were like the pioneers, all living and sleeping in one room, and in the dark Uncle Robbie talked about the ship he was on in the war, the first war, and how it was even hotter than this, down in the heart of it. Everything soaked with the sweat that ran, stinging, into their eyes. Other than that time he rarely mentioned the war he'd been in, said nothing at all about what happened when his arm was ripped off; a shell, Alan supposed, or some kind of explosion. Though Uncle Robbie did say once that the worst thing he'd ever seen was a man on fire in a burning sea.

Those stifling nights they talked, before they finally fell asleep, about things that needed doing the next day, or the latest report from Mrs. P. About the way everyone lied to Nick Carter, Master Detective, but he figured it out, and when he explained things to Patsy Bowen, his Girl Friday, it was as if he'd known all along. Aunt Edie thought that Patsy only pretended to be surprised, that she was as smart as Nick Carter any day, and hadn't she provided the final clue that led to the unmasking of the imposter who was after the inheritance? "How did it go again?" she asked, and Uncle Robbie explained, and Alan was still thinking about it as he drifted into sleep. *How did you rumble me?* the imposter had said, and then he said that in a strange way he was relieved. That it was hard to fit into a life that wasn't your own, to remember what to say and not say, how to be.

Alan's mother was always saying that he told time by his stomach, but he knew even she would be amazed at how much he ate now. The extra servings of potatoes and thick-sliced bread, the cakes and pies Edie made from recipes on splattered cards, some of them written out, she said, by women who were long dead. Most days she did her baking in the morning, when it

was cooler, made a list and shopped for their supper. He sometimes went with her if she had a lot to carry, and stared at Patch
Coulter, the butcher; he couldn't get over the way she chatted
as if he was just anyone, instead of a man who was filling up the
space that should have belonged to her grinning boy.

Mostly she was fine, but then there were times when it was
like she'd been caught in the undertow they'd warned him about,
like something was pulling her down and away. It showed in
her eyes and he hated that look, like his mother's when she took
off her glasses, and he knew that he was nothing but a blurred
shape. Edie and Robbie called it *sleepwalking*, those times she
put her purse in the refrigerator instead of the pound of butter,
or wandered off with her trowel in the heat of the day.

Often a neighbour walked her home then, talking about
this and that as if they'd just happened to meet each other,
as if there weren't knee-shaped dirt marks near the hem of
her dress. Sometimes she seemed to remember that she'd been
kneeling in the middle of someone's garden. She made it a joke
while she held her hands under the tap at home, said, "Thank
goodness I didn't go after the begonias!" She told Alan that her
mother used to sleepwalk, really sleepwalk; from what she had
told Edie it was lucky she was never eaten by a bear. Leaving
the cabin where she grew up and wandering through the forest
in the middle of the night. "What a silly I am," Aunt Edie said.
"I almost asked you if she was back yet."

The heat broke with rain that lasted more days and he stayed
in with Edie, playing cards. She taught him some tricks and
a few sneaky deals; usually she made fudge so they could play
for pieces, and he couldn't get enough of that sweetness. In
the evenings, while they waited for their programmes, Uncle

Robbie gave Alan the funny page while he looked through the rest of the newspaper, reading out bits he thought were interesting. If there was still time he opened the thick book he was reading, the one with the title that made them laugh. It was called *A Short History of Greece*, and Uncle Robbie said, "Can you imagine the size of the *Long* one?"

Aunt Edie didn't like to read much anymore, but she often opened the photograph albums that were still piled from when she'd first brought them out, weeks before. Alan liked to look at the one they called *The Book of Faces*, pictures taken by Robbie's mother that they had found in a box, after she was gone. Aunt Edie told him that she'd always had a great admiration for Robbie's mother, who had never had an easy life but didn't let it drag her down. She was smiling when they found her dead, or that's what it looked like, a thing that made it a little easier to bear.

Like the picture of dead Stevie on the mantel, the ones in the face book made Alan feel they were of people he'd seen somewhere, or people he knew something about. Three old men sitting, with bench slats behind, and a very fat woman shouting. A skinny man with maybe flour on his nose, and a girl with a welt on her cheek, who looked terribly sad. Aunt Edie found them all sad, and she preferred to look at the album she'd first shown Alan, the women in their long dresses and the bearded men. One was her parents on their wedding day. "Isn't my father handsome," she said. "Don't they look fine?" Then she turned the page and sighed, said, "They're all gone now. Everyone's gone now, aren't they Robbie."

"Not everyone," Uncle Robbie said. "Young Rob's not gone, and we're going to see him, remember? And we're still here, and this fine boy."

"Yes, this boy," Aunt Edie said, and it was clear that at that moment she had no idea who he might be.

One Tuesday Alan's mother didn't call but the next night she did, and talked to Uncle Robbie so long that the phone was warm when he passed it over. She told Alan that there'd been some trouble, that it wasn't his father's fault but he'd hurt someone in the hospital, and been moved to another place, another city. *Good*, Alan thought, no more drives, no more visits, and he was only half listening, with one eye on the clock. Almost time for *The Whistler*, and his ice cream was melting in the bowl. "Do you understand?" his mother said, and she told him again, told him they'd be moving too, that it had been quite a scramble but she'd found an apartment in the new city, and a job for herself. She said she needed him home right away; Robbie would buy him a ticket and she'd meet the train. There was so much to do and it would be good, wouldn't it, to have a few weeks to settle in before school started. She went on about painting his room any colour he liked and the big tree outside his new window, the public pool at the end of the block, but he could hardly hear her for the rushing in his head.

At some point he hung up the phone, and maybe she was still talking or maybe she said, "We miss you," as she always did. He walked down the hallway and out through the kitchen and the screen door bounced behind him, but once he was outside he didn't have a clue what came next so he walked around and around the house, thinking of all the things he wouldn't have a chance to do. Thinking he'd be gone when Bet and the others came back and they'd never see how he'd changed, never follow him through the dark night and wait for the ghost train, never know he was someone they'd miss. And he wouldn't be here for the fair, to see if Edie's pie won the prize. Wouldn't help Robbie fix up the old shed, wouldn't stand inside it with him while he smoked his pipe, listening to the rain drumming on the tin roof. Through the open window he heard the first notes of *The Whistler*, saw Robbie and Edie who were saying something to each other, and there was no sign that there'd ever been anyone else there. "It's not all about you," his mother had said on the phone, and he'd thought, *Why not? Why not.*

Alan's mother made a fuss about how much he'd grown, said she was glad of his strong arms when it came to carrying boxes and shifting heavy furniture. Aunt Edie sent a postcard from their trip west, a picture of mountains and the ocean, and later letters came too. Her pie got a blue ribbon and young Bet had been asking about him, Mrs. P. fell down some stairs and had to have her jaw wired, and couldn't he just imagine the torment. For Christmas they sent him a pocket knife with his initials etched on it and he sat on his bed while snow fell through the bare branches outside his window, opening and closing the sharp blades. He told his mother that of course he'd written to thank them, but he never did. His father was behind a locked door now, that opened onto another dull corridor; he still didn't say much but the place was filled with shouting and banging, and people with cloth mittens tied onto their hands so they wouldn't claw their own faces.

He did well enough at school and went away to the optometry college; he was too busy and it was too far for him to go home very often. He had friends there, he supposed, and they said the right things after the fire in the hospital that killed his father, the scandal and the settlement. They all went out together after their final exams but he left before things got rowdy, a little tipsy, perhaps, when he stepped into the beam of the headlights that were rushing toward him. He'd always heard that your life flashed before your eyes, like one of those movies where everything makes sense just before the screen goes black, but it wasn't like that; he woke with a sense of a slow unspooling that had gone on as long as that far-off summer itself, though he was told he'd been unconscious less than a day. The nurse told him that, right after she told him her name. "Jane. Plain Jane," she said, with a little laugh that sounded like part of the sentence. When he said something about the drinks in the bar she whispered, *"Least said soonest mended,"* and bent down to arrange the pillows beneath his bandaged head.

His leg was badly broken, heavy in plaster and strung up with weights and pulleys, and it should have been humiliating, the way the nurses had to do every intimate thing, but they were so matter-of-fact that he soon got used to it. They talked about practicalities and the future, the way he'd progress to crutches and then a cane, the way he probably wouldn't even have a limp in six months' time. "It will be fine," they said, "and you have your whole life ahead of you," something he'd been told before, that he knew was supposed to be a good thing.

He got used to Jane too, and looked forward to when she was on nights, with time to sit and talk for a while. Both of them keeping to a whisper so as not to disturb the rest of the ward, and that made everything they said seem like secrets they were sharing. She had a fierce need for order, that he would learn carried on outside the hospital doors, but for now he noticed it in the way she kept the sheets smooth and straight, adjusted the vase of yellow flowers that sat on the bedside table and angled the little white card that just said, *Get well.* He knew she had bought them herself, and had them delivered with the daily cart; he'd told them not to call his mother and there was no one else who would send him flowers. When Jane denied it he said, "Well, I guess it's another case for Nick Carter," and then had to explain, because she told him she'd never heard a radio until she was in the nurses' residence. He asked if she'd grown up with some strict religion but she said, "Not exactly."

Jane had days off, of course, that she seemed to spend cleaning her room, ironing her uniforms and sewing on loose buttons. *"A stitch in time,"* she said, and she said that was the only thing her mother taught her that was of any use. He wondered what she'd looked like as a girl, and she told him she was a scrawny little thing, wearing her sisters' made-over dresses to school and one year, to her great mortification, her brother's shoes. She said with the chance to get away she'd never looked back, why would she?

Another time they had a meal together, his cane hooked over the back of the booth, and he misheard something she said, told her he used to believe he was a changeling too; she gave him a look and said, *"Changing,* I said changing my curtains, I'll never have to, they'll go with anything." Then she said, "You're a strange one," and when he said, "Maybe I could say the same," it felt like a handshake. When they married, months later, he looked down at her flushed cheeks and felt dizzy with hope, and when his daughter wrapped her baby hand around his finger, her grip so strong for such a tiny thing, he thought that with two of them now on the lifeline, there was no chance he'd ever drift away. He opened his own office and got used to wearing the frames with the plain glass lenses that had been Jane's idea. "Of course you don't need them," she said. "But even if they don't know why, people will trust you more."

It was all right for a time, in the apartment and later the small house. Little Clare learned to walk, ride a bike; she went to school, and they did the things families did, had picnics and went every year to the circus, stuck their heads through cut-out holes above cartoon bodies. Once they rented a tiny cottage near Inverhaven, but didn't go into the town. He thought the next year he would but they didn't go back; Jane said it was fine, but she couldn't bear all that tracked-in sand. Years went by and he mowed the lawn and scraped and painted the trim, took storm windows off and put them on again. Jane kept the inside tidy, everything in its place and the weekly menu stuck to the side of the fridge. His name was stencilled boldly on the opaque glass door of his office and he was content there, with the soothing click of changing lenses in the dark. He still marvelled at the view he had, deep behind people's eyes, and the magical way that angles and numbers turned into clear vision.

In the evenings he sometimes went walking, to help him fall into a clean sleep. In the house he left behind, Jane was making the next day's lunches or scouring the kitchen sink while his daughter did her homework, and he knew they'd be there when he came back, and there if he never did. *I walk by night*; he tried to remember the whistled tune that opened that old show but he couldn't get it started, and he thought how strange it was, how you could go years without thinking about a thing, but then it popped up.

Usually he walked the path that ran beside the last row of houses, and carried on into the long grass of the open fields.

Fireflies flickered, like stars fallen down from the sky, and the damp, weedy smell made him think of Edie, blinking in the harsh indoor light. He thought he understood it now, the instinct and the quiet bravery that sent her out with her trowel in her hand. There were flashes in the distance, the lighted windows of the late train, trailed by a mournful wail, and he remembered the coins he'd once laid on the track, remembered how they'd emerged, pressed smooth and shiny and new.

III

. . . whatever
returns from oblivion returns
to find a voice
          —LOUISE GLÜCK

WISH YOU WERE HERE

I

When the rains came, they all moved on, skipping from island to island like smooth stones over water, looking for the sun.

A sentence she read in a waiting room magazine, from a story by someone she'd never heard of. That was months ago, but perhaps Clare thinks of it now because rain is falling outside the tall window, because the CD has finished and there's silence in the room where the overhead lights burn. The room where the rug is rolled and tied with strong cord, where boxes are piled everywhere, most taped and labelled, but a few with gaping mouths. Things have reached that stage where order has broken down and random, unrelated objects are tossed, unwrapped, together. The key rack in the shape of a house, hooks jutting out from a picket fence, and the mosaic trivet they bought on their trip to Greece. Three pens that still work, a battered frying pan, an old egg-shaped paperweight. "Too much stuff," she says aloud, a thing she's been doing more and more. So far it hasn't happened outside these walls, except for once pushing a cart in the grocery store. Something she said about the price of coffee, in a crotchety, startling voice.

There *is* too much stuff, even after all her sorting and weeding, but she knows how it happens, the longer you stay in one place. Things of your own and things that have passed down. In her parents' little house every inch of space seemed to be filled. So many things it was hard to turn around, hard to take more than a tiny step.

She's told herself that she must keep things for Lizzie, no way she can know what her daughter might miss in five years, or ten. Maybe John's telescope, or the silver napkin rings that came from his great-aunt. Maybe the old quilt made with such tiny stitches, or the flattened coins Clare's father had put on the train tracks when he was a boy. Lizzie travels light but she's already taken the thumb-worn telegraph key, a perfect prop for a play, and the faded photograph that hung in the spare room. Two groups of people sitting on the steps of two joined, peaked houses, names written on the cardboard backing in a spiky, old-fashioned hand. When Lizzie wrapped it up she told Clare that she used to try to imagine herself inside that photograph. A girl with a long dress and button boots, a girl with a large, happy family.

It feels as if this day has been coming forever. Notes on the calendar these past months, red steps marching as the pages turn faster and faster: time to start collecting boxes, to buy markers and string, to disconnect the phone. Clare made up notices for a garage sale and tacked them to telephone poles, trying not to cover up the other, faded ones. So much loss, dogs and cats, car keys and necklaces, and even a photocopied woman, her smudged features difficult to make out.

Lizzie missed her bus, so that windy Saturday Clare stood alone behind the piled table in the driveway while strangers picked things up and turned them over in their hands. Someone's grandmother scooped up the board games, and a short man bought all the Halloween decorations; before he took out his wallet he flicked the switch on the toy broom and everyone started at the sudden witchy cackle. Clare was glad to see it go, along with the flashing plastic pumpkin and the wadded mass of fake cobwebs. The older she gets the more uneasy she is at opening her door to whoever has thundered up the steps, the youngest children baffled and the older ones loud, most with the barest suggestion of a costume. Packs of them, jostling under the yellow porch light.

When almost everything on the table had been sold, a thin-shouldered woman appeared from around the corner. A girl, really, with wispy long hair and a filmy skirt tangling around her calves. She was pulling a rattling wooden wagon, a small, unblinking boy riding on top of a mound of floral curtains, clutching a spoon and a cheese grater. "Have you got any TVs?" the girl-woman said, in the most wistful voice Clare had ever heard. And as she watched them making their slump-shouldered way down the street, out of sight, she thought that it could easily have been a young Lizzie, half-heartedly waving the wooden spoon in the scented air. It could have been their life, trailing through more fortunate streets, with a squeaky-wheeled wagon nipping at their heels.

The day after the sale she walked the neighbourhood and pulled her notices down, leaving little white flags fluttering. She sent a cheque to Lizzie inside a card with a picture of blue shutters, an explosion of red geraniums. She stripped the beds and filled bags with clothes to donate to places, thinking of one of her mother's rules: *Not worn for a year, doesn't belong here.* Clare long ago extended the rule to five years but still always finds herself missing the donated skirt, the sweater, the week after it's gone. Sees it in her mind and knows it would be just the thing and she wonders if that's the real point of the rule, to teach you that life is like that.

There seemed to be rules for everything in her parents' house, and she still hears *blue and green should never be seen* when she pulls on John's old sweatshirt with her jeans. There was another rule about hangers in the closet, although it didn't have a rhyme; something about them facing one way or another, in case your house burns down. There's a family story about children dying in a fire, but so long ago that the details are lost and besides, Clare thinks, what kind of person would spend time scooping clothes from a closet, when everything around them was in flames.

In the room with the rain-streaked window there's a couch with a pillow and a tangle of sheets, and an old wicker chair that used to sit on the porch. When she wants to sit in the chair she softens it with the pillow from the couch; when she wants to sleep she moves the pillow back again. One of the packed boxes makes a table where she can put her mug and her ticking travel clock. The last box she seals will contain the sheets, the pillow and the kettle. The mug and spoon, the small Bodum pot she hates cleaning out, and Lizzie's old Discman with the tiny yellow speakers. Clare thinks she should label it: *All I really need.*

Lizzie calls her a dinosaur, sometimes lightly, sometimes not, and she says that Clare is literally—*literally*—the only person she knows without a cellphone. When she came to help, weeks ago, she kicked the box of CDs and said, "You could have all these on an iPod, I'll even do it for you. You could sell these, and all that old vinyl, you could give away the cassettes to others of your species." There was a time when things would have veered off then, and settled in the grooves of familiar and pointless arguments. A time when Lizzie would have said it was *ridiculous*, the things Clare held on to, when she'd packed her own mother off to a *Home*. But both of them are older now and when Clare said, "I don't see the need," as she always does, Lizzie let it go and turned to open another dresser drawer. "My God, how many sweaters do you have?" she said. "And you taught *me* the packing rule. Remember?"

Lay out everything you must pack, then be sure to put half of it back. Of course she remembers, both the rule and the day. The lowered blinds and the squeaking fan pushing at the thick air while she helped Lizzie get ready for her first overnight camp. She remembers being ambushed by tears, going into the bathroom more than once to splash her face with cold water. And she remembers that while they were arguing about how many pairs of shoes, she told Lizzie about living for almost a year with what she could carry in a pack on her back. But her daughter's lips were set in that way and she carried on cramming things into the small flowered suitcase, her hot hair stuck to her forehead.

What she told Lizzie that day was true, she did once live for a year with what she could carry on her back. Hitched around Europe with two friends, using most of the money her father had left her, as she thought he had intended her to. So long ago but there are still times, when she's standing at a busy intersection and the weather is just right, that the smell of exhaust fumes sweeps her back to that wide open feeling. So many places, so many people they met along the way, some of them popping up again at a hostel or outside a post office in a completely different country. They made their way through Spain, through France and Germany, Switzerland and Italy. And then to Greece, where it rained, though not at first.

When it was time to deal with the basement Clare found her old backpack, stashed behind the heavy wooden doors in a web-covered corner. The doors she and John took off when they first moved in, to make the rooms flow. The metal frame still bright and solid and the tough green nylon barely damaged, just a melted hole on the flap where someone had dropped a cigarette, and a few streaks of tar from the beach in Naoussa, or wherever it was. The small Canadian flag sewn on with her neat, tight stitches, although the white is now marked by rusty brown streaks where water must have dripped. Or maybe just all those years in the damp basement, chilling and warming, all those changes that were going on while her footsteps crossed the floor above. She and John used the pack the only time they went on a canoe trip, in Algonquin Park. On the second day, John knocked himself out, his head hitting a rock when he tripped on the steep portage path. The weight of the falling canoe dragging Clare to her knees.

Because she had to start somewhere one of the first boxes she packed held the photo albums from the shelf in the spare room. There were faded pictures of houses and people whose names she's not sure of, and a few black-and-white snaps of her parents, looking so young. One in their wedding clothes, and another in a driveway on a treeless street, holding baby Clare beside an enormous finned car. There's one of her dressed up for her first day of school, one of her holding a bicycle, and another of her gowned for graduation. Then the books she filled after Lizzie was born, all the birthday parties, the outings, the friends. Lizzie has the same big grin every time, although she's told Clare more than once that mostly she felt sad and all alone. The last picture of John was still loose at the back of an album; he's sitting in a lawn chair, looking off to the side, a blanket around his legs and the summer breeze ruffling his patchy hair.

There weren't as many photos from that long-ago trip as she'd thought, and most of them could have come from any post-card she'd sent home. The entrance to the Prado, gondolas in Venice, a rough-hilled island rising from the sea. There were several looking down from the path to the broad cres-cent sweep of beach, but only one of the ragged group sit-ting around a table in the bar called Plato's Cave. Ashtrays overflowing and bleary eyes, heads together and a cluster of empty retsina bottles. Gerard, who owned the bar, played Pink Floyd over and over, and the bracelets on his wrist chinked as he popped the tops off bottles. *Breathe, breathe in the air*; there was always music and always laughter, and the French girl who might have been his wife flicked her hair back when she stood with an empty tray, her long skirt drifting and a yellowing bruise high on one cheekbone.

The camera Clare had then was a cheap one, and all the photos are a little hazy. Not out of focus, exactly, but not sharp and clear either. The colours muted, the blue skies nothing special; even Jackson's bright red shirt is a washed-out maroon. It's as if the years have spread them with a softening glaze, and the thought reminds her of the old people she interviewed for her thesis, all the stories they liked to tell about dances and picnics and loving, loyal animals. Many of them had trouble with her questions about what day it was, what year or which prime minister, but could describe every detail of their first dance. The dress their mother had made, right down to the colour and shape of the buttons, the fancy stitching around the neckline. The way the school was transformed, streamers and sweet punch in a bowl, and the smell of all that pomade and flowery talcum powder. The whorl of hair beside the small mole on the neck of the boy who was dancing with someone else.

She learned though that if she let her tape recorder run long enough they would talk their way back through the skating parties and hijinks, past the ponies with bright ribbons braided in their manes. Back to what happened with that boy with the mole, to betrayals, large and small. Back to deaths and unjust punishments and pain that was just as sharp as when it was fresh and unexpected, pain they had felt and pain they had caused. She saw it so clearly then, how sometimes the smallest-seeming hurt can have an enormous effect. Can still tip you right over, even if the weapon is long gone, like the dagger of ice in that guessing game she tried to remember for Lizzie. The game she used to play with her fellow travellers on docks and beaches, and in peeling rooms filled with the sound of rain.

On the phone, when there was still a phone, Lizzie asked about the packing and Clare told her that she'd become an archaeologist after all, that she had scraped off all the top layers and was getting down to the evidence of earlier civilizations. "I even found the key to your Peter Rabbit bank," she said. "The one we had to break. It was in the toe of one of your baby shoes. You must have hidden it there, I don't see how else."

"Maybe," Lizzie said. "I sort of remember that."

And Clare told her about the fine white dust that covered the tops of the boxes on the high closet shelf, said, "How long ago was it, when your dad tried to drywall the bathroom? You probably weren't even old enough to remember."

"What was in the boxes?" Lizzie said, and Clare said, "Old stuff, just more old stuff. But that dust, I can't believe it. It must take years to settle."

Lizzie offered to come for the last day, said she'd skip the audition, she probably wouldn't get a callback anyway, but Clare said, "Don't you dare." She said, "I'm playing that CD you gave me, can you hear it?" and Lizzie said, "It's that 'Time' song, isn't it? I didn't think you had that many clocks." It was ridiculous, the way Clare had cried when she got out the old record and found it so badly warped. She tried anyway, hooking up the turntable, but the needle bucked and skipped, spitting random smacks of sound. The CD Lizzie bought the next day had been digitally remastered, had a slightly different cover, but it was close enough.

Clare kept the Peter Rabbit key, dropping it into a pouch with a jumble of single earrings. It will be in one of the *Misc.* boxes, maybe the one with Lizzie's small handprints on a sheet of faded construction paper and the tissue-wrapped ivory hair combs. The one with her father's fake glasses and a sea-stained leather bracelet, a picture of an octopus draped over a hanging line. What would someone make of that assortment, if they opened the box, like a time capsule, in a hundred years?

As baffling as the things in the small wooden chest she came across when her mother was moving. Underneath the tax receipts and documents were more of those train-flattened coins and a sheet of paper with sunset times from some long-ago year. A rusted penknife and a few ticket stubs, and a small photograph of a man holding a laughing baby on his knee. "Your father's things," Clare's mother had said. "They're no earthly use to me."

It was like that after he was gone, as if the way he died erased everything else about him. His things bundled up so quickly, her mother's hangers spread out in the closet, as if there'd never been an empty space. "He made fools of us," she said once, her lips a sharp line in her face.

Lately he's been popping up in Clare's mind, but only in bits and pieces. When it happens she thinks of random synapses firing, flashes like lightning that are all that are left from the pathways she should have tended better. The straight part in his hair and his kind eyes, his strong arms lifting her up at the circus. The scent of his aftershave when she buried her face in his neck, frightened by the trumpeting elephants. When she tries to remember more she usually thinks of him in his office, the easy way he talked to people, the little jokes he made, and the way they thanked him. She remembers spinning in a black chair, and watching how lightly he settled glasses on a small boy's face. How he adjusted the arm and the nosepiece and then settled them again, said, "Oh that's very good."

She has one clear memory of her father and mother together, an unlikely one, and that has always convinced her that it's real. She's not very old and she's digging in the sand with a red shovel, making a house, she thinks, for the seagulls who strut along, tipping their heads and staring with their blank, black eyes. There's laughter and she looks up through the dazzle of sunlight, sees her parents waist-deep in the lake. They are windmilling their arms and splashing each other, and the water hangs between them in arcs, in separate, glittering sparks that are suspended before they fall.

In the same box with the handprints and the woven bracelet there's also an old address book with what's left of a wild paisley cover. On the first few pages there are random contacts, doctors and dentists and Lizzie's old piano teacher, friends and colleagues. But the rest are filled with older names, some written with a stub of pencil, faded to grey smudges, many with the green felt pen Clare used to carry in a special pocket in her backpack. There are entries decorated with peace signs and flowers, with drawings of trains and tiny houses, smoke curling from chimneys. On one of the inside covers there's an ink sketch of figures diving from a decrepit, sinking boat, although that never actually happened.

She had a brief thought, the day she came across it, of writing to all those people she hadn't thought of for years. Like a message from the future; she would buy postcards, and she pictured them dropping through mail slots all over the world. No picking and choosing, that would be the rule; she would send a card to every one. Even the soldier who gave them a ride from Malaga, a wild guitar tune sweeping them along the coast road. Even that crazy Scot they met, when they were stranded in Lyon, and the girl who had cried in the youth hostel in Geneva. But as she turned the pages, counting how many cards she would need, the flare of the idea fizzled out. So many of the entries were completely mysterious, even the addresses giving no clue, and she thought of all the places she'd written her own green name. Thought of how many people would pick up her postcard, turn it over and shrug. How many would say, as she was saying, *I wonder who that was*.

John gave her a new book, the one she still uses, their first Christmas in this house. She remembers the tall tree with its coloured lights, can imagine it in the corner of the room where she now sits. Thick snow falling past the bare windows and the rolled rug spread out, soft and new and covered with scrunches of red and green paper from Lizzie's frantic tearing. There was a gritty feeling behind her eyes, "Jingle Bells" playing on the tape deck, and she remembers thinking how silly it was, the time and care spent on wrapping, tucking the corners in just so. She remembers too the stab of anger when she opened John's flat box, the way she assumed it was not a gift but a demand, his way of making her draw a line through her life and set aside all that happened before they met.

It was unfair, of course, and even at the time she knew it was unlikely he was sending her a hidden message. John was the most straightforward person she'd ever met, genuinely baffled by any kind of subterfuge, by people who said one thing but meant another; in those days, if she was sure of anything, it was that. Probably he had been looking for a number and noticed how little space was left in her old book, noticed the tears and ripples, the coffee stain that had seeped through the alphabet. Probably he thought she'd be pleased that he *had* noticed, that he'd chosen a new one with a sturdy leather cover. When they first met they walked down city streets with their fingers enlaced, and while Lizzie was being born she squeezed his hand so tightly that she left small bruises, left crescent-shaped gouges on his palm. And it happened so slowly that maybe neither of them noticed how much that grip had loosened.

That's not anything she wants to be thinking about, though, and she wipes her face and says, "Too much time alone," in her briskest voice. It's what Lizzie is always telling her and she knows it's true, but she wonders why solitary thoughts always lead you to a dark and lonely place. Wonders if there's anyone who spends their time remembering jokes they've heard or slapstick movies, chuckling in an empty room.

Before she gave away the television Clare used it, along with a few glasses of wine, to help her sleep. Once she forgot to press the mute button before she drifted off and woke to a woman's scream, but usually it was just to the comfort of the flickering light. And the moaning and creaking of the house, sounds that have become more sudden and mysterious as it slowly empties and make her think of that crazy play Lizzie was in once. The tiny theatre dark except for one tall candle at the edge of the low stage, and nothing but sound to tell you what was going on. Ticking clocks and a tinny bell, a motorboat, or maybe it was a chainsaw. Bird calls, a crying baby, smacks that might have been a fist fight, and every so often a different voice intoning: *The white lilacs. Flame. Sorrow.*

It was a very long play; beside her John slumped into sleep, while she fought with her bobbing head. Jerked upright at a sudden snort that might have been her own, or might even have been part of the play. Could that be it? she wondered in the dark. Were they all supposed to be characters? "Oh honey," was all she could think to say afterwards, hugging Lizzie who had been revealed at the end in a black cape, two clownish red circles on her cheeks.

Sometimes now Clare did a parallel thing when she opened her eyes in the dark and tried to work out what was unfolding on the silent television screen. It wasn't so difficult, the same few stories playing themselves out in different times, with different actors. "Don't go into the basement," she said to the woman whose hand was closing on the doorknob. "Don't believe a word he says," when a slick-haired man appeared with a sheaf of black and white roses. Once there was a news bulletin flashing, a shot of a huge airplane tilting into a ravine, flames from the cockpit and the tiny windows, jets of water and revolving lights. But as she watched she realized that this time it was a different story. This time, through some combination of luck and skill, everyone had made it out alive. Cut and bruised and rumpled, but euphoric, filling up her screen in vibrant colour.

If it had gone the usual way, she thought, there would have been small, blurred photographs in the newspaper, flat words on a page, and she realized that she was seeing the dead, watching them move their mouths, touch their cheeks, brush the hair from their eyes. That tanned teenaged girl, the tall man with his tie askew, the mother holding her baby. So many, more than a hundred of them, who would be able to go on, who would live out the rest of their lives; no need for her to imagine anything at all.

In the kitchen now Clare's hand slips as she pours from the kettle, and boiling water splashes. As she heads for the sink she stubs her toe on a box of books and hops and curses, reminded of needles in the doctor's office, the way her mother would pinch Clare's other arm just as the shot went in. She had been a nurse, Clare's mother, and though she gave it up when she married, it always showed in the brisk way she tucked the sheet corners tight, or shook out the thermometer when Clare asked to stay home from school. She liked to say that she had no time for sentiment, and she would have snorted at Clare's sorting and packing, the time she spent on each decision. When she had moved from her own house to the apartment she tossed all kinds of things into garbage bins with a gleeful flick of her wrist.

What's done is done; Clare's mother never saw the point of what she called rubbishing around in the past, and though over the years she told Lizzie more than Clare had ever heard about her life she still rarely mentioned the rock-strewn farm she came from, the brothers and sisters she never cared to see again. In movies and novels everyone knows that a gruff exterior always hides a soft core, but even now, when she wants to be kinder, Clare suspects that life is different. Thinks there may really be times when what the hard shell surrounds is a stony heart.

She's thought all along that this business of moving house is something like arranging a funeral. The red notes on the calendar, all these practicalities to focus on and the small, constant decisions to be made. She's been following those red steps like a sleepwalker, blank-eyed yet resolute, and sometimes she imagines them leading her on, off the page. At her retirement party there were the usual speeches, and jokes about students, and comments about how her door was always open, except when it was closed. They gave her a wheeled suitcase topped with a shiny gold bow, so someone had been listening when she said she might go to Scotland, to Ireland, might prowl through misty graveyards, looking for her roots. A better answer than "I really don't know," and an acceptable one these days, when everyone seems to be looking for connections.

People have given her books and she's read them, knows what every expert says about making drastic changes too soon. It's written down like a rule, but turn the page and you'll read that everyone has to make their own way through grief. And anyway, rules are made to be broken, as Lizzie still likes to say. John used to call that her mantra, and it was the title of her first project in film school; Clare remembers her explaining it, at the now-sold kitchen table. Something technical to do with *persistence of vision*, the way the eye sees what it expects to and fills in gaps. She remembers how excited Lizzie was that day, her hands dancing and stabbing at the air. She remembers thinking of all the moments that had brought them to that one, and she remembers thinking of a game they used to play. Not really a game, but a thing they used to do when Lizzie was small, and they walked the gravelled path through the park. Holding hands in their short line with Lizzie in front trying to pull them along, and they didn't resist but they didn't make it too easy. "That's the physics instinct," John said, as Lizzie bent her little body forward and tugged harder. Their feet suddenly shifting and beginning to move, the three of them stumbling on together.

Lately Lizzie has been doing research, starting with the names on the back of that old photograph, with others Clare remembers and her best guesses at dates. It was another of their old arguments—she could never *believe* how little Clare knew. "It just wasn't something we talked about," Clare had said. "All that family history—it just wasn't important." She knew it sounded feeble, but it was true. The last time Lizzie was home she'd smoothed out a roll of photocopies, records of births and marriages and burials, written out by a long-dead hand. "Keep them for a while," Lizzie said, "you'll get interested," and Clare thought it unlikely, but was grateful. It surprises her, always, this kind of evidence that Lizzie has been thinking about her, worrying about her maybe. That their roles have been—not reversed, but somehow balanced out. *Leave, but don't leave me*; there's a thought she can't quite catch hold of, but it's something to do with the pieces Lizzie has put together, throughout her life, with the idea that all along Clare has been leaving clues for her daughter to find. That Lizzie will have fit them together in a picture that may be very different from Clare's own idea of herself, but just as real.

On that same visit they made a lemon cake from an old family recipe and watched a long movie about a woman in a coma; they were both disappointed but Lizzie thought it was interesting, the way the whole thing was done without flashbacks. And then she told Clare about an idea she was working out, though she wasn't sure yet what she'd do with it. She said it had come to her in the library while she was looking things up, all around her people Clare's age or older who were doing the same thing. She'd been struck by how excited they got, and how they talked about their ancestors as if they were people they really knew. *Oh look, here's Thomas,* they said, *and his wife Bessie Anne. And this Thomas must be their son, who was the minister—now didn't he go to Ohio?*

Lizzie said she could see it as a one-woman show, just her on a bare stage with a heap of brightly coloured cloth, maybe dresses or maybe just wraps of some kind. And it would be about a long line of women through time, she wasn't sure how far back, and with each one she'd wrap herself in another layer until she'd be so swaddled she could barely move. "And at the very end," Lizzie said, "I'm not sure what, maybe music, some kind of music playing very fast and I'll start whipping those layers off, one by one, and they'll end up in a pile on the stage again, but it will be a different pile, do you see?"

Before she could stop herself Clare said, "You'll be *naked*?" and Lizzie gave her a look, but let it pass.

Since she did that first commercial Lizzie keeps her hair cut short, and the sticking-out ears that used to cause her such anguish have become a kind of trademark. For all the histrionics, for all her tales of woe, she is living a life that suits her, the life she wants; she has an uncanny ability to make people laugh, to draw them to her. Things happen, men come and go, but she bounces back; she's not a brooder, and Clare realizes that she'll be fine, that she *is* fine. In spite of me, she thinks, and she remembers, as she sometimes does, walking with Lizzie on a windy day. Her shaky toddler legs, one hand folded in Clare's and the other clutching the ratty grey cloth that she wouldn't be parted from. There was a sudden vicious gust, a bit of grit in Clare's eye, and she must have forgotten for a moment, she must have let go. Lizzie set loose and falling, hitting the hard pavement and rolling away from her.

It's a moment she's never told anyone about, but of course everyone has those. Moments of guilt, but also things that are too trivial to mention. The memory of dappled light through a breeze-blown curtain or a sentence a teacher once said, a brown horse dipping its head. But if they're so meaningless, why haven't they vanished completely? Why does her mind snag on them, again and again? Maybe they're not trivial at all, she thinks. Maybe those moments are clues, a string of essentials that make a story that weighs you down, like a backpack stuffed with everything you own, like an anchor heading for the bottom. Somehow they become that heavy, all these tiny things that float within easy reach.

The people who have bought Clare's house will be moving from another province and the woman, Beth, called occasionally to check a measurement, or to ask a question about local renovators. She sounded nice enough, said she hoped Clare didn't mind, didn't feel as if Beth was nudging her out, or taking over before time. She sounded nice, but of course it's hard to be sure, over the telephone. For all Clare knows she could be a vampire; there seem to be a lot of them around these days. That's the kind of thing she would have said to John, who would have put on a professorial voice and asked for her evidence, and she would have told him how Beth always apologizes for calling so early, how she claims to still be muddled about the time zones. She would have told him it's more likely because it's almost sunrise, where Beth is, that she hangs up the phone just in time to close the heavy lid of her coffin.

Those calls were a nuisance, but Clare knows it's better than if Beth lived nearby, if she dropped in from time to time with her own measuring tape. It's better than if Clare had actually *seen* her; then she would have to picture her in the house, all its spaces filled up with unfamiliar furniture, a jumble of strange shoes by the door. She would have to picture Beth flipping pancakes at the new stove she's told Clare about, carrying plates to the square table that, yes, will just fit where she wants it to go, while her husband and her rosy-cheeked sons beam up at her. *You can't judge a book by its cover;* Clare thinks about Beth and she thinks about the TV girl and how strong those skinny arms really were, how easily she lifted the set with its trailing cords and settled it into the wagon. And she wonders why she assumed a life of misery; it could be that they have great jokes and games, the mother and the shuffling boy. It could be that she twirls and dances in a sunny room while he beats out the time with his spoon and grater, until they can barely breathe for laughing.

The towels are all packed, so when Clare turns off the tap she pats her wrist dry on the bottom of her green sweatshirt, doing it gently, as if the red splotch from the boiling water hurts much more than it actually does. The CD has finished, rain falls past the tall windows, and the spoon is loud against the side of her cup. She packed the calendar too soon and has been having moments of panic, wondering if it really is Tuesday, or Wednesday, or whatever day. Moments when it seems that she could have easily lost track, that whole days, even weeks could have passed in the packed-up house without her noticing.

They've always happened, she realizes, these moments when she seems to wake up and wonder where she's been, sometimes for years. I'm a ghost haunting my own life, she thinks, and then she says, "What on earth does *that* mean?" It sounds like something her mother might have said, after her mind began to fray. When all kinds of things came spiralling out, but not in a way that made any sense. Cryptic phrases, names and fates that for all Clare knew could have belonged to characters in a book she had once read. "Promise me you'll shoot me first," Clare said, every time she came back from the seniors' home, and John poured her a glass of wine and promised he would.

She knows it wasn't a bad place, not really. Bright murals and posters on the walls and all the staff patient and upbeat.

The food was decent, even Clare's mother said that, and though she avoided the crafts and card games there was often something going on in the big day room, with its view of endless rooftops and the green hills of Moss Park in the distance. Clare remembers that room, and the way sunlight fell through the long window. The old people in their chairs, all waiting for yet another singalong, for the paunchy magician with his dusty top hat, and his patter. He had a few good tricks, that magician, but she remembers thinking how cruel it was, when he waved his wand and they had to watch more things vanish.

One day the entertainment was a storyteller, a soft-spoken woman in a hippyish long dress; she had trouble with the microphone stand and a red flush flamed out across her cheeks. She sang a song she said she'd learned at her grandmother's knee, though Clare had her doubts about that, and told a long story that had something to do with a black stone and a feather. Then another song she said they'd all remember from when they were young, and some of them did.

When the voices trailed off, the woman clapped her hands and said she'd create a story on the spot, just for them; she asked everyone to tell her one happy memory. Clare's mother raised a shaking hand, obeying some long-ago rule, and said something about skating on a river, the smell of a boy's leather jacket, but it didn't sound right, and Clare thought she must be making it up. Or if not that exactly, then maybe it was someone else's memory, slipped from its moorings and drifting until it had found a space where it could nudge and nestle its way in. A strange thought, but a thing that seemed quite possible, in that stuffy, brightly lit room.

Other people said other things, and the storyteller assembled her new story; there was a tiny baby and a warm leather jacket, there was a cake and a party and a beautiful sunset. She turned on a little silver tape recorder before she started, and Clare realized that was how it worked, that another group of old people in a similar room had offered up a black stone, and a grandmother's song about the rain. And though she knows it wasn't the same day, that's how she remembers it, the final stroke that left her mother glaring and silent. At the mercy of strangers who rolled her and diapered her, rubbed scentless creams and powders into the pale folds of her skin. Yet another thing Clare doesn't want to be thinking about now and she wishes, suddenly, that Lizzie had come anyway. Had thrown open the door and dropped her bag with a thud that filled up the empty hallway.

She's got rid of the Bodum pot to make room for Lizzie's roll of photocopies; now everything just fits in the last box, and Clare feels a brief pat of satisfaction. All along she's been waiting to feel the pang of leaving, but it seems now that it may not come at all. The street has changed, trees grown taller or cut down, houses sold and sold again. Even the doors she was always going in and out of have been painted different colours, the lives behind them no longer things she knows anything about. The heaving sidewalk where Lizzie fell and chipped her teeth has been replaced, marked with the initials of younger children who have themselves grown up and moved away. Women whose kitchen cupboards she knew, whose rueful laughter she shared every day, have become people she runs into so rarely that there's no point in even pretending to catch up. The dismantled house is not a thing there's any good reason to miss.

It was supposed to be filled with children, this house with its flowing rooms, and they assumed it would happen easily.

When it didn't they talked about tests and treatments, but while they talked their lives grew busier, and Lizzie grew older, taking up more and more space. "It's all right," Clare said. "It doesn't matter. We're fine just as we are, aren't we?" She meant it when she said it, and she still does, really. But as the house returns to what it once was, bare floors, bare walls, empty windows, she keeps catching flickers of movement from the corner of her eye. All those ghostly possibilities, with nowhere left to hide.

Checking her watch, she sees that the scalded spot on her wrist is barely visible and that she has the timing just right. Soon the big truck will come rumbling down the narrow street and it will be all noise and movement, strong men with steel-toed boots making everything happen quickly. The cleaning company she's hired will come later to take care of the dust and debris that's always left behind, and she'll become one of those neighbourhood faces that has disappeared. A background face; one day you notice it's missing, and realize you have no idea how long it's been gone. Lying in the dark these last nights, listening to the song about ticking away, she's sensed the piled boxes looming around her and thought there's probably an equation for it, the way things accumulate over time, while people disappear. Something else she could have asked John, something he would have enjoyed working out. The kind of problem he might have added as a bonus question on a final exam.

And it wouldn't be as tidy as an equation, but she wonders if there's some kind of rule for how long you keep seeing the dead, wonders if it's the same for everyone. How long before you stop following a familiar back in a crowd, before a profile no longer makes you blink and stare. She thinks it must be a progression, the way they retreat from the real world but still stroll through your dreams, fitting themselves to whatever is happening there. Sometimes they wear clothes you don't recognize, as if wherever they've come from is a place with shopping, and you wake up wishing you could ask them. And then one day you realize that the dreams have gone too, leaving only an occasional ambush.

In the story about the rains things were beginning to fall apart, but Clare had to close the magazine before the end, and next time in the waiting room she didn't think to look for it. She knows it's not important but it nags at her now, and she wishes she could know what happened. It must be on her mind because of the rain and the reminders she's uncovered, her old backpack and the bits and pieces in a dusty box of souvenirs. She barely recognizes the girl she was, who moved so easily through the world. The girl who coped with languages and currencies and climbed onto boats and trains, stepped off them into whatever was going to come next.

In the packed-up house Clare turns off lights and takes a last walk through each dim room. She trails her fingers over the tops of the sealed boxes and thinks about the magazine, wonders if it really matters how those pages unfolded. There's a rumbling sound outside; it might be thunder, or it might be what she's waiting for. And it occurs to her, quite suddenly, that she can make the story end any way she wants.

II
(1990)

On the last day they went to the more expensive taverna on
the hillside, found a place on the terrace that jutted out over a
tumble of rocks and looked so precarious, when seen from the
beach below. Their table wobbled and John reached into his
pocket for the folded bit of cardboard, bent to jam it under one
of the legs. Looking through the space he'd left, Clare saw the
rippled sea and a few faraway boats. The flaming sky caught
in the long moment before day tipped into night, before the
strings of lights above their heads took over, erasing the rest
of the world.

"You look lighter," she said, when John sat up again. His
hair was ruffled and his eyes bright in his tanned face. "Before-
and-after picture," he said, reaching for her hand across the
steadied table; Clare said, "After what?" and then was sorry.

When he'd called the trip a second honeymoon their daughter
said, "Gross," and wrinkled her nose. John told her it was a
joke, that there hadn't been a first, just one night in the cheap-
est motel in Niagara Falls, and Lizzie crushed her ears with
her hands. From the moment the airport doors slid apart Clare
had missed her daughter terribly, although she knew that she

had some younger, gentler Lizzie caught in her mind. Not the one who knew they didn't understand a thing. Not the one who had appeared so suddenly, scowling as she crumpled a misty kitten poster in her hands.

"It's normal," Clare kept telling John. The misery, the sulks and rages. "I was like that too, inside I was."

"I know, I know," he said, but he didn't, not really, and he kept on using the same steps, as if the little jokes and suggested outings would eventually produce something other than a withering look. He said he found it hard to concentrate with all the turmoil and he started going back to his office in the evenings to mark exams, work on his textbook chapters. Sometimes he woke up there in the morning, he said, with his face on a pile of papers, the red pen still in his hand. The transatlantic flight was the longest time they'd spent together in months, if you didn't count thinking.

The trip had all been John's idea; he came home with a clutch of brightly coloured brochures, fanned them out like a card trick and said, "Let's go to Greece, let's just go." She knew it was bravado, the bounce in his voice, knew that she could puncture it with a word, but where would that leave them? So she began making lists: check passports, try on bathing suit, buy new sunglasses. She arranged for her mother to stay with Lizzie, who said she'd *die* if she had to eat those casseroles for ten days, her grandmother's *Waste-Not-Want-Nots*. "You probably won't," Clare said, but she bought a stack of pizzas for the freezer, a big jar of popcorn for all the late movies she knew they'd watch, school night or not. She felt the familiar, childish niggle when she thought of how flexible her mother's rules were when it came to Lizzie, how she had always praised every cartwheel and report card, clapped loudly at school concerts and plays. But there was so much to organize that there wasn't much space for other thoughts, and then the taxi doors slammed and the familiar streets fell away so quickly behind them.

The airport itself was a dislocating swirl of colour and movement and echoing sound. Everyone in a hurry, it seemed, tapping heels and a bombardment of scents, power suits and gelled hair. In the middle of it all there was a young man, a boy, standing with his back firm to a round pillar. Not dressed for the weather, maybe that's what caught her eye, buffalo sandals and frayed jeans, a tie-dyed T-shirt and long, straggling hair. He's on a bad trip in 1969, she thought, and once she would have said it to John, but she didn't. As they settled into their seats and buckled their belts she thought about that boy, and wondered if he was still there. Thought about his absolute stillness and his stunned eyes, and how he'd seemed like someone who'd been flung through time, suddenly awake in a world where no one could possibly know him.

They landed in a diesel-scented morning, two days in Athens climbing and wandering and dodging scooters, and John bought her a silver ring, delicately fretted and wrapped in a twist of coloured paper. She bought him a pair of sandals with a loop for his big toe and his feet got terribly sunburned; the next day Clare wandered alone, in a trance, peering through iron grilles at hidden courtyards, trailing her fingers over the dusty leaves of flowering bushes while John read and made notes in their noisy room, wet towels draped over his feet. Then the ride to the port and a trim white boat gleaming against the water. The end of the journey, a room with pale walls, with blue shutters that could open or close, and nothing to decide but which beach to go to, what to order from a tattered menu. On the second day she reached for a bitter dark olive through the dappled light, and felt something surrender. Felt it as a loosening in her shoulders, down her spine, as sudden as an unexpected blow.

John swam in the early morning, hiked in the dusty hills, and sometimes Clare went with him, but more often she tucked a beach mat under her arm, along with a fat paperback she rarely opened. "Alone with my thoughts," she said, although she knew that wasn't the right word for the lazy meanderings in her head. Day after day, balanced on the edge of sleep on a mat on the hot sand. Sometimes the oily *putt* of a boat's motor, then only the water rippling onto the shore. And the sound of goat bells coming closer and then receding, a sound so particular that it brought an image, behind her closed eyes, of the bells themselves, of the goats' brown bodies in the warm sunlight, the way they trotted together and their strange, mournful faces. A sound she had first heard on this same island, maybe this same spot, so many years ago.

She thought about soundscapes then, and wondered if anyone else ever had. Tapes, CDs that could spin on a rack beside the postcards, that would bring everything back much more clearly than any photograph. Goat bells and the thump and splash of an octopus being beaten on the rocks at the water's edge. The clicking of worry beads and backgammon pieces in the little square where old men still leaned back in their chairs in the drowsy afternoons. Not the same old men, surely not, but with the same flat, vaguely hostile look she remembered from before, when she sat at a battered round table with a girl named Iz, drinking milky Nescafé and smoking Recor cigarettes and sharing every secret corner of their hearts.

Sometimes in those days, when the afternoon began to soften, a short man with a white apron would step out of a doorway, tip his head back and begin to shout. Long, rolling sentences rising and falling, and no one looked up, but the clatter of tiles stopped until he had finished, and then vanished as suddenly as he had appeared. They decided, Clare and Iz, that he must have been offering comfort of some kind. A reminder that the season was changing, that soon all these tourists, all these filthy hippies will be gone and nothing to do then, my friends, but sit back and count our money. Thinking about it now Clare wondered if it had really happened over and over, or just one time. And had it been this island, or had she transposed the man, the apron, from some completely different place? All these random thoughts; sometimes she wasn't sure what year it would be, when she finally opened her eyes.

By early afternoon the beach was more crowded, chattering families and young men batting balls back and forth, children shrieking in the water. Then she rolled up her mat, shook sand from the splayed book and began the walk to the blue-shuttered room. She kicked a ball back to a curly-haired boy and thought of Lizzie running, her ponytail switching and the fierce, rapt look on her face and how that was the point, the whole point of the piles of laundry, the rushed meals and the shouting from the bottom of the stairs. They were always on the verge of being late, always missing something, even when Clare ran through the checklist. Have you got your uniform, shin pads, shoes, have you got a headband?

Once it was water they'd forgotten and she bought a bottle at the kiosk, carried it over to the players' side of the field. The air was golden and completely still, the kind of evening when any sound carries a long way, but all Clare heard was the rasp of the short, browned grass on the soles of her sandals. She stopped, her hand cold on the bottle, and looked at the girls, all thirteen, fourteen years old in their red shirts, red shorts, with their hair tied back, their bruised knees. They were completely silent as they took out earrings or put tape over studs, as they unclipped watches and bracelets, reached behind their necks or turned their backs for another to undo a clasp, silver chains rippling as they passed from hand to hand. A ritual she had never noticed from her lawn chair at the far side of the field, and she was pierced by the way they moved through it, by their concentration and their beauty. One girl turned and it was Lizzie; Clare tossed the plastic bottle and it seemed to glow as it flipped through the air and landed lightly in her daughter's hands.

It *was* the same island, somewhere she'd been both happy and miserable, although she supposed you could say that about any place. John hadn't said and she hadn't asked, told herself it had to be coincidence. Not the kind of thing he'd remember if she'd even mentioned the name in those early days, when they still had separate pasts to exchange. She'd kept some things vague whenever she talked about her wandering year, though she knows she told him about the arguments with her mother, who thought she was too young. Knows she told him about the money her father had left, and the way his folded glasses sat heavy on the note that didn't explain anything.

"I ran her over," John always said when they were telling the story of how they'd met, and it was almost true. It happened in the parking lot of the nursing home where Clare was working, when she first came back and everything was uncertain. John had been called to collect the effects of a great-aunt he barely knew and he'd been distracted, thinking about the small size of the box he'd placed on the seat beside him. Clare was crossing behind his car and it was the smallest of nudges, but she was startled and slipped, and he helped her up and drove her home, buckling the seat belt carefully over her stomach. He went with her up the stairs and turned on lights in her apartment, propped her aching feet on a thick pillow and made her toast, stayed around.

"I was smitten," he always said, making it sound so simple, so inevitable. An easy story to tell, and why shouldn't it be? What was the point in thinking, as she sometimes did, that if the elevator she'd ridden down had made an extra stop, if John had looked over his shoulder, or thought a few seconds longer about that small, sad box—what was the point in thinking that if almost anything had happened differently, then there wouldn't have been a story at all.

It was the same island, she knew that, but after so much time it was like visiting the place as a ghost, or in a dream. Everything familiar yet somehow distorted, extra storeys added to old buildings, two shops knocked into one with a shiny new sign, layers of time. New structures choked the port and surrounded the old town, although the heart of it was much the same, twisting lanes, narrow between whitewashed houses and walls, and the square where the old men sat, the dark doorways of the shops around it. Much the same, but the tree in the centre was so much bigger, throwing down shade where she remembered bright light.

At the edge of the village, villas marched up into the hills, and John told her there was a narrow road that went right across the island, ending in another cluster of houses, a small shop and a café. On this side asphalt had replaced the path that curved up and around to the bay, but the sweep of the main beach was the same and if she stopped in the right place, looking down, she couldn't see the row of restaurants, the stacks of brightly coloured loungers. Could almost see herself instead, asleep on a thin green towel, or wading out into the sea.

She knew that people would have aged, that the waiters in the tavernas would have been barefoot boys that other time, but she did recognize one face. The woman behind the counter in the smaller bakery, where wasps struggled in the pool of honey that oozed around the last pieces of baklava. She was sure that it was the French girl who had helped Gerard in his bar, the one who moved with a dreamy sway while Pink Floyd played over and over, her long skirt brushing the strings of beads around her ankles as she cleared bottles, added smudged glasses to a round tray she didn't look strong enough to carry. The one she didn't give a thought to when she met Gerard outside, the music cut off when he closed the back door, a wash of moonlight falling on the piled wooden crates, on his confident hand moving over her silvered skin. Or all the other times she left the beach early and waited in her room at the end of the dim hall, hardly able to stand it when he appeared in the doorway. His white shirt glowing, a finger to his lips because of the muffled voices, the footsteps that crossed the floor above them. How young she'd been, thinking that only Iz knew, and only because she'd told her. Assuming that he'd also been swept away, that hers were the only eyes he sought out with that clear look.

The woman in the bakery was older, of course, with better English, with creases and a softer jawline. But she moved the same way as she slid back a tray, folded the top of a warm paper bag and counted coins into Clare's cupped hand. So this is how it all turned out, she thought. This is who she became. And she remembered that there had been children, two little girls with tangled hair who sat on the counter and sang along with "Money," and that other song about the dreamer. Girls who would be adults now and surely hadn't stayed, who would be busy in some city, some other place, and hardly ever visited. It unsettled her, this glimpse of the way other lives had carried on, and on the way back to the room she took a wrong turn and got a little lost, the pastries cold and heavy by the time she got back to John, who was waiting in the slatted light.

In the room with the blue shutters they reached for each other through the crumpled sheets, and that was real, but she didn't know how much it mattered. Still something sharp and glittering in the space between them, visible at sudden, unexpected moments. John has told her that almost nothing happened, that mostly he *was* working late those nights, or just driving around and around. "My mid-life crisis," he said once, in the dark. "You can have one too." As if it was something they'd both moved beyond, something far enough away for joking.

But it's not that far away, what she thinks of as the night of the ambush. The night of the department party, when she opened the wrong door to a startle in the dark, a smooth-haired woman who sidled past, not meeting Clare's eyes. On the drive home she stared at John's hands on the wheel, so many things chasing through her head that when he said, "Say something," she felt that she already had. They sat in the car in their driveway while the engine ticked itself cool; light glowed in every window of the house, the way Lizzie liked it when she was home alone, and Clare thought of all the things waiting inside. The clean clothes in a jumble in the blue basket, the permission form to fill out for the field trip, and it was her turn to drive to early practice in the morning. Things that wouldn't change, no matter what happened in the car, what they said to each other. She thought of another cliché then, about people who stayed together because of the children, and understood that it was the whole fabric of their life they were clutching in their hands.

Before they glued things back together there were weeks when they barely spoke, when they stepped so carefully around each other. And there were nights when John was somewhere else, nights when Clare washed the kitchen floor and all the dishes in all the cupboards. A glass of wine on the counter beside the tape player, hitting rewind again and again to hear the woman singing about walking on a wire, about the bottom of the sea. The volume turned up to cover the harsh, unreal laughter that came from the family room, where Lizzie watched shows about people getting themselves into all kinds of zany, avoidable predicaments. Sometimes she carried the bottle in there after Lizzie had stomped off to bed and drifted in the flickering light, waking hours later into the past. The black-and-white face of her mother's favourite actress or a seventies family strutting through a seventies living room, pausing to put hands on hips and shout at each other. A show that had fascinated her the first time around, watching it in her parents' house where so little was said out loud.

In the taverna on the hillside Clare realized that she'd missed that final, tipping moment from day to night; now the strings of lights glowed white and all the tables were filled, people eating and drinking and laughing, a crashing of sound. Strange to think that in twenty-four hours they'd be back in their own house, their own time, that another couple would be sitting in their place at the crooked table. Talking about people she and John had never heard of, or staring right through each other. A vision of her own house slid into her mind, empty rooms in rainy light, bare floors and the brown couch with the silky grey throw, waiting for her to sit down and reach to pick up the magazine from the coffee table, to begin again as if nothing had ever stopped.

She tried to see herself there, but like the island itself there was something askew in her picture of those rooms; they were familiar but not exact. She had the feeling that something had been torn and she had stepped through, like one of those old stories about a hidden, magic world. No wonder she surprised herself in the mirror, these last days. Gave herself little tests and tried to remember, without looking down, what shirt she'd put on, to remember herself doing it. Tried to picture the ring John had bought, in its twist of bright paper, when all she could feel was the weight on her hand. On the beach she was just a woman on a straw mat, invisible to the young ones running, kicking a ball so close that a spray of sand caught in the fine hairs on her arm. No mystery in the fact that no one met her eyes, that no one noticed when she waded out into the water, stirred it slowly with her browned hands. Days when she wandered without John she hardly spoke, although she heard things. "It's paradise," people said to each other, standing at the postcard rack, or when their steps matched on the road to the beach. "It's a little slice of paradise—I'd love to stay forever."

"Be careful what you wish for," she said once, but no one seemed to hear her. A good thing too; what would be the point in setting those words loose on a perfect, sunny day? What was a thought like that even doing in her head?

John had made a good plan. The overnight boat to save the price of an Athens hotel, the last lazy dinner, the bottles of wine to help them sleep. Much nicer, she told him, than the way they used to do it, with cheap Valium from someone's stash washed down with cheaper retsina. Walking the slope to the port they held hands at first, but had to keep letting go to switch their bags, which seemed so much heavier, even though the things they had added were very light. Hauling at her slipping purse strap Clare wished that she'd looked harder for her old metal-framed backpack, wished she hadn't decided that it would be a silly way for a woman her age to move through the world. A woman who had a house and a family and shopping lists stuck to the fridge, her mother's maxims sometimes tripping, appallingly, from her own lips. Lizzie was quite right to sneer at *Time heals all wounds*, or the one about breaking eggs for an omelette, and hadn't she done the same? There were things she'd been so certain of, in those long-haired days on this island, about where she would go and how she would live. As she watched John smooth out the last of their crumpled drachmas and tuck them into his wallet, giving it a little pat, she knew she would never have imagined herself arriving here.

She knew, of course she knew, that it hadn't all been wonderful, that earlier time. The pack that she carried had been heavy and awkward and the splinter of her father's death was still jagged and close to the surface. She'd been confused and angry, and she'd often been hungry and tired, been ill or desperately unhappy. But when she thinks of that time she also remembers a feeling of *loosening*. She remembers running with the others down a steeply winding pathway, dark and slick with rain. Maybe here—had it been here? A cruise ship had docked, blazing with light, and there was shouting, there were braying donkeys and men with sticks, and she remembers the panicked, lined faces of the passengers in their bright clothes as they were hoisted onto those donkeys and carried away. All that colour and noise, that confusion, and she knows it's not likely, on that crowded, rain-slicked path, but she remembers them holding hands and running right through it, as if nothing could ever stop them. And she remembers so clearly that it was like running in a dream, the feeling of those long strides, her feet barely touching the ground.

She knows that it's been studied and proved, this thing that's obvious to everyone about the memories of youth and how clear they are, how real. Researchers with tape recorders sat down with the elderly, pretending to have a visit, a chat, feigning interest in the content when really it was all about measurement. About producing charts and graphs of the number of adverbs and adjectives, the only importance of the details being their number. All that time and trouble to conclude that the reason for the vividness of those memories had something to do with *intensity*. Strange to think that if she lived to be very old she might forget her daughter's face but remember leaning on the chipped rail of a ferry boat, her hair tied back with a shoelace, and the sound of a strummed guitar. That she might remember a moment running through night rain while every trace of John and Lizzie vanished, as if they'd only been imagined, all the years of their lives.

The boat was late, two hours, then three, and if it had been more comfortable she would have fallen asleep on the bright yellow bench, leaning on John's warm shoulder. "I'm regretting the wine," he said, rubbing at his temples. Clare started to tell him about a game they used to play, to pass the time, but realized that she'd forgotten most of the details. "Something about a detective," she said. "And he sees something, or knows something, and there are clues. But just tiny clues. And then you ask me questions until you know the truth. Or not that exactly, but until you've figured it out."

"Sorry—what?" John said, when she nudged him.

Looking up from the dock it was impossible to tell where the rough hills met the night sky. Only a few circles of light marked the road, marked the tavernas and the guest houses that were themselves invisible, even under the bright stars. There had been faint music for a time, but it had stopped and the others waiting, six or seven of them, were mostly silent now too. They had all passed beyond jokes and complaints, had entered that state of waiting that feels eternal, although flickers of hope ran through them at every flash far out in the dark. Once there was the unmistakable sound of an engine coming closer, then cruelly fading. John began to explain the formula for calculating the horizon's distance to a man in a plaid shirt who had said something about it. "I don't get it," the man said, and turned away to peer again into the empty ticket office.

"Might be worse than, don't you think?" John said when he sat down again, and it took Clare a moment to remember the holiday that had been *her* idea. The place they'd rented on Lake Huron when Lizzie was four or five, a stretch of beach Clare remembered from a holiday when she was about the same age. Though they only did it once she still thought about the endless sand and the glittering stones she collected in a plastic pail. The tented kindling her father had set up so carefully and her parents' faces lit warm by that crackling fire.

She should have known, of course, that it wouldn't be the same. Their own time was a week of foul weather, a few crashing thunderstorms that knocked out the power, and it didn't take long for them to turn into a different family. A couple who bickered about who had forgotten the flashlight and the coffee, with their unreasonable, fractious child. When John said another game of Snakes and Ladders might actually drive him mad Clare found a deck of cards and tried the waterfall shuffle. Tried the Mad Hatter's trick that her father had taught her, but the cards were old and sticky and it didn't work properly. Lizzie said it was stupid, everything was stupid. She jumped down from her chair, landing on a stray green Monopoly house; there was a tiny bead of blood, and she would not be consoled.

That week had become their benchmark for the unbearable, their shorthand for occasions when something happened to time itself, each moment stretched out to an age. On the dock Clare thought that must count for something, the fact that there was no one else in the world John could say that to, and have it be really understood. No one else who could answer, "Oh, worse than. Definitely worse."

When lights finally did appear on the horizon, growing steadily brighter and casting shivers on the dark water, John helped her to her feet, moved his shoulders around the way he did before setting out on a long run. The boat chugged closer and it was like something sailing out of the past, rust-covered and smaller than it had seemed, gouges and bits broken off the gangway the sailors threw down with a crash that made them all jump. They were in a great hurry, the sailors, shouting to each other and nudging everyone up onto the deck that was slick and slippery, as if it had come through some completely different weather. Clare had imagined herself leaning on the rail, feeling the last Aegean air on her skin and saying some kind of proper goodbye as the darker huddle of the island fell away. But the sailors herded them all toward an open doorway, she and John the last to make their way down the vibrating metal stairs, descending into murky yellow light.

The noise of the engines grew louder as the boat began to move and they rocked into each other, bouncing apart again. John's face was a sickly colour, sweat on his forehead and a sudden look in his eyes. "Go, go," Clare said, and he dropped the bags at her feet, stumbled away into the gloom. Her fault; in the taverna she had teased him about the Gravol, another moment of exasperation that they both knew had nothing to do with seasickness, and he had tucked the package back into the first aid pouch. Said, "Here I am, then, taking a chance."

The boat began its shuddering turn and Clare lurched, recovered and looked for a familiar face, comrades from the waiting time who had come down the steps just before them. They would roll their eyes at each other and one of them would help her find seats, a place to put the awkward bags. But there was no one standing, no one looking to recognize her as a fellow traveller. The sides of the space were filled with short rows of seats that looked as though they might have been salvaged from a train crash. Each heaped with something or someone, asleep or feigning sleep, and she wondered what the point was, of all that waiting, if this was where it brought her.

In the centre there was a raised area, a waist-high platform, covered with a rubber tarpaulin. A group of women had occupied it and they also seemed to have stepped out of time, long dark dresses, and scarves wrapped tightly around their heads. She realized that the drone of sound was not just the engines; the women were talking to each other in a language she didn't recognize, a nasal, complaining tone although some of them were smiling and one was rocking and laughing, her hands pressed to her mouth. There were baskets and cloth-wrapped bundles that some were using as pillows, their legs drawn up with only the dusty toes of their shoes showing beneath the folds of black. Food spread out on creased paper, olives and bread and strong-smelling cheese, little round cakes dusted with sugar.

The women were talking and laughing and eating in the space they'd claimed, but a few shifted and beckoned to her, making shooing motions at a younger woman who had Lizzie's sulky look. One nodded and patted the cleared spot at the edge and Clare climbed up, curled up, her head on the pillow of her canvas purse, turning her back on the train-crash seats, on their bags and the neatly printed labels. She closed her eyes and listened to the rustling and chewing, the women's circling voices, and thought that if she'd taken a different degree she might know things about them. If she even knew what the language was she would be able to imagine exactly where they had been and where they were going, who was waiting to hear the stories they were bringing back.

The engines rumbled and the voices webbed around her and she had a sudden crazy thought that she'd been waiting for these women, and that she was meant to go with them. They would welcome her as they had when they made her this space, right on the edge, and maybe wherever they were going was a place she was meant to be. Somewhere away from all this *better than* and *worse than*; she saw herself moving with them through a timeless landscape. Long skirts rippling as they made their way along a winding track, a faint sound of music leading them on through a hole in a deep green hill.

Something touched her shoulder and she came back to herself with a start. She turned her head to see John standing beside her and though it took a moment, in the dim light, she saw him clearly and completely, saw him just as he was. A kind and serious man, her daughter's father in every way that mattered. Whatever had blown through their life would have rocked him just as violently; she realized that now, just as she knew that nothing he ever did or decided was done lightly. And she saw that he was so much braver than she was, though it seemed such a simple thing. Putting one foot carefully in front of the other, and carrying on.

She noticed that the women's voices had stopped just as John said, "Can you shift a bit?" His face close to hers, and one knee already on the platform. There was a sudden hissing, a rasping cackle, and they seemed to rise together like a great black wave, the hissing louder and louder. "It's all right," John said, in his calm and reasonable voice. "It's all right," he said, straightening up, his palms facing out. But it made no difference; the sound rolled on and a bit of thrown food hit him on the cheek, leaving an oily streak that glowed dully in the murky light, just beneath one startled eye.

The noise subsided as he backed away, as he said her name,

wiping at his tired face, and Clare wondered if there would be
even a trace left of this long, still moment, should she live to
be very old. And she knew that she was clinging to the shreds
of something, that whichever way it went, any minute now she
would have to open her hands.

III

When the rains came, we moved on, skipping from island to island like smooth stones over water, following the sun. A time of rusting ferries and sunburned shoulders, matches flaring and frayed bell-bottoms and always someone, somewhere, strumming a guitar. Everything fluid, people came and people left and some we minded losing more than others, but it was fleeting. This was 1974 and we had no idea how young we were. Still trusted anyone with long hair and a bouncing walk.

In Athens we stayed in hostels in crumbling buildings and places that were even cheaper, rooftops where we spread out sleeping bags and the night sky was the only thing hanging over us. We made connections everywhere, on those rooftops or waiting at bus stops, in the American Express office or among the expensive rows of tables in Syntagma where waiters in white shirts popped out of dark doorways and wove their way through traffic, balancing plates on heavy round trays. Have you got a light, have you got a good place to stay, where have you come from, where are you going; in those days we were always moving and always talking, choosing the details to share from our ordinary lives and leaving out what didn't matter, shaking off what didn't fit and thinking we could really do that, draw a line before and after and have nothing trailing along behind.

We were looking for the sun but not the city sun, nothing like tourists, we thought, and some of us didn't bother to make the steep climb to the Acropolis. What felt right was watching grey Piraeus fall away from the deck of a boat and then turning to face the open water. One boat, one place, and then another and another and we began to recognize each other on beaches or in ferry lines, outside cafés, we began to move along together, sharing cigarettes and bits of food, cheap Valium to help us sleep on those long and noisy voyages. People came and people went and we knew them for a while, knew the stories they brought with them and the ones that happened when we were together. Sometimes they left bits of clothing behind and that kept them as close as skin, at first, but mostly it was just those stories left and as time passed they thinned out, didn't mean the same to someone new who hadn't been there and anyway had their own stories, patches to add to a pattern that was always changing. We sailed from one place to another, sometimes separating at the dock where women held up signs and plucked at our sleeves but always finding each other again, and the days and nights slid into their rhythm, the beach, the square, the bar.

———

Sometimes a tiny moment is all that it takes, and braided time begins to unravel. It was Halloween and the streets were filled with wet brown leaves, with ghouls and tiny angels, and on her front porch three children stood in a pool of light. Tangled long wigs held on with flowered headbands, tie-dyed shirts and strings of bright beads, medallions around their necks. *Peace, man,* one said, making the sign someone had shown him, guaranteed to get a laugh and an extra handful of candy.

The children clumped back down the steps, their wigs askew and their fluorescent peace signs bouncing. All of it as remote, as dated for them as those movies that pop up on television in the middle of the night. The ones with cardboard scenery and improbable dialogue, a conniving woman with sharply drawn eyebrows and an innocent one in soft focus. She thinks now about how time does that, by moving on; you glance back and so many things seem as ridiculous as the ancient belief that the sun was a fiery chariot, dragging the night across the sky. That a person could sail to the edge of the flat world, and just disappear.

She still has her own, real beads and they're very different; they made a delicate rattle in the bottom of a box when she lifted it down from the closet shelf. It's not very big, that box, but it holds a lot. Those tiny black and blue beads and the frayed string that once held them, a hard-covered notebook and a sifting of flimsy tickets from buses and boats, sugar cubes crumbling in their wrappers. There are several matchboxes, one filled with soft sand, and a dried-out leather bracelet. A handful of washed-out photographs, the harsh wake of a boat and rough hills set against a clean sky, the blue shutters that frame a window with a long view to the sand and the sea. Things the girl she was had thought were important to capture, and she tries to imagine herself looking through the lens of her cheap camera. The sun hot on the top of her head and a slow clatter of goat bells the only sound.

There aren't many interiors or night shots, because of the expensive square flash cubes. There's a peeling, whitewashed room with a fluttering curtain, and a picture of a group of long-haired people in a bar, flashed bright and clear and smiles on all their faces. Behind them a tray seems to float in the air, the person who holds it lost in the shadowy background. For a long time her memories were tied to these frozen photographs and she would have thought, if she'd thought, that the rest had faded to nothing. Then a boy flashed a cheeky peace sign under her yellow porch light and they began to stir. Rousing like a ragged ghost army and falling into place, the whisper of shuffling feet taking on a marching rhythm.

The last place was a small white village on a small island, twisting narrow lanes that all somehow ended at the tiny square where the old men sat, saying things in a grumbling tone. Some of us had rooms in Adelpha's house at the edge of that village, the main floor a long corridor with doors opening off, rusting metal bed frames where we were always stubbing our toes and a tiny room somewhere in the middle with a toilet and a shower, a drain in the floor. The water a thin spray that was never more than warm and with our long, salt-crusted hair, everything in the room dripped wet by the time we were done, and when we wiped the crooked mirror our sun-browned faces startled us, made our eyes seem so much brighter, looking out, looking in.

Adelpha knew some German but most of us didn't; she carried paper and a fat green pencil in her apron pocket and wrote

down numbers, sometimes drew stick figures to explain that
we should never take our clothes off on the main beach or that
the taverna by the port was not a good place. Every *Freitag* we
climbed the outside stone steps to the rooftop, through the
hot buzz of wasps that hovered over a spread of drying figs,
and Adelpha smoothed out our crumpled drachmas and made
checkmarks in a little book. She lived up there in summer,
behind a curtained doorway, with a family we could only guess
at by the things they left behind, a school book splayed open
or an abandoned glass of coffee, part of a small footprint in
a mess of squashed fruit. Sometimes we saw her in the village with other women dressed in black, crusty bread or paper-
wrapped packets in the string bags that dangled from their
hands. *Kalimera*, we said, or *kalispera*, and sometimes they
nodded, but there was a way they turned their heads, just the
tiniest bit; we noticed that but didn't think it was anything that
really mattered.

The place she's rented in this little beach town is more like a
cabin than a house, tucked in behind cedars and facing a quiet
street. Out the back door there's a clump of tall bushes, their
leaves already fallen and blown away. There's a tangle of garden
and scruffy grass, and a short flight of steps that leads down
to the beach where she walks, in all kinds of weather. She's
been told that the town is bustling in summer, but it's hard to
imagine that now. Hard to picture bright towels spread out on
the sand, and women bending to squeeze water from their hair.
Children squealing and jumping in the waves, slapping at the
surface with the flats of their hands.

She came here on a whim, that's what she said. A name that popped into her head when there were complications, a gap between closing dates and a burst pipe in her new place, all the damage the previous owners left behind. It made sense to have the repairs done before she moved in, and though she agreed with her friends that it was so *frustrating*, in a way she'd been quite relieved. Glad of an in-between time when she could finally deal with things and work out how to go on, but that hasn't happened yet. Instead she's surrendered to the place and the season, to the thoughts that float through as she walks the long shore, or looks out at the changing lake. They're not the thoughts she expected to be having, and she doesn't know where they'll take her. All these stirred-up memories of what it was like, to be young, with a brimming heart.

When she was first here she fell heavy into sleep at any time at all, waking sweaty and confused like someone with a terrible fever. No more tasks, no more lists and no pattern to anything, the days and the nights. Once, through a window, she saw the moon moving quickly through the black sky. Watched it slip into the water, a last silvered bubble on the ruffled horizon drawn down like a setting sun. It didn't seem like something that should happen, but there was no one to ask, and in the middle of the night it seemed quite possible she'd arrived in a place governed by completely different rules.

That's a hard thought to shake even now, when she's made herself a kind of routine. She sleeps soundly through the night and wakes just before dawn, coffee poured as the first gulls wing out over the lake. They come in groups, maybe families, another thing that she hadn't known before. Snowy white, or darker, or streaked, in quite separate bunches with pauses between, always moving in the same direction. If the wind is against them they just flap harder, and their shed feathers are scattered along the shore.

Things call to her on her beach walks and she picks them up, bits of water-smoothed wood and those feathers, smooth stones that glow richly, then fade. She drops them in a pile by the back steps and thinks one day she'll spread them all out. See how they fit together, these shapes and textures that for some reason have caught her eye. Back inside she makes notes on the calendar each day, just the weather and the colour of the water. Slate grey, as a rule, but once a dazzling Aegean blue.

———

Every day on the island the sun was hot and the water barely rippled. Every day the same, waking late, a cup of coffee, then the winding path to the main beach where we spread our fraying towels on the sand. It was hard to imagine that there had ever been anywhere else, that we hadn't always known each other, and sometimes we talked about that, how it was quite possible that we'd once sat on different benches in the same station, or passed each other on a narrow sidewalk without even a flicker.

There were no clouds in the sky but there were other patterns, lazy smoke rings rising and thinning or the way Douglas and Robert moved chess pieces on a swollen fold-out board. Even the puckered scars running up Robert's right arm that we thought were from Vietnam, though he never said. He didn't say much, ever, but Robert really hated to lose, crashed a fist that sent chess pieces flying and once a white queen splashed and sank to the bottom of Jen's tall glass. She brushed droplets from the fringed vest she swore Jim Morrison had given her, warm from his own body, drained the glass and caught the queen between her straight white teeth.

Jen hooked up with Carly and Jackson in Marseilles after a bad ride, her palms and shoulder still scraped from hitting the gravel road. She had silver rings on every finger and rows of bangles, an open look, and the room they shared was the biggest one, chained cupboards on the wall and a chipped stone sink that had a pink tinge, when the light was strong, from when one of them rinsed out Jackson's favourite red shirt. Jackson said he'd once played an angel in a movie and we could see it, his smooth cheeks and his flowing cornsilk hair. He and Carly met on a commune, maybe in Vermont, but something happened and they flew away. They travelled light, worked in bars and on farms and picked things, sold things—earrings made from twists of wire and the strips of leather he plaited into bracelets that stained and tightened in the sea. He said he knew all kinds of knots from those years he was in the navy; that was after the time in jail and the summers in the fire tower but before the movie and the ranch, and the year of riding freight trains. It was hard to believe he was old enough for all that, but when someone said no way had he run away with the circus Jackson jumped up on the narrow stone wall by the graveyard and walked it backwards, finishing off with a perfect handstand, a deep bow.

Carly may have known the truth of it, but she was hard to reel in. Everything about her seemed to float, her long skirts and trailing sleeves. Stray cats rubbed against her, caught their claws in the filmy fabric when she crouched down to give them bits of food she'd been saving for them. Once she stood between a man and a pus-eyed dog he was kicking, and she cried when the fishermen beat small octopus on the rocks near the water's edge, though Douglas told her they were already dead, and it was just a way to make them tender.

Douglas knew things like that, and about the Muses and the Furies, but he said he wasn't really that kind of teacher anymore. He dropped acid at a concert in Hyde Park and it changed everything, and he'd had to leave his wife and son behind too. Whenever he could he came to the islands with a portable easel strapped to his back, because he'd learned he had an artist's soul. Mostly he sketched but sometimes Douglas painted flowers on our cheeks, bright colours that wore away slowly until they looked like bruises. He went for long walks with Iz and sometimes with Clare, to the end of the white beach and out of sight, and he was always writing down the titles of books they should read, things about the soul, and how to be OK. "Here comes your father-figure," Hans used to say, but Iz told him it was nothing like that.

Hans said he was in a band back in Yde, and if only he'd brought his guitar we'd be amazed. Sometimes he pretended, moving his fingers in silent chords and stopping and starting again. "I *always* have trouble with that one," he said, and Robert did the spooky chuckle, *The lun-a-tic is in my head*, and it may have been true. Hans called himself The Joker, but no one laughed much at the things he did and said, passing on fake messages and making up stories about people he'd seen, sneaking around places they shouldn't have been. Sometimes he offered a box of matches with a little shake to show it was full, nothing but burned ends inside and he thought that was so funny. He did it again, saying, "For real this time," and we took it again and he laughed even more; we kept on falling for it, so willing to be convinced each time he said, "No, this time I really do have some, I swear it's not like all the other times, I swear."

Maybe it was a similar thing, the way we kept going into the water although the sea in the little bay was not much cooler than the air and it only made us thirsty, whatever bottles we'd brought with us always almost empty. Someone said that if we had money we could open a café right here, just a little one, just essentials, and even though we knew that would spoil everything we made lazy plans for the Bare Minimum Café, and everyone had a different list of the things they couldn't do without.

———

On the spindly hall table there's a guest book going back years, signed by brief summer renters who write *Fabulous!* and *Those sunsets!* after their names. On some pages children have drawn pictures, stick figures jumping from boats and fat yellow suns, and some of them have printed their names in crooked, wavering letters. One snippy entry mentions mice but she hasn't seen any signs, not even in the tilting shed that's filled with fishing poles and beach chairs and old cans of paint. A bicycle with a rusty chain leaning against the far wall, plastic shovels and pails and even ice skates hanging from a hook, damp red mittens wadded up inside.

Most of her things are in storage but she has what she needs, and the cabin is furnished with the kinds of things people move up from. There's a bed and a kitchen table, there are chairs. There's a heavy old couch, and a bookshelf with a few glossy magazines and fat paperbacks, and war stories and books on sailing. There are crosswords, mostly filled in, and a collection of fairy tales for children, some battered board games that release a musty smell when she lifts the lids. On top of the bookshelf there's a clunky old radio; it looks as if it would play music from the 1940s, if it actually worked.

A small room at the back gives the best view of the lake, through a new, long window. She's not the first one to notice; there's an old armchair pulled up to it, draped with a bright quilt, and a strange low table, shellacked plywood on a wobbly driftwood base. Sometimes she reads there but mostly she just sits looking out, the soft cushions moulding around her and her feet propped on the shallow, cold sill. Lately she's been wondering what it would be like to stay on here through the winter. To find out if the whole lake freezes over, and to see, really see, the small changes that lead into spring. She mentioned it to Bonnie, who gave her one of her squint-eyed looks, as if she were hearing a foreign language and it took time for the meaning to filter through. "Put that thought right out of your head," Bonnie said. "Winters are terrible here, you have no idea at all."

Bonnie is the woman in large sweatpants who met her with the key. It's not her house, but she's something like a caretaker, she said, for an old woman who's been in the Lakeview for years. "You know, the retirement home, though Lord knows why we call them that, those places. As if they're somewhere people look forward to, can't wait to be." Bonnie cleans at the Lakeview three days a week; she says it isn't bad but really, wouldn't you rather be dead?

From the start it was clear Bonnie is someone it would be hard to edge away from. She loves to talk and to find things out, asks questions that need some kind of answer, mixed in with details of her own that would be confessions, if they weren't so casually said. Already she knows much more than she wants to about Bonnie's husband and his bad back, her son's piercings and her own *female troubles*, and how she's been here fifteen years but there are still people who won't give her the time of day. Even worse is knowing she herself has a place now, an existence inside Bonnie's head. *Think I'll check on the widow tomorrow,* she imagines Bonnie saying, as she serves up the family supper. Probably some kind of patterned paper on the kitchen wall, and a clock with knife and fork hands. Maybe there's a grunt from her husband, who's not much interested in conversation, while the pierced son asks if there's any more bread.

Some of the mismatched furniture must belong to the old woman in the Lakeview, maybe the radio. Some perhaps dumped by the feuding nephews and nieces Bonnie's told her about. "They're just waiting for her to pop her clogs, and then there'll be fireworks," is what she said. It could be that some of the touches are Bonnie's, the plastic flowers in the vase with the smudged flea market sticker, the dusty bowl filled with scentless potpourri. A few pictures on the wall seem likely too, a girl with a watering can and bonnet, a brown horse in a misty field. There's another of a shouting woman, just her face and her wobbling chins. Maybe some kind of joke, that one, and somehow it fits with Bonnie's contradictions. Her rough red hands and her blunt way of talking, the frills on her blouses and the pink earrings that shiver when she moves her head.

———

In the hot afternoons we climbed back to the village and some of us slept and some of us lay down together. A faint smell of drains in all the dim rooms and thin curtains hanging limp, the loudest sound the rasp of a sandal outside, someone moving carefully through the narrow white streets. Later maybe voices and the rattle of iron grilles sliding up and we drifted back to the square, feeling hungry and rested and so easy in our bodies. Most times we took the path to the best place to watch the sun go down and stayed there until the sky was dark, all those stars like a flung-out net, and we talked about the universe and our tiny place in it, said that everyone ever alive had probably done the same, seen the same, and how amazing was that.

We talked and we shared things as if we were all in the same place, but Iz knew that Douglas had a thick wad of traveller's cheques and the place Hans and Robert stayed was almost a hotel, served them breakfast at a table with a patterned cloth. It didn't really matter and most things were cheap enough, a twist of souvlaki from the fierce man in the grubby apron, plastic sandals from the dusty shop and the lined notebooks Iz bought to fill with all she was thinking about. When she and Clare made their list for the Bare Minimum Café they decided it had to have a lending library, and Iz said that some time before, on a boat or a train, a girl had given her a fat paperback, so many pages the cover could barely contain them. "You can imagine how excited I was," she said, and Clare could, the two books she herself had packed long finished and traded for a warm green sweatshirt.

The girl who gave Iz the book said that someone had passed it on to her in a youth hostel in Germany, saying, "I couldn't finish it, you're welcome to it." A story about models in New York or Los Angeles, and uppers and downers, parties and schemes and betrayals, all kinds of shallow thoughts. Desperate as she was, Iz said she couldn't finish it either, left it in a dark room in Venice for someone else to pick up. Clare said she'd thought it was a rule, said she'd never left a book unfinished, no matter how much she didn't like it, but Iz said, "Not this one. Not even you." And they imagined that book moving around from place to place, hand to hand, the back-stabbing models living out their crazy, drama-filled lives, their story not completely known by anyone. Maybe for years, even decades, the pages more worn and damaged, the book split into smaller sections and the people who came across them having to make up their own stories about what came before and after.

Sometimes they did it themselves, that way they talked with their thoughts bumping into each other and bouncing off, ending up in some crazy place. "This is the story of Celeste," Clare said, "this is what happened. It was terrible, she got leprosy somehow," and Iz said, "No, that's not it. She was in a fire and left terribly scarred, but it made her a better person. And what about Auburn?" "She bumped her head," Clare said, "and had amnesia, so she didn't know any better when she ran into a creepy older guy who said that he'd make her a star. But she must get her memory back." "Of course she does," Iz said. "She bumps her head again when Jade trips her on the catwalk, and remembers everything about the life she was meant to be living. And she goes back to her kind, patient husband and lives happily ever after, because someone has to, don't you think?"

———

Clare's father had left her some money, a note that said, *See everything*, so she tried to. She started out in Spain with two friends from school, more friends of each other than of hers, but she was used to that. On the ferry from Brindisi the friends met two boys from Calgary and she settled her pack on her back, shifted her shoulders and walked off in a different direction. She met Iz in the clinic on Dedalou Street where people went to sell their blood, neither of them really that broke but who could pass up cash for something that could be replaced so easily. They started talking and just kept on, blew half their payment on a meal in a real restaurant, an arbour stretched over them covered with vines, with tiny, flickering lights.

Iz said she'd been working as an au pair in Basel, with the sweetest children, who cried when she left. She hitched south with a boy named Michel who could always make her laugh, taught her the French words for body parts and emotions, miming fear and sorrow and joy. He was gone when she came back from the market in Thessaloníki, a wilting flower on her rolled-out sleeping bag and a note that said, *Sorry but I must to leve,* and she said she felt so foolish, not realizing it was the same old story.

Making her slow way down to Athens, Iz kept thinking she'd see him, that they'd meet in each town she passed through because he was on his way back to her, wearing his exaggerated expression of regret. When that didn't happen she found herself remembering the chewing sounds he made when he ate and the ugly nylon shirt he often wore, the one that made him look like someone else. Although mostly she still thought of the way his hair fell softly back, after he'd shaken it out of his eyes. The way his jeans and wide leather belt sat on his bony hips. Halfway through the second bottle of Demestica they decided, Clare and Iz, to take the first boat out in the morning, and when they met at the ticket office they felt like sisters or long-lost friends, easy together, but with so much to catch up on.

Iz and Clare didn't look anything alike but there were so many coincidences, and they made up a story and talked as if they really believed it. A feud or a curse long ago and a family divided, splitting off to the east and the west. They both carried things in their right pockets as charms, Iz a tiny teacup and Clare an old, flattened nickel, and the same names popped up going back in their families and really, how likely was that? But Robert said that names went with different times after all, like styles of clothing, ways of thinking, and it meant nothing. There were stories about fires in Jen's family too, and in Carly's, and did that mean they were all related? Jackson said he had a twin brother, but they'd been separated at birth and adopted in different states; he hadn't mentioned it before because it made him sad.

Douglas said anyway it was just a distraction, trying to make connections that way—we should all be trying to move forward, instead of wandering around in the past. But Carly was certain that they'd lived before, maybe in the same family or at least the same town. Or maybe they were really the same person, what about that, arrived here from completely different times. She was never bothered when people laughed, just said, in her calm, breathy voice, that if a man could actually walk on the moon surely anything was possible.

———

She finds the tiny library just past the cenotaph, at the end of the short main street. Finds the atlas she wants to check, and then a history of the town that she carries over to the only long table. She's not much interested in the pioneer section, though she knows she should be. Their hard journeys and all that hewing, that chopping. All the clearing they had to do before they could begin to build something modest and new. But after the sketches of the first shack and the first tavern there are early photographs of buildings she's walked past. Two churches and the courthouse and the boarded-up station, some of the grand houses on the bluff. There's a picture of that retirement home when it was first built as a hotel—a *completely modern* hotel, according to the caption. Empty doorways and windows and several workmen posing for the camera, holding up paintbrushes and hammers. Behind them one has turned his back and perhaps he's actually working, bent over a little, his suspenders a dark X against his shirt.

The book is surprisingly thick and she skips most of the text. Turns past newspaper headlines about shipwrecks and wars, all the pictures of soldiers as they march away, and then back home again. There are other parades, and sports teams and church picnics, a circus tent. Clearly Bonnie was right about the winters; there are snowbanks that reach the tops of hydro poles, and the lake is a tumble of ice. The last pages are filled with all the town councils, looking much the same until the seventies arrive. Sudden long wedges of sideburns and wide patterned ties, silly moustaches; she knows she's probably walked past some of them too.

There are two girls at the other end of the table, maybe doing their homework, their heads bent and their smooth hair glowing in the sleepy light. The sound of their laptop keys reminds her of something, and she tries to work out just what it is. Thinks of long fingernails, impatient on a Formica table, strips of plastic in a doorway, clattering in a sudden breeze. Neither is quite right and then she wonders why she makes it complicated, why she tries to connect that noise to something that's already known. She thinks of other sounds that you recognize without even realizing, the ping of a microwave, or the beep when a truck backs up, the grating whir before a CD starts to play. *The past is another country*—is that how it goes? She thinks about how every sound in the world was once new, a train whistle slicing through the night or the tick of a clock, the crackle of the very first fire. What it would have been like for those shapes huddled around it, feeling suddenly safer, and warm.

She knows she could turn that into a good essay topic, something to do with new sounds, with learning and associations. *The past is another country: discuss.* But of course she doesn't do that anymore. The right choice to hand in her keys, to roll the poster of Lorenz and his rubber boots, and sweep up the paint chips it had pulled from the wall. The last time she stood in a lecture hall she kept losing her place, distracted by the same sound of tapping, and by things she was keeping at bay. It didn't matter; except for those few in the front, she knew no one was listening, and she thought of tossing her neat notes in the air, thought of sending them all away.

She's certain that she didn't really do that. She hopes not; it wouldn't have been fair. Not their fault that they stay the same age while she just gets older; not their fault that they don't yet know all that they don't know. And she thinks of another time she walked a long beach, holding a small child by the hand. She remembers the silvery light, the pause they walked through between rain showers and how quiet it was, only the sound of the waves as they washed up, leaving their wet loops on the sand. "We can't go far," she said, or something like that, and just then the child pointed and said, "Look!" A duck up ahead, followed by the skittering, matchstick legs of the ducklings that trailed along after. As they watched, the duck took to the water, struggling to get over the breakers but then swimming calmly while the ducklings tried so hard to follow. Bowled over and tossed back on the shore in a wet tumble, again and again, and she couldn't hear it, over the water, but she imagined their peeping and wailing. Thought, Yes, it's difficult for her. But look how impossible for them.

———

Iz had a grandmother who lived with them when she was growing up, one who rocked in a chair and told stories. She said she knew that made her sound like one type of grandmother but it wasn't like that, and all of her stories were terrifying. Filled with ghosts and demons and punishments, and people singled out for tests and torment that they didn't deserve, but couldn't escape. She said she still had nightmares about the horse that lunged out of the water and snatched up children, left their parents weeping on the pebbled shore.

Once her grandmother told Iz that she might be a changeling baby, because of her strange ears that stuck out, and when she went crying to her mother she said it was only teasing, such a big fuss she was making over nothing. Iz still had faint scars from the operation to pin those ears flat; she said she'd become obsessed and her parents thought it would make her life easier and for a while it did, and she felt transformed. Her brothers found other things to tease her about, but nothing they came up with bothered her as much, and they got on better anyway as they all got older, united against their youngest sister who was a tattletale with big blue eyes and screamed the place down if she didn't get her way. Such a noisy house she grew up in, filled with tantrums and the sound of her brothers' heavy feet as they thundered through.

But lately, Iz said, she'd been thinking that she'd made a mistake, that she'd messed with the order and wasn't the person she was meant to be. One who wasn't so sad, one no one would want to walk away from. She knew Douglas would say that was nonsense, it was up to everyone to decide their own life, but Iz told Clare she kept thinking about her grandmother's stories. The one about the tailor's vain daughter who stole a jewelled cloak, and paid such a terrible price. Forever after invisible and condemned to float at the edges, watching others live out their happy lives.

Clare told Iz once that she envied the crowded rooms and the noisy family; she said her own father could go days without speaking, her mother too, and in her memory she grew up in a house that was silent, except for the clock in the hall. "Ticking away," she said, "like the song." Clare's mother liked things ordered, lists everywhere and always the same meals on the same nights, and if Clare looked for one word to describe her it was *sharp*, like the knitting needles that clacked together in her busy hands. She said her father was softer and his cheeks were always smooth, gleaming from his electric razor. He was an optometrist with his own office and every morning he buffed his shoes, took his lunch bag from the counter where it sat beside Clare's and put it into his black briefcase, snapped the locks. Her mother opened that briefcase after he died, nothing inside but a newspaper folded to the crossword and a salami sandwich with two bites gone, and Clare thought that must have marked the exact moment he had made up his mind.

Once a year, near her birthday, Clare's father said, "Welcome to my kingdom," and he checked her eyes and showed her how everything worked, the charts and the clicking lenses and the bright circle of light. "Perfect vision," he said once a year, and one of those times he told her a secret, said that he had perfect vision too. Nothing but plain glass in the frames he changed every year, but it was what people expected; after he died Clare's mother said of course she'd known, and it had been her idea in the first place. She didn't like to talk about him but Clare thought she had to be sad, and she tried to keep her company, sitting up late and watching old movies on TV, even though they were so boring she could have screamed. Her lunch already made, she could see it from the couch, the folded bag sitting by itself on the counter.

At the round table in the sunlit square Clare told Iz that it was terrible how quickly he had vanished, and how she'd let it happen. How soon she got used to waking up without the sound of his razor, the staccato slaps of Old Spice. She said her feelings were so jumbled that she tried very hard to feel nothing, though she took his striped scarf from the closet and wore it around for a while. She lost track of it, but when she asked all her mother said was, "That old thing? That's no loss at all."

Usually she has the beach to herself when she walks, but occasionally there's a figure in the distance. Sometimes coming toward her, and maybe also working out how to manage the approaching interaction. How long to appear lost in thought, how soon to look up and the proper distance to begin to acknowledge each other. Either way they risk looking like fools; too far apart and they're smiling at nothing, but wait too long and it's ridiculous to pretend not to notice when it's just the two of them on the empty sand. It feels like a small victory, the way they manage the calculation and the connection, before moving on in their different directions. Two people in exactly the same place, for an instant, but with completely different thoughts, and for different reasons.

If it's a day when she's feeling particularly untethered she does an exercise, once they've passed each other, and tries to remember each detail. Gloves or no gloves and the colour of the jacket, buttons or zipper. Height, weight and age, size of nose. It was one of her favourite lectures, the one on eye-witness testimony, on *attention*, and she always started with that short video, young people in some kind of hallway who are passing a ball back and forth. "Count the white-shirted passes," she told her students, "count carefully," and when it was done she had them call out their answers. There were always a few who suspected a trick, a few clever ones who had counted black passes too, and how many girls, how many boys, how many with long hair tied back. But they gaped just like the others when she said, "Yes, that's fine, but did anyone notice the gorilla?"

It can only work once, that video, but it works astonishingly well, the gorilla so obvious, when the students watch it again, they can hardly believe it. Year after year they still talk about it as they gather their books, as they zip up their backpacks. Still shaking their heads at how much you can miss, paying attention to what you thought was the important thing.

We knew every crooked lane in the small village on the small island and our days and nights had a lazy rhythm. But content as we were they sometimes caught up with us, those empty moments where there was nothing new to say. Then we played a game of questions and answers, *yes* or *no*, a game that always started with someone saying, *A detective walks into a room . . .* There was always a dead body in the room, no obvious cause or weapon, a few strange clues. There might be a man with a damp shirt front, or a woman on a cot, a thin broken stick on the floor. An open window and a few shards of glass, a suffocated couple. The detective says, *I know what happened here,* and the point is to arrive at the bizarre solution he has instantly understood. A man who has stabbed his own heart with a dagger of ice, two goldfish and a broken bowl.

It was a game that could go on for hours, stopping and starting and carrying on in the bar in the evening, while Pink Floyd played and Gerard's little girls sang along and we thought how lucky they were, growing up free with no rules about homework or bedtimes and the whole island their playground. *Us and them, us and them;* the little girls sang and sometimes they danced until their mother brushed the tangled hair from their eyes and led them off to wherever they slept. Some nights she came back but mostly she didn't, and then Gerard pulled a chair up to our table and Hans said, "Here's *Romeo,* here he is." And Gerard smiled as he set down his bottle, and gave Clare his sleepy-eyed look.

For a while Clare stayed on after he'd turned out the lights, and in the dead afternoons they met in all the secret places he knew; she told Iz everything and said she hadn't known she could be so happy. Other times Iz listened while she fretted because he hadn't appeared. Had something happened or was it her fault, it must be, she must have mixed up the time or the place. Until one night she watched Gerard watching Jen as she raised her tall glass. Her bracelets jangled as she swept back her shining hair and Clare felt such a fool, the last to see it, the last one to know. "How could you not *tell* me?" she said to Iz as they walked through the empty square, and Iz said, "How *could* I—put yourself in my place." The next days weren't easy but then Clare caught her balance, steadied by the sun and the beach, by that rhythm, and she told Iz, "I think it's working, what you said." Carry on and pretend it doesn't matter, and one day you'll open your eyes and find that it's the tiniest thing.

Someone had heard something about a secret path to a secret bay and we tried to ask Adelpha about it; she said, *"Schmugglerin,"* and mimed an eye patch, and that made it even better. We imagined a flag in the wind, a white-sailed ship and a wooden chest spilling treasure, and set off the next day with the rough map she had drawn, an X near the graveyard marking the start. A narrow track that wound through dust and scrub, that circled small groves of twisted trees and sometimes climbed steeply and we wiped our faces with shirttails, with the ends of patterned scarves, stumbling and tripping and Iz banged her knee hard, and had to limp the rest of the way. Adelpha had drawn the wandering path and a few scattered squares that maybe matched the lone huts we passed so she must have known it well, this baking centre where people lived differently, out of sight of the circling sea.

We were talking about turning back but then like a puff of magic the beach was there below us, a rush of sand flowing out to meet the waves as they crashed in, rolling white and much bigger than anything we'd seen in the place we'd come from. There was a building of some kind and we thought of water running down the sides of cold bottles, platters of olives and oil-soaked bread, and it seemed like a cruel joke as we got closer, and then a marvel. A puzzle without an answer, a room for the detective to walk into, except that it wasn't a room, that structure, nothing more than the *idea* of a room. No roof, just a concrete floor marked in large squares and one white wall with a wide window set in, blue-painted shutters that could fold closed but now were open, framing the long run to the sea. On one side there was a line strung between poles, draped and sagging with small, dried octopus, and there was no way to know, in the bright sun, if they'd been there for hours or months. No way to tell if the place itself was the beginning or the end of something, the real window in the imaginary room. We held on in a ragged line and felt the pull as we waded through the waves, rode them back to the rippled shore until it was enough. The white wall cast a narrow shadow and we closed the blue shutters and stretched out, our heads and shoulders cooler in the shade; Hans said that if there was music it would be perfect but we told him it already was, and that was exactly how it felt.

The way back should have been easier with the heat of the day past, even for Iz who was still limping. But the path twisted and things looked different in the fading light, and suddenly we weren't sure of anything, not which rocky hill, not which far-off hut, which stunted tree was the landmark. Then the night fell down, only a paring of moon, and we stumbled and cursed and felt the chill. It wasn't far, we knew that, but the ground was tricky underfoot and we had to pay attention, stop talking, and that silence left space for other thoughts to slither in, with the dark hills looming all around. Until we saw the first warm lights, more and more of them, and the smaller shadows of the place we'd started from. We moved faster then, almost running as we pushed our way through the narrow streets, and our feet were so light on the solid ground, heading for the music, the bar and the long table where we would sit and laugh, turn it into a story and share all our crazy fears. That out there in the dark we'd really thought we might be wandering forever, and how we'd remembered every campfire and every old tale we'd ever been told. The way we'd realized how close they really were, those things that roamed through the night, and the ones that swooped in with a terrible cackle.

———

She's read books, she's seen movies and plays, the medallions, the rings and the bells. The music and dancing, psychedelic swirls and free love, the communes and Turkish prisons and blown minds. It's always more comic or more dire than anything she remembers, more *authentic*, somehow, and the stories are often said to be true ones. But she knows how that works, those true stories and how we all tell them. In even the simplest recounting, a conversation in a shop, or a walk through the park in the evening, you alter a phrase, or give yourself words you should have said. You make the dog growl louder, you make it a Rottweiler, though really you have no idea what it was. Little tweaks in the details that surely don't matter, until you think of how many there are, in a lifetime.

And she knows that memory works something like this, no matter how it seems. Not a file in a drawer but a fluid thing, which changes each time you recall it. She's taught that too in the lecture hall and she knows that it's tricky, that it just doesn't *feel* right. "It's not like a photograph," she used to say to her students, "it's not like a movie." And then she'd say, "Think of a time, I'm sure you've had them, with family or a friend, a time there was disagreement about something that had happened. What it was or when it was or who was there. You're probably quite certain they were wrong and you were right. But what does it open up, when you think that really you both were?"

Every few days she walks to the store and the shush of the waves falls away, as she climbs the slight hill to the main street. It's not far, but there's a different quality to everything, the sound of her feet on the sidewalk, and the way slamming car doors shift the air. Even the light, where it falls through the trees, instead of on the endless lake. Maybe that's why her own voice sounds strange to her, saying things she's expected to say. Why everything she overhears seems significant—a mother who tells her child, "It's a bridge, not a tunnel," or an old man who mumbles, "But what was it he *didn't* say." In the checkout line two women talk about poor June, about how she doesn't get out at all, now Alvin is gone. "Such a shame," they say, "but you can understand it, can't you. It's just not the same, doing things on your own." She knows that's true, but she doesn't think that if Alvin came back June would take him to the mall, to the casino or out to a movie. She's quite certain that if the dead came back you'd just want to sit down with them; she thinks that would be enough. To sit quietly with them, breathing the same air, so close that it's as if you are touching.

———

It wasn't that same night, but not long after, that a cruel wind blew up in the dark. Shrieking and roaring through all the narrow alleyways, shutters banging off white walls and all kinds of debris careening through. By mid-afternoon it had blasted off again but nothing was the same, not even the colour of the sky, the paler sun not quite strong enough to warm anyone who still went into the white-capped bay. We pulled sweaters and jackets from the bottoms of our packs, smelling of wet canvas and diesel and other places, and we looked different to each other, wearing things that had been packed away for so long. The remnants of that wind clattered the bright plastic that hung in doorways, fluttering the corners of the clipped-down plastic cloths on the outside tables and finding every fissure, drawing in the rain that trailed after.

Inside the cafés it was steamy, sound was different and time was too, stretched out longer but not in any good way. We talked about Marrakesh and about Kathmandu, and about the things that were calling us home, while we waited for the rare boats to appear. Jackson and Robert dealt out cards and Carly threaded the beads she'd poured in a dull mound on the battered table. She called Hans a brat when he puffed out his cheeks as if to blow them away. And Douglas taught Clare to play chess and Iz had to watch it as it happened. Their heads bent together while pieces tapped in set moves on the board and their conversation growing into a different kind of attention. Later she said what did it matter, that it wasn't something they'd planned. Or that no one owned anyone else; she knew that. She was tired of the long conversations, everything out in the open as if that would make it easier to bear. Tired of them both being *sorry* and expecting her to say something that would make Clare feel better when she curled up with Douglas in her stolen space. Rain fell in the long afternoons and Clare ran through it, trying to think only of the splashing sounds her feet made. And somewhere else in the white village Iz wrote down how it felt. She closed her notebook and wondered if anything would ever change.

Different boats came and we moved on, the white wake fanning out until the island was just another mound in the sea, until it was gone. We left some things behind and there were others we carried with us, tiny beads and flimsy tickets and threads of memory that would fade, twist and change when they were drawn back to the light. Clare stood on a windy deck while time folded back, the grey buildings of Piraeus getting closer, until they were all she could see. She didn't know it yet, but inside her, new cells were growing, twitching and dividing. A careless, random combination becoming someone who would appear, months later, in a space no one knew was there, until it was filled.

And whatever way Clare thought her life might go, it went this way, even if she didn't deserve it. A kind man opened his arms wide enough, and they were more together than they would have been apart. Sometimes things were easy and there were times they were so much harder. But they held on to each other until they couldn't, anymore.

———

It seems the world she's stepped out of is waiting to welcome her back. Her contractor leaves a message with Bonnie—all the repairs have been done, pipes replaced and the stained floors refinished. Her boxes are waiting, old things to unpack into a new, clean space. Bonnie drives down to tell her and holds out a plate of fresh muffins, the ploy so blatant it would be cruel to turn her away. While they drink coffee Bonnie looks around, takes in the piles of paper and the dirty dishes, the wet clothes draped over most of the chairs. She says, "I heard that—that you like to walk," and then she laughs her hoarse laugh, says, "What did I tell you, you can't have any secrets around here."

Rain hits the window with a slap and keeps on coming, and Bonnie keeps talking. She says the old woman in the Lakeview took another stroke; she's holding on, but everyone knows how those nephews are rubbing their hands. The hardware's closing, and that dress shop too, not that she could ever afford it. Her husband's cheques have been cut back and her son sleeps every day away, Lord knows what he gets up to at night. And then somehow she's talking about high school, about the Nature Club and all those great hikes they used to take. The teacher who gave her his old camera, and the photographs she hasn't looked at for years. Blades of grass that sort of *glowed* with the dew, she remembers, and a small deer just before it startled and leapt away. Bonnie says she was quite sure back then and that was her plan, to travel the world and take pictures, perfect pictures that she'd sell to magazines.

There's a little pause then, and maybe they both see it. A different Bonnie, crouched and holding her breath under some foreign sky. Waiting for the right moment, her finger so steady on the button, waiting for the soft click that will catch exactly what she wants. "Kids' stuff," the real Bonnie says, shaking her head, and her earrings glint and tremble, as they always do. She looks at Bonnie and sees the ghosts that trail everyone; mostly they mumble, but sometimes they roar, and they can cluster so thickly that it's hard to peer through.

In the morning the gulls wing out in their set direction, and if the wind is against them they flap harder, that's just what they do. By the back steps she blows to warm her cupped hands, then scoops everything into an old bucket. The small stones and bits of wood, the sleek feathers she collected; they don't weigh much at all and she dumps them in a damp trail at the water's edge. A wave rolls in, rolls back, and what's left is a random scattering; already she's not sure what she's added and what was already there.

The dark sand is rain-pocked but shows lighter and softer in all the places where her footsteps have broken through. When she looks back they make a line that shows clearly, and leads right to the place where she now stands. And she thinks maybe these are the thoughts she was waiting for, while she walked the cold shore and looked out at the misbehaving moon. While she traced a path through other times and other places, like someone looking for the familiar shape of one lost thing, an outline as clear as a lucky coin or a misplaced key. While she rummaged through one room, then another, picking up other things she'd quite forgotten, had set aside. Maybe it's those things themselves or just the time it took her to find them; what matters is how steadily she now stands, as the waves roll in. Knowing that something has formed a counterbalance to the surprising weight of it, this vague need for forgiveness she understands she's been carrying so long.

It's still early and the beach is quite empty. She has things to pack up and things to tidy but not many, and then she'll move on without leaving any trace. She told Bonnie she would, but she knows she won't even sign the guest book. Won't join that line of strangers who happened to be in the same place looking through the same windows, names that mean even less than the ones that hang from a family tree. She tips her head back and it's cold enough to see her breath, before it vanishes beneath the enormous, shifting sky.

And she's quite certain that other girl sailed off into her own happy life, happy enough. A usual kind of life, with the usual thoughts and worries, regrets. They could still run into each other, maybe in an airport or on an unfamiliar street. Or maybe one day she'll bend to pick up the mail that's scattered on the smooth slate tiles. Everything damp from the rain that's been falling, her blurred name on a postcard sent from somewhere that's not, after all, so very far away. Of course they arrange to meet and they arrive at exactly the same time, as if they've been moving in step all along. If it's summer they'll choose a place with a patio and it will remind them. They'll think of long afternoons and other tables set on uneven flagstones, the legs levelled with crushed matchboxes and folded paper, with whatever someone thought they could spare.

But it's not summer, she knows that; instead it's quite a different season. Snow swirls beyond the wide window, and they watch people hurrying home through the cold early dusk. Inside where they are, though, it's perfect. Not too bustling or quiet, and just the right music underneath. The earth-coloured walls like a small, warm cave, and between them a white candle flickers in a glass bowl. It's a little awkward at first, as she'd imagined it would be, and they both fuss with their reading glasses, take their time with the oversized menus. But they begin to talk and the wine comes, one laughs, then the other, and very soon it's clear that everything is all right. Because that's what she does, isn't it. She imagines it all.

ACKNOWLEDGEMENTS

With thanks to my agent, Dorian Karchmar, and my editor at Knopf Canada, Anne Collins, for their encouragement, their patience and their humour. And to all the librarians and archivists, the family members, friends and perfect strangers who have answered my sometimes bizarre questions—I wish I could name you all.

MARY SWAN's first novel, *The Boys in the Trees*, was a finalist for the Scotiabank Giller Prize in 2008 and for the Amazon First Novel Award. She is the winner of the 2001 O. Henry Award for short fiction and is the author of the novella *The Deep*, a finalist for the Canada/Caribbean Commonwealth Prize for Best First Book, and the collection *Emma's Hands*. Her work has appeared in several Canadian literary magazines and anthologies, including *Malahat Review* and *Best Canadian Stories*, as well as in American publications such as *Ploughshares*, *Harvard Review*, *Zoetrope* and *Harper's Magazine*. She lives with her family in Guelph, Ontario.